THE
BOOMERANG
EFFECT

THE BOOMERANG EFFECT

A NOVEL BY
GORDON JACK

An Imprint of HarperCollinsPublishers

HarperTeen is an imprint of HarperCollins Publishers.

The Boomerang Effect

Library of Congress Control Number: 2016936186
ISBN 978-0-06-239939-7 (trade bdg.)

Typography by Aurora Parlagreco
16 17 18 19 20   CG/RRDH   10 9 8 7 6 5 4 3 2 1

First Edition

*To my parents, who helped me survive my teen years
with a lot of love and just the right amount of attention*

THE
BOOMERANG
EFFECT

ONE

By the time they called me into the principal's office for my disciplinary hearing, I had nearly sweated through my Meridian High hoodie. I figured it wouldn't hurt to show some school spirit at the meeting that could get me expelled, but I had no idea these things were made of insulation fiber. Of course, the excessive perspiration could be the result of being deprived of pot for three days. They say that sweating is one of the ways the body cleanses itself of toxins. Either way, I looked nervous and guilty, which wasn't the impression I wanted to create.

I entered Principal Stone's office and found him sitting behind his enormous desk, his bald, pockmarked head looking like an oversize cantaloupe. Positioned in a neat semicircle in front of the desk were Stone's secretary, Mrs. Darwipple; our campus security guard, Mr. Riddel; and my guidance counselor, Mr. Lunley. Lunley acknowledged me with his traditional namaste prayer bow. All the others sat rigid and expressionless, not wanting to form attachments to the animal they were about to slaughter.

"Where are your parents?" Stone asked.

"They couldn't make it," I said.

"They couldn't make it?" Stone said, shaking his head. "This is a disciplinary hearing to determine whether you will be allowed to stay at Meridian."

"My mom's out of town and my dad had an important conference call," I explained. "He asked me to give you this." I handed Stone a sealed letter, now stained with my hand sweat. The envelope was embossed with the logo of my father's law firm—Barry, Yu & Singh, an appropriate name for a ruthless pack of attorneys. Walter Yu was actually senior partner, but he settled for second billing so that the firm's name would evoke fear in opposing counsel.

Stone took one look at the letter and sneered, his unibrow wrinkling to a *V* on his forehead. My dad had represented Stone's ex-wife in their rather ugly divorce, and I think he's never forgiven my family for costing him his Jet Skis. He slapped the envelope on his desk and said, "Take a seat, Mr. Barry."

I lowered myself onto the rickety fold-out chair, designed, I assumed, to throw me off balance.

"Let the record state that the disciplinary hearing to determine Lawrence Barry's enrollment at Meridian High School began at two oh one p.m. on Monday, September ninth, in Principal Howard Stone's office. In attendance are Principal Stone, Hugh Riddel, Gerry Lunley, and Lawrence Barry. Notably absent are Lawrence's parents."

"You want me to include 'notably' in the record?" Mrs. Darwipple asked.

Stone closed his eyes and massaged his temple with his stubby fingers. "Strike it," he said, after giving it some thought.

"Must we take such a formal tone?" my counselor said, removing his John Lennon glasses and placing them on my file folder on his lap. "We're here to help Lawrence, right?"

Stone and Riddel exchanged glances. As adults, they had clearly learned to control their eyes from rolling, but I could tell the reflex was still there.

"We're here to determine how to best respond to Lawrence's actions at the diversity assembly. Mr. Riddel, please share your observations."

Riddel flipped open his notebook, just like he was a real police officer and not a mall cop in training, and began reading. "Friday, September sixth, ten oh seven a.m. Lawrence Barry and Alex Tran were observed dancing shirtless with rolls of toilet paper at the school assembly."

"We were performing a traditional Chinese Ribbon Dance," I clarified.

Riddel stared at me, his possum face revealing nothing. I wondered if he had been beat up a lot in middle school and quickly concluded that he had.

"Barry and Tran stumbled across the gymnasium floor, clearly disoriented."

This struck me as a bit of editorializing. My memory, fuzzy though it was, was that we were quite graceful.

"When asked to leave the gymnasium floor, both Barry and Tran only increased their spastic movements, inciting the crowd and creating an unsafe environment for the assembly."

"People loved us," I interjected. "And Alex is the treasurer of the Asian Student Union so he had a right, as an Asian person, to share an important aspect of his culture. Isn't that what the diversity assembly is all about?"

I thought this was a pretty good defense, even though Alex is Vietnamese and really has no business dancing like a Chinese person.

"Alex Tran has already confessed to using the ASU's funds to buy marijuana. He's been transferred to Quiet Haven alternative school." The effort it took for Stone to keep a straight face while saying this was epic. If I didn't know how overjoyed he was at sharing this news, I'd think he was having a stroke.

"Really?" I gulped. "That is shocking." I had no idea Alex had stolen from the ASU. Alex liked to think of himself as hard core, like the gangsters in the Hong Kong action films he was always watching, but his dad was a software engineer at SurveyMonkey. If he needed money to score weed, he didn't need to steal from his own people to get it.

Riddel continued. "As I escorted Barry and Tran off the gymnasium floor, I smelled the odor of marijuana on the boys."

"That is so not true," I blurted out. Riddel was just making stuff up to get back at us for gluing the student driver sign to the back of his golf cart. Electronic cigarettes don't produce odor. Do they? Actually, I'm not clear on this point. This technology is kind of new to me.

"It was obvious the boys were high, so I brought them to Principal Stone's office for disciplinary action."

Riddel flipped his notebook closed and stuck his golf pencil behind his ear. I fought the urge to grab the Scotch tape off Stone's desk and use it to rip off his scrubby mustache. Sudden fits of rage are another by-product of pot deprivation, I've heard.

"I think Lawrence was pressured into performing by Alex," Lunley said.

"It doesn't matter why he did it," Stone said. "And we can't have different punishments for the same crime."

"Alex Tran was sent to Quiet Haven for stealing club funds, not for dancing at the assembly," Lunley said. "I don't think transferring Lawrence is appropriate. He's got a B average and wants to go to college." My counselor looked at me for confirmation on this point.

"Yes. College. For sure." I tried to sound enthusiastic, but the words sounded like something from a patrol-car loud-speaker.

Lunley went on. "Outside of some attendance issues his freshman year, his record is pretty clean."

"You're forgetting the streaking incident," Stone said.

"Those accusations were never proven," Lunley said, a little weakly in my opinion, and closed my file.

"What about the fire in the science building?" Riddel said.

"That was an honest mistake. Lawrence didn't know those chemicals were combustible."

"Then there was the Jell-O fight in the cafeteria."

"Lots of kids were involved in that. I think it's unfair to single out Lawrence."

I had been involved in enough "incidents" in my two years at Meridian that we could go on like this all day. Eventually, Lunley would get tired of making excuses and Stone and Riddel would get the transfer they wanted. I shifted in my seat and felt a drop of cold sweat travel down my spine. I was going to Quiet Haven, the place where they distributed ankle bracelets instead of student ID cards. I had only one chance left.

"Maybe you should read my father's letter," I offered, pointing to the envelope on Stone's desk. I had no idea what it said, but I hoped it was legalese for "quit hating on my son."

Stone took out a rather menacing-looking letter opener and stabbed the envelope with a flourish. Watching him tear it open, I was reminded of someone skinning and gutting a fish. He removed the single page and read it silently. The only clue we had to the letter's content was Stone's face, which grew a deeper shade of red the longer he stared at the page. When he finished, he slammed the paper down on the desk and breathed heavily through his nose.

"What would you recommend, Mr. Lunley?" he asked through gritted teeth.

Mr. Lunley looked surprised to be asked this question. Guidance counselors are probably never given authority to punish students. Their job is to make kids look good for colleges, not make it easier for admissions officers to reject them. Lunley centered himself through some deep cleansing breaths and then smiled like the Dalai Lama. "I'd like to sign Lawrence up for the Buddy Club," he said, tucking a loose strand of gray hair behind his ear. "I think he'd really benefit by mentoring one of our freshman students."

"But would the freshman benefit?" Stone asked.

Lunley nodded his head. "Lawrence has a lot to offer if only he channeled his energies in more positive directions."

Stone took another look at my father's letter on his desk and then slammed his open palm on it as if it were a fly he was trying to crush. "Fine," he bellowed, his tone at odds with the spirit of the word. "But let the record state that I object to this lenient sentence."

"As do I," Riddel said.

"And if Lawrence so much as breathes in a mouthful of secondhand smoke—pot or otherwise—or embarrasses himself or this school in any way, he will be joining his friend Mr. Tran at Quiet Haven. Are we understood?"

We all nodded our heads in agreement. I peeled myself off my chair and followed Lunley back to his office.

"That was a close call, Lawrence," Lunley said, once we were seated on the yoga balls on opposite sides of his desk.

"Tell me about it." I was dying to see what my father had written in the letter. Maybe Dad blackmailed him with some shameful secret Stone's ex told him during the divorce proceedings. I wouldn't put it past Dad to fight dirty. He's a pretty competitive guy and doesn't like to lose at anything. When I was six, he told me to fuck off when he got sent back to the starting tile in what I thought was a friendly game of Chutes and Ladders. We stopped playing board games after that.

"How are you feeling?" Lunley asked.

"Great."

"Really?"

"Uh-huh."

Lunley folded his hands and looked at me like I was the sound of one hand clapping. He may have thought he was breaking me down with his stares and his silence, but I've faced better psychologists than him without confessing.

"You know you can talk to me if you're struggling with addiction."

"I'm good, Mr. Lunley," I said. "Thanks."

Lunley reached into his top drawer, pulled out a pamphlet, and handed it to me. "Drug Free: The Way to Be," the headline read. Underneath the purple block lettering was a cartoon squirrel wearing sunglasses and a leather jacket. It was an outdated look, even for a rodent.

"If you can look past the stupid cover, you'll find a lot of good information inside," Lunley said.

"Thanks," I said. This was the second time today an adult had handed me printed material instead of talking to me. Suddenly, I wanted to grab my yoga ball and hurl it against the wall to watch it ricochet around the room like an exploding kernel of popcorn. Instead I pulled the summons out of my pocket and started folding.

"Mr. Lunley," I said, not looking up from the scrap of paper in my hands, "have you ever gotten high?"

There was a loud squeak as Lunley squirmed on his yoga ball. Looking up, I saw him blinking spastically behind his glasses. "We're not talking about me, Lawrence," he said, pulling on his gray ponytail.

I went back to my folding. "I'm just asking."

"Yes," he said. "I've gotten high."

"Do you think it's as bad as this pamphlet says?"

"I think it can be," he said. "For some people."

"How do you know if you're a person it's bad for?"

Lunley stood up and walked over to his window, seemingly recalling some memory in which he saw the best minds of his generation destroyed by madness. (We read "Howl" in English class last year and for some reason that line had stuck with me.) "I think you have to ask yourself *why* you're getting high," he said finally. "If you do it occasionally to relax and have fun, that's one thing. If it's to cope with everyday stress, that's another."

"What if it's a little of both?"

"Then that might be a problem."

This seemed ridiculous to me. My parents end most of their days with Scotch and Pinot Grigio. (Not mixed, mind you. In separate glasses and separate rooms.) If I handed them a pamphlet with a greaser squirrel and the slogan

"Drinking Wine Is Not Fine," they'd laugh in my face and tell me to grow up.

"The point is, I guess, that you should have other things in your life that bring you joy. If the only thing that makes you happy is getting high, then you need help." Lunley returned to his yoga ball and sat down. "What brings you joy, Lawrence?"

Getting high, I thought. Also, hanging out with friends. Playing video games. Complaining about how unfair things are. I decided not to share this list. Instead, I placed the origami squirrel I had folded out of my summons on his desk.

He picked it up and exclaimed, "Lawrence, this is amazing."

I shrugged. It wasn't really that amazing. The paper was a bit heavy and the wrong shade of pink. Plus I hadn't made a squirrel in years. The proportions were good though, even if the animal lacked detail.

"Where did you learn to do this?" Lunley asked.

I shrugged again, not wanting to reveal my true passion. For a guidance counselor, that kind of information is like blood to a shark. If Lunley picked up the scent of a genuine interest, he'd attack and find me an after-school job at Hobby Lobby.

"Well, this explains your A in geometry last year," he said, rotating my work of art in his hands.

Ah, geometry. My brain had never met a more compatible subject. I didn't even have to think in that class. The information seemed embedded in my DNA, like my preference for dark-haired girls and weakness for Reese's peanut butter cups.

"Why aren't you taking an art class?" Lunley asked, looking at my transcript.

The television in my head changed channels abruptly, moving from my favorite episode of Meridian High to an awful middle school rerun of Ruben Valdez setting my origami peacock on fire with his lighter. "Look at the flaming homo," he screams when my attempt to rescue my animal results in my sleeves catching fire. The laugh track reaches high decibels.

"What's this Buddy Club you talked about?" I said, bringing my focus back to the present.

Lunley turned his attention away from the computer and back to me. "The Buddy Club is a mentor program that pairs upperclassmen with new students," he said. "I think you'd be great at it, providing you take the responsibility seriously."

"I can do that." A few meetings of showing a clueless ninth grader how to avoid ending up facedown in a trash can? Easy. It would keep Stone off my back and I could list it as an extracurricular on my college applications.

Lunley spun around on his yoga ball and pulled a manila

folder from his filing cabinet. He removed a spreadsheet that had a list of names, addresses, and phone numbers and wrote one name down on a sticky note for me.

Spencer Knudsen.

"His name sounds a little dorky," I said. "Think he'd mind if I shortened it to something cooler, like 'Spence' or 'Wolverine'?"

Lunley ignored my question. "He's a transfer student from Norway."

"Does he speak English?" I asked.

Lunley nodded. "He's pretty smart. His dad's been nominated for a Nobel Prize in Physics and is now a visiting scholar at Stanford. His mom was some famous cellist before Spencer was born. He's been homeschooled until this year."

"So, he's a major geek."

"I think you'll like him." Lunley wrote down Spencer's address and phone number. "He lives really close. You know that apartment complex by the fire station?"

"You want me to go visit?"

"Why don't you start with a phone call?"

"I'll text him."

"That's his home number," Lunley said. "You're going to have to talk to him." He mimicked holding a phone to his ear.

I sighed. I really didn't like talking to people on the phone.

Lunley stood up, clasped his hands together, and bowed.

"Thank you, Lawrence, for agreeing to do this."

"Do I have a choice?"

"Spencer needs someone like you to help him with this transition."

"Someone like me?"

"Someone cool, but with a warm personality."

"So, I'm tepid."

"You know what I mean."

I stood up. "Thanks for saving my ass today," I said, grabbing Lunley's hand and shaking it vigorously, as my dad had taught me to do. "I promise not to let you down."

TWO

My friends Adam, Will, and the two Nates passed me the vape pen when I met them in the student parking lot after school. Whoever designed this device must have seen us filling our parked car with smoke and thought, "There's a problem that needs fixing." The vaporizer could be filled with pot, provided you liquefied it down to its essential THC goodness. The gadget was also shaped to look like a pencil, so when you took a long drag, it appeared as if you were chewing on the eraser while struggling to compose your next line of poetry.

I inhaled like a drowning person reaching the water's surface and leaned back against my car. What a relief to have that disciplinary hearing over and done with. The stress it caused was considerable, I'll tell you. It wasn't everyday stress either. It was "your life could become seriously fucked if you don't fix this" kind of stress.

I waited for the guys to ask me about the meeting, but they were too busy looking at their social media feeds to notice anything except the vape pen when it was passed their way. I was pretty sure I told them about my expulsion hearing. Our friend Alex had just been kicked out of school a few days ago. They must be wondering if I was the next one to be voted off the island.

"Let's get out of here," Will said, "Alex is waiting."

"Who's the designated driver?" I asked.

"You are," Adam said.

"But I . . ."

"You'll be fine," Will said, opening my car door. He hurled my copy of *The Odyssey* into the backseat, where it was tossed around much like Odysseus is in the story. We had been reading the book in English and I was totally into it. Most of the books we're assigned in class were written to make us better people. Frankly, I prefer reading about guys who battle one-eyed giants and have sex with hot witch goddesses.

I started the car and reversed out of my parking space. Will plugged in his iPod and cranked the latest from Da ReFlux. The thumping bass pulsated through the car like an amplified heartbeat. The guys rapped along, broadcasting their complaints about ghetto life to the residents of our upper-middle-class white community. I wasn't feeling especially gangsta today, so I took another hit off the pencil and tapped my fingers against the steering wheel.

"So, I had my expulsion hearing," I said.

"Oh, right!" Will said. "How'd that go?"

"They gave me mandatory community service."

"No Quiet Haven?" Nate asked.

"Not yet," I said. "Stone said one more fuckup and I'm outta here."

"That sucks, man," Adam said, offering me the vape pen. I declined.

"Alex thinks he's going to be the only Asian there," Will said.

It wasn't often that you heard of Asian students getting expelled, unless you counted that badass from Malaysia who got kicked out for stealing people's Adderall, but Alex had always bucked his cultural stereotype. He was the one who first got me high when he saw me alone at the Art of Origami show at the Asian Art Museum. I was staring at a beautifully detailed beetle, trying to mentally unpack all its tiny folds, when Alex sauntered up and asked, "Dude, are you high?" When I shook my head, he asked, "Do you want to be?" And that was it. We sneaked outside, rolled a joint using the origami paper I always carried with me, and I never looked back. My dad was happy I had made a new friend who wasn't, to use his word, "different." Mom was happy to see that my "compulsive" origami folding had been replaced with an interest in Led Zeppelin.

I was happy too. Two years into middle school and I had begun to realize that origami wasn't going to win me any popularity contests. In seventh grade, I'd tried to start an origami club after being encouraged by a well-meaning art teacher. Two girls showed up and promptly left after I handed them each a paper crab ("You gave them crabs!" Alex howled when I told him this story.) But pot smoking connected me to all kinds of cool people. Through Alex, I met Adam, Will, and the two Nates, and we had been a solid crew ever since we started at Meridian.

Now here we were, coming to say good-bye to the guy who brought us all together. Alex was currently under house arrest until his transfer to Quiet Haven went through. He was having the time of his life though, alone at home with access to the family liquor cabinet and online pornography. When I pulled up in front of his house, he stepped outside with a beer in hand and waved us in. My friends spilled out of the car and raced to join him. When he saw me hesitate, he shouted, "C'mon, Lawman. Just hang with us for an hour."

My hand hovered over the door latch. I had a ton of homework to do and I should really follow through on my plan to become a more responsible person. But then I thought about going home to an empty house with its cold, polished floors and giant abstract paintings my mother made during her years of postpartum depression and thought, Fuck it. One beer by the pool couldn't hurt.

I woke up four hours later on an Adirondack chair next to Alex's pool. The sky had turned the shade of pink I associate with undercooked chicken. I was alone, except for a couple of squirrels perched on the fence that surrounded the Trans' vegetable garden.

"Didn't you learn anything from my pamphlet?" one of the squirrels asked. I didn't recognize him without his sunglasses and leather jacket.

I dug around my pockets, looking for the info Lunley had given me. I must have lost it somewhere between the counselor offices and my car. "Shit," I said.

"You'll never be accepted into the squirrel community unless you get your shit together," the other squirrel said.

"But I'm not a squirrel," I moaned.

"Oh, in that case, blaze it up, homie."

I sat up and stared at the fluffy-tailed creatures. What was I doing with my life that I was alone at someone else's house, hungover at 7:00 p.m. and talking to squirrels?

A leaf floated down and rested on the surface of the Trans' pool, a clear sign that summer had ended. I leaned over and puked onto the Trans' immaculate lawn. It was time to go.

I walked over to the sliding glass doors that led to the

Trans' living room. The lights were on but it was empty. Had Adam, Will, and the two Nates gone home already? Maybe they were smarter than I thought and arranged rides home with more sober drivers.

Before opening the door, I walked over to the kitchen window to assess the situation. I didn't want to stumble into the house and be confronted by Alex's parents asking me all sorts of uncomfortable questions about why I chose to come to their house after school to take a stoner's nap.

Staying close to the stucco wall, I peered into the kitchen window and saw the Trans squeezed around a kitchen table eating dinner. Mom and Dad were listening to Alex's little sister, a cute girl in pigtails, talk excitedly using wild hand gestures. Even Alex, who normally doesn't respond to the adorable, seemed engaged in her story. Maybe she had stood up to a bully or performed the winning move in the school's four-square tournament. When the girl was finished, both parents shook their heads in mock disapproval, but you could tell by the way they did it that they were proud of their plucky little daughter. The mom refilled the girl's glass with milk and tucked a loose strand of hair behind the girl's ear.

I blinked in disbelief. This was not the portrait Alex painted of his family when he talked about them to me. Part of the reason we bonded was because we both felt abandoned by our hardworking parents. At least Alex's parents made time in their day to eat with him. Here he was, a convicted felon, and the dinner scene looked like something you'd see in a sitcom, the kind where the sane family lived with a wacky grandfather or had crazy neighbors visiting throughout the day. I glanced back at my puke on the Trans' lawn and quickly came to the conclusion that I was that crazy neighbor and left quietly by the side gate.

My car was chilly when I got in, so I cranked the heat. Before I pulled away from the curb, I caught sight of my reflection in the rearview mirror. On my forehead was the word "LOSER" printed in black Sharpie. I had to hand it to the guys. They knew enough to write the letters backward and reversed so they would look right in the mirror.

THREE

I pulled into our garage just before eight. As soon as I entered the house, my dad pinged me with a message saying he was working late. He'd installed surveillance cameras throughout the whole house so he and Mom could "stay connected." I threw my backpack on the kitchen table and waved to the camera above the refrigerator. A few seconds later, my phone rang.

"What's on your face?" Dad asked.

Oh shit. The Sharpie. I forgot to scrub it off. "Nothing," I said. "Just some prank my friends pulled on me."

"Your friends are idiots." My dad's enthusiasm for Alex and the others had waned considerably since ninth grade, when none of us made varsity anything. "How was your meeting with the principal? Did he like my letter?"

"He did not. What did you say to him?"

I could hear the sound of ice clinking against glass as my dad took a sip of something. Probably Scotch. "I informed him that suspending you for a harmless prank would jeopardize your education and that was something my firm took very seriously."

"It wasn't a suspension hearing," I corrected. "It was an expulsion hearing."

Dad harrumphed. "It was a waste of time is what it was," he said. "Nothing was going to happen. Not if Stone knows what's good for him."

"Well, I'm now a member of the Buddy Club."

"What's that?"

I explained the mission of the club as best I could.

"Sounds like you're a dog walker," Dad grumbled.

"My counselor says I need things like this for colleges."

"I'll talk to someone about getting the name changed to something that might actually impress someone. Something like 'Leadership Team' or 'Operation Rescue.'"

"Sounds great, Dad." I didn't see what either of his proposed titles had to do with the club's purpose, but I didn't feel like arguing.

"Your mother left you a video message on the website."

"Ugh."

"You better respond or things will get ugly."

"I will. I'm going to eat now."

"Tell Estrella to leave mine in the microwave. I'll heat it up when I get home. Oh, and Lawrence?"

"Yes."

"No more screwups. This year is too important for college. If you don't get your shit together, we *will* send you to Langdon Military Academy."

I gulped. Langdon was a year-round boarding school in North Dakota, which actually used the term "correctional facility" on its About Us page. According to their website, they specialized in helping troubled teens find acceptance with themselves and elite colleges. My parents had been threatening to send me there since August. "Don't worry, Dad," I said, and hung up the phone.

I opened our family website to watch Mom's message. She was in New York promoting her book *The Connected Clan: A How-to Guide for Virtual Parenting*, and looked stressed out and tired. Apparently, she had run into a bit of criticism from the hosts of the morning news shows. "These people refuse to accept reality," she complained from her hotel room, checking her email on her phone. Even on camera she couldn't stop multitasking. "If you want a relationship with your kids, you've got to meet them where they live. Am I right?" I would have to respond to this question with my own video, which would require scrubbing my face clean first.

Estrella, our cook, brought me my dinner, which I ate at the bar that separates our kitchen from our living room. She looked at me strangely, probably trying to figure out the meaning of RESOL and why I had the word printed on my forehead. I felt bad for giving her another reason to hate the English language, but I didn't have the energy to explain the prank. Instead, I told her about my plans to mentor under-privileged youth.

"Voy a ayudar a un chico nuevo en mi escuela," I said.

Estrella did that thing she always does when I share a piece of good news—she moved her finger in a crosslike fashion across her massive chest and began talking to God as if he were sitting with a beer on the couch in the next room. After thanking the Lord for this blessing, she turned to me and asked, *"¿Quién es el chico?"*

"No sé," I said. *"Creo que es un poco . . ."* I didn't know the word for "weird" so I used the closest word in my Spanish vocabulary. *"Estúpido."*

Estrella pressed her doughy hands against my cheeks and kissed me on my forehead. *"Tú eres un buen hijo, ¿sabes?"* I nodded and politely excused myself from the table.

I went upstairs to my room and closed the door to block out the sound of Estrella's telenovela. Sometimes I watched the shows with her. Our favorite was *Secretos Subterráneos*, a soap opera set somewhere in Chile. Every week an unfortunate miner gets trapped two hundred feet underground and needs to be saved by a rescue team, headed by the sexy scientist Lana Elena Graciela Jimenez Rodriguez.

Before cracking the books, I went to the bathroom and used a sandpaper sponge to wipe off my face tattoo. Even after repeated scrubbings the lettering didn't disappear completely. Looks like I was stuck with this label for the next couple of days.

It was too late to Skype Mom, so I recorded a video message telling her about the expulsion hearing and my sudden interest in philanthropy. "I'm really looking forward to giving back to my community," I said, trying to keep the sarcasm out of my voice. This took a couple of takes. Like, thirty. When I was satisfied with the results, I posted the video on our website for Mom to watch tomorrow.

I closed my laptop and emptied my backpack on my desk. *The Odyssey* landed on top of the pile of textbooks, handouts, and notebooks, which I took as a sign that the gods wanted me to prioritize English over math. I grabbed the book and hopped on my bed to continue reading.

> They started at once, and went about among the Lotus-eaters, who did them no hurt, but gave them

to eat of the lotus, which was so delicious that those who ate of it left off caring about home, and did not even want to go back and say what had happened to them, but were for staying and munching lotus with the Lotus-eaters without thinking further of their return; nevertheless, though they wept bitterly I forced them back to the ships and made them fast under the benches.

Sometimes a writer is so good it can feel like he's talking directly to you. Homer was basically describing my day here. My friends and I were Lotus-eaters. All we did was sit around, smoke pot, and play video games. Lunley was trying to get me off this island, only with less aggressive tactics. Maybe what I needed was for someone to tie me up and drag me under a bench. That is essentially what Stone did to Alex by transferring him to Quiet Haven. For the first time since we got in trouble, I was a little jealous of Alex's punishment. Now that he was kicked out of school, he had no choice but to get his shit together. As long as the decision was up to me, I would always take the easy way out.

I needed to be more like Odysseus—a man with a purpose. Odysseus overcame the obstacles in his life because he had to get back to Penelope. What purpose did I have? I hadn't a clue. All I knew was that I was never going to find it hanging on this friggin' island with all these lotus plants. I needed something else to focus on.

Glancing over at my desk, I saw the slip of paper Lunley had given me wedged between my trig and Spanish textbooks. I reached over and pulled it free and saw Spencer's name and phone number. Here's a small step in the right direction, I thought. Colleges love to see applicants devote themselves selflessly to community service. Maybe Spencer would have some terminal disease that I could turn into an inspiring personal essay.

I dialed the number written below his name and hoped the call went to voicemail.

"Hello?" a dull, monotone voice said.

"Is Spencer home?"

"This is Spencer."

"Really? You sound like you're forty."

"I'm fourteen."

"I'm your mentor. From Meridian High."

"Excuse me?"

"Your mentor."

"I didn't ask for a mentor."

"You didn't?"

"No."

"Well, I guess they're just assigned. Like lockers."

Silence. I hated talking on the phone.

"So, I was wondering if you want to get together tomor-row."

"What is your name?"

"Oh, sorry. My name is Lawrence. But you can call me Lawman."

"I think I'll call you Lawrence."

"That's cool. So, tomorrow? How about lunch?"

"Okay."

"In the cafeteria."

"Okay."

"So, I'll see you then."

"Okay."

"See ya."

"Good-bye."

I leaned back and started folding the piece of paper with Spencer's name on it. I wanted to come up with the right symbol for my mentee, something that would represent the metamorphosis he was about to experience through his work with me. A tadpole was an easy shape and would allow me to get back to my homework sooner. But tadpoles change into frogs, which didn't seem like much of an upgrade. Cat-erpillars required more complicated folding and changed into beautiful, soaring butterflies—the perfect metaphor for my little protégé. I worked on the piece for nearly an hour.

Origami always relaxed me, like pot without the paranoia. When finished, I took it to the shoebox in my closet and gently placed it with the other works of art I keep hidden from my parents. With a clearer focus, I returned to my reading to see what troubles Odysseus encountered next.

FOUR

Mom pinged me with one of her surveys the following morning as I was leaving for school. She sends me these questions throughout the day and will respond with a phone call or a website link depending on my answer. Today's question was: *Are you experiencing shortness of breath or choked feelings?* I clicked the "no" option to avoid the follow-up questions, added a smiley face emoji, and got in my car. I imagined her showing my response to a skeptical reporter covering her book tour. "See?" she'd say, holding up her phone. "He's fine."

To be honest, I was experiencing some choked feelings about my first meeting with Spencer. I knew *I'd* make a good first impression, but I had no idea how lame *he* was going to be. Walking into the cafeteria at lunch, I immediately regretted picking this as the spot for our first meeting. The place was packed with people waiting in line to buy food or eating their lunches at the round tables scattered across the room. What would my peers think when they saw me eating with a freshman? I wished I'd brought a little sign that said *Do Not Disturb—Mentoring in Process* to put on our table.

I scanned the area for someone who matched my mental image of Spencer Knudsen, who I pictured as a pudgy boy in lederhosen, like the kids in *The Sound of Music*. Did that take place in Norway? I now regretted not brushing up on my geography prior to this meeting.

Someone tapped me on the shoulder. I turned and saw a mini adult wearing a white button-down shirt and black trousers, which still looked freshly pressed and ironed. With his violin case, he might as well have been on his way to a concert at our performing arts center. The pasty boy extended a hand for me to shake. "Mr. Barry, I presume," he said without looking me in the eye.

"Spencer?" I said. My first thought was: Fuck!

We found space at a table and sat down. I looked around and was relieved to see no one I knew. Yes, yes, I know. This makes me a shallow prick. I totally own up to the fact that it matters what people think of me. For as long as I can remember, my dad has drilled it into my head that the real three *R*s of school are Relationships, Reputation, and Real Estate. For him, being successful means a) knowing the right people; b) having them think highly of you; and c) owning the most desirable space on campus. (Although, I think this last point is not meant to be taken literally, unless it's possible to buy the section of the quad where all the cool people hang out.) Currently, I was failing in all three *Rs*. I was in the cafeteria eating lunch with a freshman who looked like he had memorized the periodic table of elements in the first grade.

Spencer dug into his rolling backpack and removed a mini ice chest. His food was housed in tiny plastic containers, which he arranged carefully on the table in front of us. There was something goopy that looked like homemade yogurt, a small bowl of pasta covered in Alfredo sauce, and a peeled and diced pear. Nothing he ate had any color. It was like his mom had killed his lunch and packed its ghost in Tupperware.

"How did you know who I was?" I asked.

"I Googled your name. The only picture I found was of you vomiting in a toilet."

"Good to know." Eventually, I would have to clean up my digital life as well as my actual life. Baby steps, I reminded myself, baby steps.

"So, Norway huh?"

"That is where I'm from, yes."

"I bet it's cold there."

"Oslo is negative four degrees in January."

"Yikes."

"Of course, that's Celsius. In Fahrenheit it would be . . ." Spencer paused. "Twenty-four degrees."

"Which are we?"

"Fahrenheit."

"Right." Boy, did this guy need help. I took a deep breath and dove in with another question.

"So, you play the violin?" I nodded toward his case.

"Viola," he corrected.

"What's the difference?"

"A viola has a deeper sound than a violin."

"Like a cello?"

"A cello is an octave below the viola."

"Other hobbies?"

"I enjoy astronomy."

"Seriously?" I mumbled. Was this kid in training for the nerd decathlon? He was hopeless. If he were looking through his telescope, he wouldn't be able to see Planet Cool from where he was standing. He reminded me a little of me, back before I met Alex. Back when I went to origami conventions and tried to learn Japanese so I could read all of Akira Yoshizawa's books.

But I didn't want to turn Spencer into a pothead, not that he seemed the type to go in for that kind of thing. The problem was he wasn't an athlete, funny, or good-looking (unless you were attracted to young Harry Potter types minus the scar and magical powers). You needed at least one of these attributes if you were going to be cool and didn't want to smoke pot. He was a musician. That was something. But he played the viola, not the most popular instrument for garage bands. I did a quick Wikipedia search on my smartphone and only came up with one violist who was remotely cool. John Cale used the viola in some Velvet Underground songs, but I was pretty sure he also used heroin, which made him less than a perfect role model. This was going to take some time.

"I think we should meet twice a week," I said.

"Hey, Lawman," Will said, sneaking up behind me and whipping off my baseball hat. "RESOL" could still be seen on my face so I slapped a free hand over my forehead.

"Give me back my hat, you fucker," I said.

The guys took great delight in watching me dance between them as they tossed my hat around the circle. I glanced over at Spencer and saw him frozen like a statue amid the mayhem.

"You have something on your face," Adam said, imitating someone politely warning an unsuspecting person of an unsightly food particle wedged in his teeth.

"What's RESOL mean?" Nate asked.

"Is that some kind of Satanic cult?" the other Nate asked.

"Ha ha. Very funny. Can I have my hat back now?" Will tossed me my hat. "Assholes," I said as they all grabbed chairs and sat around our table.

"Who's your friend?" Adam asked.

"Is he your math tutor?" Nate asked.

"What do you guys want?" I said.

"We need a ride to Taco Bell," the other Nate said.

"I'm kinda busy here," I said. My mind scrambled to think of a way to explain Spencer. If I told them about the Buddy Club, there'd be no end to the hazing.

"C'mon, dude," Will said. "We're starving."

"You can copy my trig homework," Adam said.

"Give your tutor a break. I'm sure he's exhausted explaining polynomials," Nate said.

"Polynomials are covered in algebra, not trigonometry," Spencer said.

"Oh, snap!" Adam said. "The little dude just out-mathed you."

"Nerd alert, nerd alert," Will shouted.

I wanted to shield Spencer from more comebacks coming his way. The only way I knew to end their taunting was to give them what they wanted. "Fine," I said. "I'll take you to Taco Bell."

The guys whooped and hollered and stormed out of the cafeteria.

"Sorry, Spencer," I said, standing up. "Mind if we continue this tomorrow?"

"Tomorrow is fine."

"Can we change our meeting time though?"

"What time would you prefer?"

"How about we meet for breakfast instead?" There'd be less douchebags in the cafeteria then, I assumed.

"That's fine, but it has to be at seven, since I have orchestra at seven thirty."

"Works for me," I said, grimacing. I hadn't woken up before 7:00 a.m. since my dad's regular golf caddy got a concussion from a wayward line drive. After today's embarrassment, though, I owed it to him.

"Later." I held out my hand for a fist bump. Spencer looked at me like I was offering him a bruised apple from the cafeteria fruit bowl and left me hanging.

FIVE

It was tough waking up at 6:30 the next morning, but one thing you should know about Lawrence Barry is that he honors his commitments. I knew a 7:00 a.m. meeting would be difficult, given that my faulty alarm clock always shuts down with repeated fist pounding. So I placed the clock in my underwear drawer about thirty feet away from my bed. When the alarm sounded, I had no other choice but to leave my warm bed and dig through my boxers to shut the thing off.

Mom had posted another video message on our family website. She had filmed it in the back of a cab, probably on her way to another talk show. She looked a bit like one of those Real Housewives, the ones that border on crazy. Maybe she was just overcaffeinated or nervous about her interview.

"Hey, honey, it's Mom," she began, not realizing this

kind of introduction was unnecessary in a video chat. "I miss you. Hope you're doing well after all that funny business at school."

I assumed the "funny business" she was referring to was my near expulsion.

"Send me a video and tell me how you're feeling. I'm going to be swamped all day, but I want to hear from you. People here are still having trouble with our site, so the more emotional you can make the post, the better. I need it by noon your time. Okay, honey. Kiss, kiss."

The video ended. I instinctively gave her puckered face the finger. Mom had taken an awesome piece of technology and turned it against me. Now I was going to have to find time during the day to cry in front of the camera so she'd have her proof of concept. Maybe instead of sadness, I could express how I was really feeling. That would require hurling my phone against the wall though, which would hurt me more than it would her.

I was five minutes late when I arrived at school, so I parked in Mrs. Coolidge's space in the faculty lot to cut my walk to the cafeteria down by a minute. Mrs. Coolidge's out on maternity leave so the prime parking space would be vacant anyway. My convertible BMW stood out amongst the teachers' Priuses and electric cars, but hopefully no one would object to me classing up this section of the lot.

Spencer was in the cafeteria when I arrived, dressed in the same white shirt and black pants as the day before. His jet-black hair looked almost toupee-like in its perfection—not a strand out of place. He was reading a giant brick of a book titled, *Quantum Mechanics Non-Relativistic Theory Volume 3*. "WTF, dude," I said, pushing the book aside and sitting down.

"Good morning, Lawrence," he said.

"'S'up," I said. I placed the list of discussion items that I had brainstormed the night before in front of him. "I thought this could be our syllabus for the next couple of weeks."

Spencer examined the list. "What's this word?" he said, pointing to the first lesson.

"Pantsed," I said.

"I wasn't aware pants could be used as a verb."

"It's when someone pulls your pants down in gym. There are ways to avoid it."

Spencer continued reading.

"Why must I pretend to know karate?" he asked, referring to agenda item four.

"Well, you're not going to win any physical fights, so you have to appear like you're trained in some lethal martial art you only use in self-defense."

"And this lesson about my belt?"

"That's easy. Don't wear one."

"Why not?"

"It's not cool," I said, lifting up my T-shirt to show him my belt-less cargo shorts. "You want your pants to hang off your butt."

"That doesn't look comfortable," Spencer said.

"Being cool isn't about being comfortable," I said. "It's about creating an image. Speaking of which, you've got to lose those cuff links. It looks like you're going to a funeral."

"Who died?" a deep, hoarse voice said from behind me.

I could tell by the sudden eclipse of the sun that Zoe Cosmos had entered the cafeteria. She was only a sophomore, but she had the soul of an ancient Greek witch. We were in the same art class last year and she only drew pictures of dark orbs and serpents.

What was she doing at school so early? Shouldn't she be getting back into her coffin by now? I hadn't anticipated defending my mentee against this she-devil. I squeaked a response to her question but even I didn't understand the sound that came out of my mouth. Truth was, I was powerless when it came to Zoe Cosmos. Her jet-black hair, narrow eyes, and sharp cheekbones looked like they were designed by a Disney animator to scare small children. The best thing I could hope for was that one of her ravens would beckon her to some fresh roadkill on the other side of campus.

"Who's your friend, Lawrence?"

"I'm Spencer Knudsen." My mentee spoke up when he saw I was having trouble breathing.

"Nice to meet you, Spencer," Zoe said, extending her claw. Spencer stared at her hand but did nothing. Maybe Norwegians have some other form of greeting, like the kissing French or the bowing Japanese.

"We're kinda busy here, Zoe," I managed to say.

"Fine," she said. "See you around." And she slithered away.

I should probably explain my rudeness lest you come to the inaccurate conclusion that I am some woman-hating misogynist. I am not. I love the ladies and strongly believe we need to break the glass ceiling to help them ascend into the stratosphere of equality.

With that said, I must confess there are some women who frighten me. I get chills whenever Nancy Grace is on television, and I failed freshman algebra because my teacher, Ms. Helman, had these froglike eyes that shot lasers. (Full disclosure, I was often high when I went to algebra.)

With Zoe Cosmos, though, things are more complicated. Have you ever stood on the edge of a cliff and had to resist the urge to jump? Or wanted to accelerate into the car ahead of you on the freeway? Then you have some idea of how Zoe makes me feel. I guess you could say I'm simultaneously attracted to and repelled by her. If I'm Odysseus, then she is my siren, the girl who tries to lure me to my death by singing on some craggy shore. The best thing I can do when she's around is plug my ears with beeswax and keep moving.

"So that was Zoe," I said.

"Okay."

"Why don't you shake hands?" I asked.

"I don't like touching people."

"Okay, normally, I'd think that's weird, but in Zoe's case, it's probably good policy."

"She seems nice," Spencer said.

"She's not. Trust me on this."

We sat in silence. Zoe had seriously interrupted my mentoring flow. I looked at my list of discussion topics, hoping to find my place again. Was it too early to start my lecture on body spray etiquette?

"I noticed you arrived from the south today," Spencer said.

"Excuse me?"

"The student parking lot is located on the north side of campus, but you arrived from over there." He pointed toward the faculty parking lot.

"Yeah, I was kinda late, so I grabbed an open space in the teachers' lot."

"Mrs. Coolidge's spot?"

"Yeah. How did you know?"

"I just saw her walk past with Principal Stone. She looked . . . upset."

"Shit!" I said, pushing my chair back and bolting for the door.

"You might want to give Mrs. Coolidge this," Spencer said, handing me his blueberry muffin, still wrapped in cellophane. I took off toward the faculty parking lot.

Sure enough, my car was surrounded by Mrs. Coolidge and Principal Stone, both looking grumpy and bloated. Apologies flowed from my mouth like beer from a poorly tapped keg. The food offering appeased Mrs. Coolidge. "Thanks. I'm starving!" she said, regarding the muffin as if she had just birthed it.

"Lawrence," Stone said, shaking his bald head and furrowing his shaggy eyebrows. "I should have known."

"I just had to run into the cafeteria to tell my mentee I was running late."

Stone muttered something about no good deed going unpunished to Mrs. Coolidge, who couldn't respond due to the muffin in her mouth. He pointed a stubby finger in my direction. "You just can't stay out of trouble, can you?"

"I'm sorry," I said. "I really am meeting my partner from the Buddy Club. You can ask Lunley if you don't believe me. His name's Spencer Knudsen. He's a freshman. From Norway. I'm helping him."

"Why don't you help him understand our policy on student parking?" Stone asked.

"Well, he doesn't drive, so it's probably not necessary. Believe me, he's got more pressing issues we need to tackle first."

Stone walked over and rapped his knuckles against my skull. "Maybe you should cover the consequences of repeatedly breaking school rules and pissing off the principal? I can arrange for a 'scared straight' tour of Quiet Haven if you think it would help."

"Not necessary," I said, getting the gist of his message. "This won't happen again."

After moving my BMW to a space in the more distant student parking lot, I hiked back to the cafeteria.

I found Spencer flipping through the pages of his *Quantum Mechanics* book and collapsed next to him.

"Phew," I said. "That was a close call."

"Are you sure these morning meetings work with your schedule?"

"My what?"

"If we are going to meet regularly, I'd like it to be on the same days at the same time in the same place."

"I'm more of a spontaneous kind of guy. Why don't I just text you?"

"I don't text."

"What do you mean?"

"I don't have a cell phone."

I stared at him. Mouth agrape, if that's the correct term. "You. Don't. Have. A. Cell phone?" Spencer could have said he didn't have one of his testicles and it would have surprised me less. "You mean you don't have an iPhone?" I whipped mine out and showed it to him as a visual aid. "That's cool. You got an Android?"

"I don't have a cell phone."

"TracFone?"

Spencer shook his head.

"Oh my God." I don't know if I said these words aloud, but they were echoing in my head, along with that ominous music that signals the death of every minor character in horror movies. "You have to get a cell phone."

"Why?"

"Why? Why? Because, it's, like, everything." There was no single reason I could articulate. It's like trying to answer why you need oxygen. Well, no, that's easy. How about sight or hearing? Sure, you could survive without one of your senses, but think about all the amazing things you'd miss out on. Cell phones were like that.

"Can we schedule our meetings at this time and place?" Spencer repeated.

"Uh, sure," I said. It probably wouldn't hurt me to start

out each day in the company of someone who reads about quantum mechanics at breakfast. These morning meetings would also help me avoid my wake-and-bake routine at home. Plus, there were fewer people at school this early who could hassle me for spending time with such a nerdy freshman.

"Can I ask you a question?" Spencer said.

"What's up?"

"Why did your friends write that word on your face?"

"Oh that," I said, instinctively touching my forehead. "It was just a joke."

"I don't get it."

"Get what?"

"What's the joke?"

"Oh, see, I passed out and they thought it would be funny to write the word 'loser' backward on my face so I would see it in the mirror."

Spencer stared at me, expressionless. "I have trouble understanding humor," he said finally.

"That's okay," I said. "It's not really funny."

I pulled out a map of the school I had printed from home. I was in the middle of highlighting the safest bathrooms for freshmen to use at lunch when the bell rang. Spencer packed up his belongings, nodded curtly, and walked off with his wheeled backpack. I followed closely behind, not saying anything about the rolling monstrosity he dragged behind him. First period was about to start and I needed to make the transition from teacher to student. We could address the backpack issue at our next meeting.

SIX

The rest of my morning proceeded without incident, which made conjuring a satisfactory emotion for Mom's video challenging. My hope was that I would come up with something in fourth-period Yearbook, which was a class with minimal supervision. All Mr. Koran, our "adviser," did during the period was grade his English papers and bid on baseball cards on eBay. Occasionally he'd confer with Crystal Nguyen, our editor in chief, about an approaching deadline, but other than that, the class was an opportunity to chill with my former best friend, Eddie Salgado.

Eddie was the main reason I looked forward to fourth period. He and I had been tight in middle school, but moved into different social groups when we came to Meridian. We weren't athletes or nerds or musicians, which left us with no real crowd to join. I was adopted by the stoners, and Eddie joined the cheerleading squad after falling in love with its hottest member, Dawn Bronson. "It's so *not* gay," he argued when I said the sport was hurting his image. "You know how much strength it takes to catch a falling one-hundred-twenty-pound girl from a pyramid? A lot more than catching a stupid football, I'll tell you."

"Yes, but those uniforms."

"What? If I were holding a tennis racquet instead of a megaphone, we wouldn't be having this conversation."

He was right on every count. But still, there was something decidedly girly about the whole concept of cheering, right? Teenage boys aren't supposed to be enthusiastic about anything. We're supposed to snort and scoff and call things gay even when we secretly like making macaroni portraits of Katy Perry. Forget I said that.

As you can imagine, the stoners and the cheerleaders rarely socialized with one another, which meant Eddie and I drifted apart. Truth is, we were both embarrassed to be associated with the other. Eddie would see me emerge from a smoke-filled car and look the other way, just as I did when I was forced to watch him perform a handspring at school pep rallies.

Being in Yearbook helped us reconnect and remember how much we liked hanging out. Eddie never drank or got high, so we talked about things that mattered, like which girls in our class were on birth control and which teacher was headed for a nervous breakdown. Today, we were working on our layout for the football team pages, which was hilarious because we thought most of the players were major dicks. We were struggling to find the perfect caption to a photo of two football players kissing on the bench at the last game. The players weren't actually kissing, but through some genius Photoshopping, Eddie was able to make the image look like a scene from a gay Viagra ad.

"How about 'Jerry Tortelli Completes a Pass,'" Eddie suggested. Jerry was the quarterback of our team and the king of the major dicks.

"Too vague."

"'Jerry Tortelli Fumbles the Balls.'"

"Too specific."

"'Jerry Tortelli Loves His Tight End.'"

"Perfect," I said, typing the caption into our layout.

"No, no, no," Crystal said. For someone so stealthy, she certainly had a rigid appearance and demeanor. Everything from her bangs to her moral judgments was cut precise and straight, leaving no room for mystery. With a swift move learned at Mac Camp, she highlighted the image and deleted it from the screen.

"What?" Eddie said.

"The yearbook is not the place to push your personal

agenda," Crystal said.

"What personal agenda?" I asked.

"Your 'everyone is gay' agenda. This week it's Jerry Tortelli. Last week it was Principal Stone."

"You have to admit that photo of him and Officer Hetrick was suggestive."

"They were demonstrating the Heimlich maneuver!"

"Yes, but with such enthusiasm," Eddie said.

"This has got to stop. Eddie, as a gay Latino, you of all people should see that these jokes are offensive."

"I am not a gay Latino!"

"You're not?" Crystal stepped back, struggling to squeeze Eddie into a new mental box. "Isn't your last name Salgado?"

"It's Portuguese. I'm European-American."

"Oh, sorry. What about the whole cheerleading thing?"

Eddie made one of those exasperated grunts people use to indicate they want the conversation to end, pushed his chair back, and stormed out of the room. Crystal looked at me and mouthed the words "What the fuck?"

"Eddie's not gay," I explained.

Crystal recovered from her shock quickly. "I knew that," she said. "I was just making a point about hurtful stereotypes. Maybe now you two will be a little more sensitive." And with that, she stormed off, her short black hair bouncing behind her like an overexcited puppy.

I walked outside to see if Eddie was okay. He was nowhere in the hallway, so I went to the place where everyone goes when they want to cut class: the library. He was sitting in the stacks where they shelve the books on sexually transmitted diseases.

"'S'up," I said.

"You know the worst part about being a male cheerleader?" he asked.

"Having a penis?"

Eddie punched me in the shoulder. Hard. "I've been cheerleading for two years hoping Dawn Bronson would notice me and I'm no closer to dating her now than I was when I was a freshman."

Eddie had been in love with Dawn Bronson ever since he met her at orientation. At the time, she was a sophomore in charge of leading the new students through a school scavenger hunt to help them become more familiar with the campus. The way Eddie describes their first meeting, it sounds like Dawn floated down on a cloud of cotton candy and handed him a scented map, saying, "Use this guide to find my secret treasure." Even though she was older and Fox News beautiful (the legal commentators are my dad's favorites), Eddie convinced himself he had a chance with her. So he joined the cheerleading squad and participated in student government and basically followed her around like a sick puppy only to have her develop an allergy to dog hair and throw him in the pound with all her other abandoned admirers.

"Now that she's a senior, this is my last chance to get her to notice me. I was hoping to ask her to homecoming."

"Isn't she dating Jerry Tortelli?"

Eddie moaned and banged his head against a book called *Sex, Lies, and Hook-Ups: What Teens Need to Know.*

I patted Eddie on the back and tried to think of a solution to his problem. It seemed impossible, though. Dawn was the president of the senior class, head cheerleader, and in charge of any hurricane relief effort. She was way out of Eddie's league. He'd have better luck with one of the girls who form the base of the cheerleading pyramid rather than the girl standing at the top.

"Homecoming's lame anyway," I offered, trying to make him feel better.

"Homecoming's not lame. It's the one week that unites our school around our shared values of achievement, community, and respect."

I backed off, seeing I'd touched a cheerleading nerve. Apparently, Eddie could mess with individual football players, but school spirit was off-limits.

"Sorry," I said. "I've been kinda moody since I gave up weed."

"Really?" Eddie said. His mood did a complete 180. "Good for you!"

"And I'm going to college," I said, hoping to pump him up even more.

"That's awesome!"

I could probably say I was going to cure cancer and Eddie would be supportive. It made me feel good to have my own personal cheerleader helping me fight the angry gods who were out to destroy me.

It suddenly occurred to me that Eddie was on his own odyssey back to Ithaca. Dawn was his Penelope and he had sacrificed everything to connect with her. Despite all the trials and tribulations he had experienced, he never lost sight of his goal: to hook up with the hottest girl at Meridian. Maybe he could teach me something about focus and commitment.

"Wanna go to the taco truck?" I asked. We had five minutes until the bell rang. Just enough time to pick up our stuff from Yearbook and head to the moving health code violation parked in the back of the school.

"That would be great," Eddie said.

This felt good, I told myself. Like I was moving toward something instead of driving around in circles.

"Want to help me with a video?" I asked on our way back to class. "My mom wants me to share something personal."

"Tell her about giving up weed."

"She doesn't know I smoke weed. Okay, she probably does, but she's never wanted to talk about it."

"What's the point of the video then?"

"To show that families can still be close even when they're far away."

"Sounds like a slogan."

"That *is* her slogan, actually. She's promoting her book now in New York."

"Talk about who you're going to take to homecoming."

"I'm not going to homecoming."

"Then talk about someone you like."

"I don't like anyone."

"That's sad," Eddie said.

It *was* sad. Incredibly sad. Here I was with all these friends, and I'd never felt so alone. Was this the detox talking? Two days without weed and my emotions were all over the map. I felt tears well up in my eyes and there was nothing I could do to stop them.

"Dude, you okay?" Eddie asked, pausing in the hallway.

"Fine," I said. "Actually, this is perfect." I held my phone at arm's length from my face and started recording. "Hey, Mom. Just thinking about how fast things are changing. I can't believe I'm a junior. Pretty soon, I'll be graduating and leaving for college. I wish I could just slow things down, you know? Go back to a simpler time when you used to bring me to your office and let me play with your fax machine. Anyway, enough of this moping. Can't wait to see you. Bye!"

I stopped recording and posted the video on our family site.

"Dude, that was amazing."

"Yeah. My mom will eat that shit up." I sighed. "Now let's go get our lunch."

SEVEN

After a very satisfying taco platter, Eddie left me to attend a junior class meeting in the science wing.

"You should come," he said. "We're brainstorming homecoming float ideas."

"That's okay," I said. As much as I liked hanging out with Eddie, I wasn't quite ready to join his crowd of pep-squad enthusiasts. Don't get me wrong, I liked Meridian just fine; I just didn't see the need to celebrate it during the precious few hours in my day when I'm not being lectured or tested.

"Besides, I have homework to do," I said, giving him a fist bump and heading toward the center quad.

On my way, I passed a group of football players huddled around their quarterback, Jerry Tortelli. Jerry was standing on some elevated platform, holding court like he was Coach Harkness running through a complicated play. I steered clear, careful not to draw any attention to myself. I wasn't a target for these guys, but I knew it didn't take much to piss them off. Some of them responded to eye contact with a punch in the face.

I was hugging the opposite wall, keeping my head down, when I noticed the object Jerry was standing on to address his bloodthirsty crew. It was Spencer's rolling backpack. My little mentee's hand was still clinging to the elongated handle, and he looked agitated and uncomfortable.

What's a mentor supposed to do in this scenario? My mind quickly ran through my options. I could bravely stand up to a bunch of assholes hopped up on Red Bull and steroids and demand they release my little buddy from captivity. This didn't seem advisable, however, unless I didn't mind spending the rest of the year in a body cast. I could run and snitch to the administration, but this might also lead to bodily disfigurement. Besides, no one in the front office would believe me after the number of pranks I had pulled. That left me with one other option: keep walking and silently pray for the gods to intervene.

I picked up my pace and kept my eyes focused on the ground, trying not to feel guilty. My hands started to sweat, making me smell like moldy cheese baking in the sun, another stinky side effect of my detox process. I made a quick detour toward the parking lot so I could douse myself with the Axe body spray I kept in my car for just such an emergency.

After freshening up, I closed the top of my convertible for some privacy and reflected on my actions. Should I have intervened? I mean, who was Spencer to me anyway? We'd met twice and exchanged a few words. Did we have the kind of relationship that required me to sacrifice my life in order to save him from embarrassment? Is that what good mentors do? I didn't see anything in the Buddy Club charter that required me to damage my reputation and/or face in order to help my mentee "more fully integrate into the Meridian school community."

Normally I wouldn't get this worked up over something so minor. I mean, being picked on by jocks is a rite of passage all freshman boys go through, right? At least they weren't dumping Spencer headfirst into a trash can or toilet. If I were still getting high, I'd be able to forget about the incident or at the very least find something hilarious about it to share with my friends. But I wasn't getting high, so now I had to deal with all these big feels, which sucked.

A squirrel paused in its dash along the fence that separated the parking lot from the football field. It turned and looked at me. "You did well to run away," he said, giving me a tiny thumbs-up.

I shook my head. I thought these visions only came when I was high or hungover.

"Heroes' lives always end in tragedy," the squirrel said. "And snitches get stitches."

Then he darted off.

I rolled down the window and released the toxic cloud of Axe body spray that had polluted my car and brain.

Despite the squirrel's pardon, I still felt bad for leaving Spencer to fend for himself. So after school I drove to REI and bought Spencer a normal, shoulder-strap backpack, which I presented to him at our breakfast meeting the following day.

"What's this?" he asked.

"It's a backpack," I said.

"I see that, but why are you giving it to me?"

"It's standard issue. All new students get them. Don't feel obligated to write me a thank-you note or anything."

Spencer glanced at my peace offering and said, "Thank you, but I prefer this model." He pointed to his rolling suitcase, now cleaned of Jerry's footprints.

"But the other one you don't have to wheel around."

"Those wheels relieve the stress on my neck and back," Spencer said.

"Yes, but they damage your reputation," I said.

Spencer raised an eyebrow.

"Your freshman year is when you create the impression that will last the four years you're in high school," I began. "Just ask Freddy Wilmington. He snarted in class his first year and graduated with the nickname Stinky. You have to take control of your reputation early or others will define you by their terms." (I could have used myself as an example here—some people still refer to me as "Snore-i-gami" in reference to the numerous origami presentations I made in seventh grade—but I didn't want to lose face in front of my protégé.)

"Are you referring to the incident with the football players?" Spencer asked.

"What? No. Did you have an incident? That's weird. I had no idea. What were they doing? Like, harassing you?"

"It was upsetting, but it ended as soon as I directed Mr. Tortelli's attention to something of greater interest."

"Which was?"

"Miss Dawn Bronson's flirtation with a wrestler."

"Dawn was flirting with a wrestler?" Maybe there was hope for Eddie after all. "You think she and Jerry broke up?"

"I believe they are in a period of transition. Miss Bronson recently removed the photo taken of them at last year's winter formal from the cover of her binder."

"How do you know this?"

"Miss Bronson is in my calculus class."

"Can you give me a minute?" I took out my phone and texted Eddie the news. Within seconds my phone rang.

"Holy shit," Eddie said by way of greeting.

"I know."

"Are you sure?"

"That's what Spencer said."

"Who's Spencer again?"

"The kid I'm mentoring," I said, resisting the urge to ruffle Spencer's hair. "He and Dawn are in the same calculus class."

"He's a freshman?" Eddie asked.

"Yes."

"And he's taking calculus?"

"Uh-huh."

"And you're his mentor?"

"Yup."

There was a long pause.

"You still there?" I asked.

"Yup," Eddie said.

"Let's talk more in Yearbook," I said, and hung up. "Thanks for that bit of information, Spencer. You've made one male cheerleader very happy."

Spencer didn't acknowledge the compliment. He was too busy trying to figure out how to fit the new backpack in his rollaway bag.

"Don't worry about the backpack," I said, taking it off his hands. "I can return it."

Eddie and I spent most of Yearbook doing a close reading of Dawn's Facebook page. She had 3,050 friends, not an exclusive group by any means. There were some powerful names in her circle, including a couple of Steve Jobs's kids and a Coppola. Dad would be happy if I were included in this network. I made a mental note to have Eddie help me with a friend request.

"Her relationship status changed to 'it's complicated' two days ago," Eddie said.

"She sure posts a lot of Bible verses," I said, scrolling through her feed.

"She's very devout," Eddie said. "Like an angel."

"If she's so religious, why was she with an asshole like Jerry?"

"What's this about Jerry?" Crystal asked, appearing out of nowhere. Seriously, the girl has mad ninja skills. And that's not racist, because it's a compliment. I wish I could be as sneaky and aggressive. Okay, now that I hear it, it does sound kind of racist. I don't like Crystal very much, to be honest.

"He and Dawn broke up," I said.

"I knew that," Crystal said.

"We don't know it for sure," Eddie clarified. "Dawn hasn't said anything at practice. This seems like the kind of thing she'd bring up for discussion."

"I'm sure Jerry dumped her and she's, like, totally embarrassed," Crystal said.

"Jerry dump Dawn," Eddie scoffed. "I don't think so."

"Jerry could have any girl in the school he wanted. Why

waste his time on a Goody Two-shoes like Dawn Bronson."

"Just because someone is good doesn't make them a Goody Two-shoes," Eddie said, rushing to Dawn's defense.

"Dawn's a future trophy wife," Crystal said. "She might as well be gold plated."

"You take that back!" Eddie said.

"Why? Do you love her?"

"Dawn does more for this school than anyone. She'll be remembered more than you."

"The yearbook decides who gets remembered and who doesn't, and who's in charge of the yearbook? Oh, that's right. I am."

"Come on, Eddie," I said. "Let's go work on our clubs pages."

We were halfway to our workstation when Crystal repeated the line she always says when she's looking to motivate people. "He who controls the past controls the future. He who controls the present controls the past!"

When I got home that afternoon, my dad's Porsche was parked in the garage. This was unusual for four o'clock, so I checked our family website on my phone to see if there was a business trip I had forgotten about, but the week was clear. Mom had a few more author appearances and then she was scheduled to come home this weekend.

"Dad?" I yelled, entering our home. "You here?"

"In the kitchen," he said.

I found him sitting at the table with a venti-size Starbucks cup and his laptop. Estrella hovered nearby, nervously wiping a spotless counter.

"What's up?" I asked.

"Your mom's had an accident," Dad said. "Sit down."

I threw my backpack on the floor and slumped into the first available seat. This was all my fault. I didn't even know what happened and I blamed myself. I had made that stupid, phony video and it probably caused Mom to have a heart attack or something. God, I was such an asshole. Why couldn't I just do the things my parents asked me to do?

"Your mom broke her hip," Dad said.

"What? How?" I asked.

"She wasn't paying attention and walked in front of a cab," Dad said.

"Was she on her phone?"

Dad shrugged. "Probably," he said. "Isn't she always?"

I pictured her watching my video on a busy Manhattan street, mesmerized by the emotional confession I had bullshitted. What if she had been hit by a bus? Or fallen down a manhole?

"I want to see her," I said.

"That's nice, Lawrence, but now's not the time. She's

scheduled for surgery tomorrow. After that, she'll be recu-
perating at Aunt Lucy's on Long Island."

"How long?"

"Don't know. It depends on her recovery. The doctors say
she can't get on a plane for at least three weeks."

"She's going to be at Aunt Lucy's for three weeks?" I asked.
Mom had avoided her sister's house during her visit because
she had only three bedrooms and four out-of-control kids.

"She's going to need help with her physical therapy, and
Lucy's a nurse. There was really no way out of it."

"When can I see her?"

"Do you think that's a good idea? The school year's just
started, and you've already gotten in trouble. You were nearly
suspended."

Expulsed, I wanted to correct him, but didn't think that
was an actual word.

"I don't want you missing classes and falling behind.
This year's too important. You've got to turn things around if
you're going to have any hope of getting into a good college."

"But she needs us. Doesn't she?"

"She's not dying, Lawrence. She's going to be fine. How
about we do a Skype session after surgery? Mom would love
that."

"Fine," I said.

"In the meantime, why don't you post a get-well-soon

video for her to see when she wakes up? I know she'd appreciate that."

I picked up my backpack and trudged upstairs to my room. I would make Mom's video in a little bit, after I had calmed down. Right now, all I wanted to do was sit at my desk and get lost in some extreme origami. I took out a dollar bill and started working on a cockroach. It represented how I felt right about now. Maybe after I was done, I could crush it with my fist.

EIGHT

Mom's accident only fueled her drive to spread the gospel of virtual parenting. After being offline for three days during her surgery and recovery, she returned to our family site with a vengeance, bombarding me with videos, blog posts, messages, and surveys. "This is the best thing that could have happened to me," she said in a video post from Aunt Lucy's place. "I'm doing a conference call with the president of VirtueTech next week. He thinks our family website can serve as the prototype for something much bigger. Can you imagine? Our site could be the next Facebook." Mom's enthusiasm was extinguished by the appearance of my cousin, who stuck her jelly-smeared face in the frame and waved hello. In the background, I heard Lucy scream, "Juniper! Leave your aunt alone! She's working!"

If Mom's website went global, I'd be the most hated guy

on the planet. I'd have to go completely off the grid, which was the virtual equivalent of running away from home. Spencer managed to live without a cell phone, but he had only one friend so it was easy for him. If I went offline, I'd be depriving thousands of friends and followers of my daily tweets. Still, it might be worth sacrificing these relationships if I could get away from my parents' surveillance. Better to be an orphan than to be parented by Big Mother.

Speaking of Spencer, our breakfast meetings were quickly becoming a nice routine. Unlike my parents, I actually made an effort to be physically present for our morning meal. The hardest part was getting out of bed at 6:30 a.m., but I solved that problem by buying Estrella a bullhorn and giving her explicit instructions to use it as my alarm clock. She was so invested in seeing me become a good person that she sneaked into my room every morning and blasted my eardrums with the thing. I had become so fearful of the sonic boom that now the sound of her tiptoeing across my carpet was enough to get me out of bed and into the shower.

Sometimes Spencer and I worked on our homework, but most of the time we just hung out. I would explain to him why American high school students don't say the word "dubiously" and he would predict the future. Seriously, I was beginning to think my mentee might have superpowers. In the past two weeks alone, he accurately predicted that:

- Stone would object to my T-shirt of a gun-toting panda.

- I would get sick if I ate the jelly doughnut I found in the back of my car.

- The party at Sally McGovern's house would be canceled because her parents would not be taking their vacation to Aruba. (He figured this one out by monitoring the stock price of Mr. McGovern's biotech company.)

In addition to keeping me in good standing with Stone, our meetings also helped me break my wake-and-bake routine of years past. Between breakfast with Spencer and lunch with Eddie, I managed to be drug free for two whole weeks, a personal record. It was painful at times, what with the dull headaches, excessive sweating, and rubber-cement balls of phlegm coming out of my mouth, but every day the craving for the lotus plant lessened. Unfortunately, this decrease in smoking was accompanied by a decrease in communication with Will, Adam, and the two Nates. They still responded to my texts, but they rarely initiated conversation anymore. I figured this was a temporary glitch in our relationship. Once they saw how much I had achieved through sobriety, I was sure they would want to join me on the wagon. Or was it off the wagon? I never understood the connection between partying and horse-drawn carriages, to be honest.

In the meantime, I enjoyed working on my two projects: making Spencer a cooler person and helping Eddie figure out a way to ask Dawn to homecoming. My two mentees couldn't be more opposite. Spencer was all logic and analysis, super smart in everything except what comes most naturally to people. He could cite the average annual rainfall in the Amazon but not have a clue about how to acknowledge someone in the hallway. Eddie, on the other hand, was all emotion. He'd write pages and pages of love poems to Dawn but never consider how this might lead to a restraining order. Given their respective handicaps, the best thing I could do for Spencer and Eddie was bring them together. I was like a neurosurgeon, uniting the right and left side of the brain to make a complete whole.

"Seriously, I think Spencer could help us," I told Eddie in Yearbook. "He's like Professor Xavier in *X-Men*."

"What does he know about girls, though?"

"Tons!" I said, although to be honest, I wasn't sure Spencer knew girls existed, except as sentient beings who move a bow against a violin. But I was desperate. Homecoming was two weeks away and we weren't any closer to getting Eddie a date with Dawn for the dance.

After the bell rang, we went to the cafeteria, hoping to find Spencer sitting at our usual table. When he wasn't there, I suggested we go to the only safe place for nerdy kids hoping to avoid seeing the bottom of a trash can: the library. Sure enough, we found him at a table, reading some French book.

"What's this?" I asked, tipping the book up so I could read the cover.

"*Cyrano de Bergerac*," Spencer said.

"I didn't know you were taking French."

"I'm already fluent," he said. "This is one of the few French language texts in the library."

"Interesting," I said, trying to put an end to the conversation. "Look, we need your help with something."

I explained Eddie's situation to Spencer, who nodded in his typical fashion. His neutral expression was oddly reassuring. Most other people would laugh in Eddie's face upon hearing his desire to take the most popular girl to homecoming, but Spencer appeared calm and thoughtful, like he was intimately acquainted with such problems.

"It appears that in his attempt to become close to Miss Bronson . . ."

"Call her *Dawn*, Spencer." Spencer had an annoying habit of referring to girls by their last names. It was a verbal tic I had been trying to break for the past few days.

"In his attempt to become close to *Dawn*, Eddie has made himself invisible to her. Like the water a fish cannot see because he's surrounded by it, Eddie has become unrecognizable from the many other admirers in Dawn's entourage."

"He's right," Eddie said. "Yesterday at practice she called me Amanda."

"Ouch."

"What he lacks right now is mystery. He needs to surprise her into seeing him again for the first time. Like Cyrano." Spencer held up the book and I instantly recognized the face on the cover.

"The dude with the big nose!" I said. When Eddie looked at me funny, I explained. "Steve Martin played him in an old movie. Cyrano's this ugly fireman who's got the hots for Roxanne, who's like a mermaid or something. Actually, I think that might be a different movie. Anyway, he knows she's way out of his league, so he puts the moves on her through his good-looking friend."

"That sounds like an adaptation . . ."

"So, I'm the good-looking friend?" Eddie asked.

"No, you're Cyrano. The ugly one," I said.

"I don't get it," Eddie said.

"What Spencer's saying is that your cheerleading costume's like a big nose to Dawn. She'll never see how awesome you are as long as you wear it. So what you need to do is find a sneakier way of hitting on her."

"Actually, that's not what I was suggesting . . ."

"I could be the mascot," Eddie suggested.

"That's perfect!" I said. "You can hide behind the mascot's

mask and tell her how you feel. After she's fallen in love with you, you reveal yourself and ask her to the dance. Ba-bam!"

"Won't Dawn be pissed that I tricked her?" Eddie asked.

"Trust me, dude. Ladies are willing to overlook a little dishonesty when romance is involved." I learned this through my viewing of *Secretos Subterráneos*, but I wasn't going to admit that to these guys.

"This could work," Eddie said.

"It's perfect! What do you think, Spencer?" I asked.

"Perhaps if you simply compose a letter telling Dawn how you really feel . . ." he began.

"Fuck that," I said. "You'll look desperate." Clearly Spencer didn't know anything about the art of seduction.

A roar of laughter interrupted our planning. Across the room, I saw Will and Adam going crazy over something on Chester McFarlane's phone. The librarian walked over to where they were sitting and removed the device from Chester's hand. After she returned to her station, Will, Adam, and Chester pulled out another phone and continued viewing whatever hilarious YouTube video had just gotten them into trouble.

I panicked. Had they seen me with Eddie and Spencer? If so, I could expect a fair amount of hazing about my new "friends." What if they weren't watching a video but filming us huddled around some French play excitedly planning

Eddie's seduction of Dawn? I had to get out of here. This place was *way* too public to be seen doing something that wasn't official mentoring business.

"Let's go talk to Coach Harkness about the mascot," I said. "We've got thirty minutes left before lunch. Spencer, you in?"

"I am not."

"Okay, see you later then."

I grabbed Eddie and headed toward the door. On my way, I picked up an issue of *Rolling Stone* from one of the tables and hid behind it so Adam and the guys wouldn't see me exit the building.

NINE

We spent the rest of the period convincing Coach Harkness to let us revive the old Viking. He seemed to like our idea of keeping the identity of the performer a secret as a way to build interest in what already looked like another dismal football season. We hadn't won any of our three games, not even against the School of Dramatic Arts, the team whose theme song was "Tomorrow" from the musical *Annie*.

"You'll have to fix the head first," Harkness said, leading us into the storage closet and removing the large, bearded costume head, split at the helmet. The sight of the gash was a bit unsettling. I remembered the bloodthirsty cheers that erupted from the stands when our Viking went down, clubbed to death by a mascot that looked like one of the seven dwarves. The harness encasing the actual human's head was a good six inches away from the wound, but the sight of a sharp, spearlike object puncturing the costume was enough to traumatize Jenny Doyle, our previous mascot, for life. I hear she only attends mock trial competitions now.

Getting the Viking head from Harkness's office to my car without anyone noticing would be tricky. In just a few minutes, the halls, quad, and student parking lot would be filled with kids on their way to lunch. If we wanted to avoid any uncomfortable questions, we had to hurry. Eddie draped a *Go Vikings!* banner over the head, stuffed the rest of the costume in a garbage bag, and the two of us ran to my car. If only Mrs. Coolidge had stayed pregnant and not deprived me of a prime parking space, this would have been a whole lot easier.

The head was the size of one of Mr. Lunley's yoga balls and blocked my vision when I held it in front of me. As we approached the parking lot, the banner slid off and I came face-to-face with the Viking, its empty eye sockets staring at me like some Nordic zombie. I hadn't felt such a premonition of doom since I opened my PSAT test packet and saw the word "ruination" staring back at me. Maybe Spencer's hesitation to fully endorse our plan was worth considering more deeply.

"Dude, come on," Eddie said, pulling me back to reality.

We reached my car, popped the trunk, and threw the head in. The bell rang, releasing students to lunch. Rather than get our things from Yearbook, we decided to head to Starbucks and continue planning. As we worked out the details of our seduction plan, we could also come up with an excuse to give Mr. Koran for why we weren't in class all period.

It's amazing what a couple of venti triple-shot caramel macchiatos will do to lift your mood and improve your work ethic. After Eddie and I consumed the appropriate quantities of sugar and caffeine, we felt no cheerleading captain/student body president/future centerfold of *Playboy*'s "Women in Congress" issue was out of our grasp.

"This is totally going to work," Eddie said, folding our brainstorming napkin and tucking it in his back pocket.

"Totally."

The plan was this. We needed a way to keep Eddie's identity a secret while he was performing as the Viking. If he disappeared from the cheerleading squad on the same day the mascot reappeared, everyone would assume he was the man behind the mask. To throw suspicion off him, I volunteered to be the Viking at the next game, which was tomorrow. When people saw Eddie and the mascot together, they'd reach the logical conclusion that they were not the same person and Eddie could take over the role for the rest of the season.

"Have you thought about how you'll transition from team mascot to Dawn's date?" I asked. "The homecoming dance is only two weeks away."

"I have an idea for that," Eddie said. "I've got, like, two volumes of poetry I've written about Dawn at home. Every night, I'll go to her house and recite one in the Viking costume."

"Won't that be a little creepy?"

"Trust me, these poems are good. On the day of the homecoming game, I'm going to reveal my true identity after I've saved her life."

"How are you going to do that?"

Eddie grabbed another napkin out of the dispenser and started diagramming his plan. "Near the end of the third quarter, the cheerleaders make their human pyramid. Dawn is always on top. I'm always on bottom."

I couldn't help but snicker. Eddie slapped me in the face, for either disparaging Dawn or the classic cheerleading routine or both, and then went on with his plan.

"With me gone, they'll probably put Susie McGannon at the base. She's built like a wrestler, but her hands are freakishly small compared to the rest of her body. All it will take is for some clueless yearbook photographer"—here he pointed at me, indicating my role in the plan—"to step on her dainty fingers for the whole structure to collapse, sending Dawn tumbling into the arms of the waiting mascot. After I save Dawn's life and reveal my true identity, I'll ask her to homecoming in front of everyone. There's no way she can say no."

"Unless Jerry Tortelli breaks both your legs for stealing his girlfriend."

"They're broken up, remember?"

"Maybe we should run this by Spencer? See what he thinks?"

"Why? It's perfect. Besides, the less people who know about this, the better. I don't see what could go wrong."

In my head, I fast-forwarded to a scene in which my decapitated head was paraded around the field by the drum major, but kept my pessimism to myself. Eddie must have seen the look of distress on my face though, because he asked, "How's the detox going?"

In the past few weeks, Eddie had become my de-facto sponsor. He was the only one I could confide in about my withdrawal symptoms, and he had been super supportive. "Caffeine helps the depression, but fuels the anxiety," I said.

"I was doing some research online and one site said hot, soothing baths help."

"I'll try that."

"Maybe next time, get only two shots in your caramel macchiato. Or try decaf."

"Good idea."

"I think it's great that you've lasted this long. You've got real willpower."

I felt my eyes welling with tears. No one had ever recognized this quality in me before. "Does any of your research say that sobriety makes you gay? 'Cause I totally want to hug you right now."

"Maybe you used drugs to cope with your gayness."

"Okay, now I want to punch you in the face."

"So, we're good?"

"Yeah, thanks for the pep talk."

And with that, I was ready to don any costume and enter any arena to help my friend win the girl of his dreams. At least now I would be making an ass of myself for a worthy cause.

TEN

The following morning I met Spencer for our usual mentor breakfast. I wanted to run Eddie's plan by him, to see if he could identify any flaws that could get me kicked out of school. I hoped our mascot stunt wasn't crossing some rule hidden in the fine print of the student manual. However, the success of our plot depended on the kind of secrecy required for CIA assassinations or Apple product launches. So instead, I talked about homecoming week, which is something they don't have in Norway.

"Homecoming is when the school unites around the most popular students in the senior class. There are six boys and six girls on homecoming court. The school votes for two of them to serve as king and queen. Personally, I'd prefer it if they competed in some kind of Hunger Games fight to the death, but I'm not the school principal."

Spencer nodded sagely, which is how he always nods. Sometimes, I get the feeling he isn't interested in my tutoring. Take now, for instance. Rather than pepper me with inquiries about the students most likely to win homecoming king and queen, he removed some sheet music from his overstuffed backpack and started tapping out a song with one of his black loafers.

"The floats," I went on, ignoring the metronomic beat of his toe against the sticky linoleum floor, "are built in secret locations by the different classes. Each class has a different take on the theme. You know this year's theme is 'Fairy Tales,' right?"

Spencer nodded again; this time his head followed the beat he tapped out with his shoe.

"Kinda lame, I know. I think the school got a lot of heat for last year's 'Zombie Apocalypse' concept and swung too far in the other direction. I'm sure Dawn Bronson was in charge of picking the theme so she could dress up as Cinderella and wave from a glass carriage or something."

Spencer just stared at me. "Hey!" I snapped my fingers in front of his face to interrupt whatever math calculation he was doing in his head. "Are you listening?"

"Sorry," he said.

"Dawn will be homecoming queen, without a doubt. Whether or not Jerry can intimidate enough voters to choose him as king is the big question."

"I have a question," Spencer said.

"Really?"

"It's about the dance."

"Yes?"

"Is it a formal affair?"

"You mean do people wear tuxes and gowns?"

"Yes."

"It's semiformal, which means you dress like you're going to your court hearing."

"I don't follow."

"Like you're going to a wedding."

"I see."

"Why? Are you thinking about going?"

"It's complicated, but there is this girl . . ."

Our conversation was interrupted by the booming voice of Chester McFarlane, a douchy friend of Will's who hijacked your food by licking it. "Wassup, bro?" he screamed, slapping me on the back of the head. I turned and saw him straddle the chair next to me. "Missed you at Kevin's party last weekend. It was epic."

I nearly choked on my Pop-Tart. Kevin had a party last weekend? Congressman Finley's son, Kevin? Why hadn't I heard about it? Those things were usually tweeted, especially if they were, to use Chester's word, epic. It didn't make sense that Chester would be invited and I wouldn't. Just last month, *he* was the social pariah after he told his father we used a thousand-dollar bottle of wine to make sangria popsicles.

I tried to maintain a calm exterior, but inside my whole sense of self was dissolving like the Pop-Tart in my mouth. "I was busy," I finally managed to say.

"I'd show you pictures, but Kevin confiscated everyone's phones at the door. I guess his dad's running for reelection and he didn't want any evidence leaked to the press."

That explained the social media blackout. I wondered if Kevin cared as much about collecting people's car keys as he did their camera phones.

"This your little brother?" Chester said, turning and nodding at Spencer.

"No," I said. There were two things wrong with this question. First off, Spencer and I were total opposites. If the story of our lives were made into a movie, I would be played by a young Brad Pitt and Spencer would be played by some actor who had emigrated from Eastern Europe circa 1930. Second, I had known Chester since the eighth grade. The fact that he didn't know I was an only child was kinda surprising, even for an idiot like him.

"Chester, this is Spencer. He's . . ." Again, I didn't know how to introduce Spencer. If I said "protégé," Chester would probably punch me. "He's new to the school."

"Well then, beat it, shrimp."

Spencer started packing up his stuff. If he was hurt or offended by Chester's command, he didn't show it. I swear, it would be easier to defend the little guy if he showed an emotion once in a while.

"You can stay, Spencer," I said.

"Seriously, bro?" Chester said, his freckled face screwing up like he'd just tasted the cafeteria's veggie scramble.

"That's okay," Spencer said, gathering his things. "I need to practice the Brook Green Suite 'Prelude' before class."

"Yeah, you do that," Chester snorted. He snatched the remainder of Spencer's dehydrated apricots and shoved them in his mouth. After giving them a few chews, he spit them out on the floor. "Ugh. What are those?"

I wanted to douse the dicktard's red hair with the remains of my latte.

Spencer walked off, dragging his suitcase behind him, leaving me alone with Chester, who gossiped about the party I hadn't been invited to. The event sounded fairly typical, with beer pong tournaments, surprising hookups (one between two people everyone assumed were cousins), and scavenger hunts in the absent parents' bedroom. It didn't sound like I'd missed anything epic, but that wasn't the point. The point was, no one told me about the event prior to it taking place.

Was this my punishment for hanging out with Eddie and Spencer? In my desire to stay sober, I hadn't actually made myself available to my friends, but that was only because they didn't do anything without getting high first. Maybe I should organize some activity we could all do together that didn't require artificial stimulants. Something like bungee jumping or hang-gliding or deep sea exploring. The point was, if I didn't balance my time better, I'd lose membership in this more important social circle. I couldn't ignore the cool people in order to help those in need of coolness. Even Mother Teresa took a break from the lepers every once in a while, right?

The rest of the day passed slowly. I had a harder than usual time concentrating on my classes. With each bell, I became increasingly anxious about performing in front of a stadium crowd. (Okay, there are usually only thirty people in the stands at our football games—we're in Silicon Valley after all, not Texas—but in my imagination that number had grown exponentially to Super Bowl–size attendance.) What does a mascot do, exactly? Was I supposed to work in sync with the cheerleaders? Rouse the fans with some crazy Viking dance? Should I know something about football rules? Because I didn't. Despite my dad's best efforts, I had never taken an interest in football, basketball, baseball, golf, or tennis. I felt like I was in one of those dreams where I show up to a final after skipping the class all semester. Actually, that wasn't a dream. That was freshman year.

By the time Yearbook class rolled around, I was in a full-stage panic attack. I was desperate for something to take the edge off. One bite of a pot brownie would do the trick nicely, and satisfy the sweet tooth I'd developed since going sober. Marijuana wasn't supposed to be addictive. At least, that's what my dealer always told me.

"Live strong," my squirrel spirit guide told me. I heard his voice the same way Luke Skywalker hears Obi-Wan Kenobi during peak moments of stress.

"That's Lance Armstrong's slogan," I replied.

"He stole it from the squirrels," my spirit guide said. "That guy was a real asshole."

"You okay, dude?" Eddie said, passing me a bottle of cranberry juice and a banana.

"What are these?"

"Cranberry juice helps purify the body and the banana gives you the potassium you might have lost through . . . excessive sweating."

I checked my T-shirt and saw two large pit stains darkening the fabric. I did a quick smell test and was relieved to find the moldy cheese odor was no longer there. Still, I must look pretty bad if Eddie was administering this kind of first aid.

Eddie repositioned the pillowcase he had wrapped around

his left arm. This was supposed to be the sling his doctor gave him for his "injury"? This plan was never going to work. We should have brought Spencer in to help us with the details.

"Relax, dude," Eddie said, walking me over to the far corner of the classroom. "I texted the squad to let them know I was injured and that Coach Harkness was bringing back the mascot. I told them he was keeping the mascot's identity a secret to build interest in the game, since the players aren't generating much fan enthusiasm on their own. The girls are psyched."

"I'm not going to get in trouble, am I? Stone will use any excuse to transfer me to Quiet Haven."

"You're not breaking any rule," he said, then added under his breath, "that I know of."

"So, what do I do, exactly?"

Eddie walked me through a couple of easy dance moves. As we were practicing the Vibrating Thumper, Crystal swooped down on us from her perch at the editor's desk. "What are you two doing?" she asked. Her oversize round glasses magnified her suspicious gaze and made you feel guilty even when you weren't doing anything wrong.

"What does it look like we're doing?" Eddie said.

"It looks like you're having a seizure."

"We're practicing dance moves," I said.

"You taking Eddie to homecoming?"

"What if he was?" Eddie asked.

"Then I would applaud your courage for finally embracing your sexual orientation."

"Eddie's going with Dawn," I said, too eager, probably, to reorient our sexual preferences.

Eddie punched me in the shoulder. Crystal laughed out loud.

"Right," she said. "And I'm going with Jerry Tortelli."

"You like Jerry Tortelli?" I asked.

"What? No. Who told you that?"

"Uh, you just did," I said.

Crystal blushed a deep red and then stormed off without giving us any orders to get back to work.

"Whoa, looks like you hit a nerve," Eddie said.

"No wonder she wigged out when we tried to slander him the other day," I said.

The bell rang. Eddie gave me one final, encouraging chest bump. "Break a leg," he said.

"Break an arm," I said.

Eddie lifted his injured arm in mock salute and we parted.

ELEVEN

I parked my car next to the football field and watched the junior varsity game from the comfort of my BMW. I didn't see the point of suiting up and performing for our frosh-soph team, as their fans consisted of stay-at-home moms and supportive girlfriends with their noses stuck in romance novels. The opposing team had an even weaker fan base. Their mascot, a lobster with a pirate's hat, sat in the stands texting—not an easy task when you're wearing large claws over your hands.

The sun and heat were strong for this time of day. I opened the windows to let a weak breeze cool the interior of my car and hydrated myself with Eddie's cranberry juice. There was no way I was going to wear jeans under the Viking costume. I was already sweating like a pig, which is something I've never seen a pig do, by the way. If I didn't want to become one of

Spencer's dehydrated fruits by halftime, I'd have to perform in nothing but this cotton suit and polyfoam mask.

My phone buzzed with another survey question from my mom. I rolled my eyes. This one asked, *Do you dwell on dark mental images?* I clicked the "no" option and stepped out of the car to retrieve my costume. As I unlocked my trunk, suddenly the world turned an ashen gray. Thick storm clouds blanketed the sky, obliterating the light and heat from the sun. A cold wind whipped through the parking lot, reanimating the lifeless trash that littered the area. I had to shield my face from the grit and dust that swirled around me. When the wind died down, I saw Zoe Cosmos standing in front of me, stroking the white fur of a lab rat. "Hello, Lawrence."

"Zoe," I managed. My throat was suddenly dry and hoarse.

"Here to support the team?"

"Yup."

"I, too, have school spirit."

"You do?"

"His name's Jason. He died on the football field twenty-six years ago."

"How?"

"Freak lightning strike."

"That sucks."

"It's why our team is cursed."

"Is Jason with us now?"

"If he were here, you'd feel it in your nether region."

"Okay, well, I gotta be going. See ya."

I ran inside to the nearest bathroom and hid in one of the stalls until light returned to the world. Once I sensed my goose bumps vanishing, I peeked outside and saw the sun quietly reasserting itself in the sky. Birds emerged from hiding and cautiously chirped an "all's clear" to the other living creatures. Before Zoe returned, I retrieved the costume from my car and hustled back to the bathroom to change.

On my way, I waved to the security cameras stationed on top of the lamppost near the entrance to the parking lot. The surveillance system was Stone's brilliant idea to catch a student who had been sneaking onto campus at night and painting caricatures of some of the older and angrier staff members. When kids started getting busted for making out in their cars at lunch, we knew Stone had become drunk with power. With the help of some hippie parents and the ACLU, the students sued, and now Stone is only allowed to film campus activity at night. I had a good three hours before the cameras would be turned on. I could make it back to my car and change before then.

The Viking costume was better suited for sensory-deprivation torture than for rallying support for a losing team. The outfit consisted of large, cumbersome boots, a dress with serrated sleeves and hem, two mittens, an over-size belt, and the polyfoam head. Imagine setting your feet in shoe boxes, wrapping your hands in gauze, and placing a paper grocery bag over your head with tiny holes cut out for seeing, and you get an idea of what it felt like to be our school's mascot. If real Vikings dressed like this, it's no wonder they became extinct.

I bumped into a bike, tree, and flagpole on my way back to my car. After throwing my pile of clothes onto the passenger seat, I stumbled toward the football field and arrived to great fanfare. At least I think it was fanfare. The oversize head amplified and distorted sound so I couldn't tell if people were cheering my arrival or testing the emergency broadcast system. I did hear the announcer of the game exclaim, "Look who's returned from the dead! It's Victor the Viking. Everyone show Victor how happy you are to see him."

A cluster of JV cheerleaders embraced me like I was a returning war hero. A few tried to peek inside my oversize nostrils to see who I was. "Is that you, Phyllis?" I heard one girl say, striking a blow to my male ego. The dress I wore did nothing for my figure, but my arms weren't covered. I flexed a bicep to demonstrate my prowess only to hear another voice say, "Megan? Have you been working out?"

I pushed the girls away and stumbled over to where the varsity cheerleaders were doing their routines. Dawn bounced over, bringing with her the smell of honey and lavender. "Hey, Victor!" she said, her voice singing rather than shouting the words. She was the antithesis of Zoe Cosmos; she brought light and life wherever she stepped. Dawn wrapped an arm around me and immediately all my worries and fears vanished. This must be what it felt like to be popular. If I were to walk onto this field in my normal attire, I wouldn't be noticed, except by administrators in the stands, suspicious that I was at the game to pull a prank or collect bets in some illegal gambling scheme (Note to self: look into starting some illegal gambling scheme for the homecoming game. Spencer can help work the odds in my favor.) But in this costume, I was embraced as one of their own.

Dawn and I danced the Slippery Pup for a bit before she returned to her squad for more cheer routines. I retreated a few steps and found a space where I could perform safely for the crowds. Throughout the first half of the game, I did a medley of dance moves, including the Sprinkle Captain, the Funky Push, and the Ping-Pong. I have to admit, it was pretty fun. Maybe I didn't have to get high to have a good time. To free the inner Lawrence, all I had to do was disguise the outer Lawrence. It worked for Batman.

The crowd cheered me on, more engaged by my antics than by the lackluster game, which stalled at a meager 7–7 tie by halftime. It took me a while to spot Eddie thanks to my limited vision and the fact that the stands had filled with fans since the JV game. Eddie was sitting in the center of the middle row, his arm covered by his pillowcase sling. He probably picked this location for its high visibility, but it also made it impossible for me to reach him without risking serious injury to myself and others. I decided to forgo our planned lap dance and just hope that enough people noticed him in the stands and me on the field and came to the logical conclusion that, given our current understanding of physics, Eddie couldn't exist in two places at the same time.

"Is that you, Eddie?" a voice from behind me asked. I spun around and saw Crystal, camera in hand. She probably couldn't find any photographers to take pictures of the game for the yearbook and came herself to do it. She would snap my photo and attach the caption, *Gay Latino performs in drag at halftime*, unless I stopped her.

"Come on, show me the Punching Screwdriver," she said, raising her Canon and pointing it in my direction. I did my best impression, but that move is really hard to pull off without parachute pants. Maybe if our mascot were a genie it would work, but not in clunky Viking boots. But I'm losing track of what's important here. Crystal thought I was Eddie. I had to convince her otherwise.

I didn't want to say anything and risk Crystal identifying me as the Viking. Our whole plan would fall apart if she figured out we were working together. Instead, I pointed toward the stands where Eddie was sitting.

"What's that move?" Crystal asked. "The Fat Travolta?"

I stopped moving.

"The Frozen Statue? I like that one." She snapped a few pictures just as the whistle blew announcing the start of the third quarter. Crystal's attention shifted from me to Jerry Tortelli. She trained her telephoto lens on him and followed him as he ran onto the field. Like I said, the acoustics inside the Viking head weren't good, but I swear I heard her moan with every completed pass.

I figured I had no other choice but to venture into the stands. Reaching Eddie was about as easy as wading through a pack of dogs in a meat costume. Everyone I passed had to push or poke or prod me, hoping to topple my Viking bobblehead into the rows below me. I managed to make it to the center without losing balance and collapsed into Eddie's lap. "Get Crystal's attention," I whispered. "She thinks I'm you."

"Crystal!" Eddie yelled. "Take our picture!"

Unfortunately, our team had been moving steadily downfield, taking Crystal with them. She was now on the twenty-yard line, completely mesmerized by our team's surprising passing attack. Eddie screamed a few more times but to no avail.

"I'll get her," I groaned, righting myself and heading back

through the stands. This time I approached the journey as one might venture into a mosh pit—all swinging arms and rushing sideswipes. I slammed others before they slammed me and knocked a few unsuspecting mothers into the lower rows. Just as I was about to exit the stands, a familiar hand clamped down on my shoulder, stopping me from moving.

"You authorized to wear that costume?" Principal Stone asked.

I gave him two big thumbs up, not wanting to reveal myself. If Stone knew it was me behind this mask, he'd probably haul me in for grand larceny and identity theft.

"Just be careful, Wendy," he whispered into my left nostril. "The last mascot nearly had her head chopped off."

Wendy? Really? I had to start working out more.

I looked at the clock on the scoreboard and saw that there were three minutes left in the third quarter. Where did the time go? The costume not only immobilized its wearer physically, but removed them from the time-space continuum.

I stumbled down the bleacher steps and landed with a thud on the track that surrounded the football field. The cheerleaders had just finished assembling their pyramid formation. I paused to stare up at Dawn standing at the top, her dainty feet positioned on the backs of two sweaty and grunting girls. The sun was behind her, and she appeared to glow in triumphant glory. With her tanned and toned arms raised in a *V* for victory sign and her blond hair blowing gently in the breeze, she looked way more powerful than any of the players on the field.

I was listening as Dawn fired up the crowds with her cries of "Let's get physical" when I heard a different kind of cry emitted from someplace near my left kneecap. I looked down and saw Susie McGannon's face contorted in pain. A quick investigation discerned that the source of the girl's anguish was my heavy boot placed squarely on her right hand. "Get off me, you idiot," she managed to grunt. I removed my foot and mumbled an apology, which was my second mistake. Without the boot to keep it in place, Susie's hand shifted from position.

You know how people are always using the butterfly effect to describe the cause-and-effect relationship of distant and seemingly unrelated events? Well, if you ever want to watch the butterfly effect in action, simply stomp on the hand of a person at the base of a cheerleading pyramid and you'll see a young man's lovelorn hopes and dreams crushed to dust. That's the only way I can describe how I felt when I watched the reverberating shock wave travel in slo-mo domino style from Susie's wobbly arm up to Dawn's frozen smile. When the entire formation collapsed all around me, I could hear Eddie's heart breaking in the stands. I had one job to do and I had blown it.

I looked for Dawn on top of the pile of cheerleaders, hoping that the enormous body pillow would have cushioned her fall, but didn't see her anywhere. Somehow, she had landed on the hard surface of the track, a good three feet away from her squad. When I tried to help her up, she just seethed in anger and pain. "I'm. Going. To. Kill. You," she said, grabbing the hem of my skirt, a poor substitute for the part of my anatomy she really wanted to grip and twist.

The remaining squad stood up suddenly, as if rebounding from a rehearsed tumble. They moved toward me and all I could see was them tearing apart the costume with their manicured hands, leaving me naked and defenseless in front of the stands full of bloodthirsty spectators. I turned and ran, but with my lack of peripheral vision, I couldn't really see where I was going. Before I realized it, I was crossing the football field by the end zone. I knocked over one of our receivers and was hit in the side of the head by either a missile or a football. Given the loud roar I heard erupting from the stands, I figured it was a football. My oversize head must have intercepted a pass meant for the receiver I had knocked down. A pass that, if completed, would have broken the persistent tie in the game. I looked over at the opposing side and saw the lobster mascot, claws raised in some kind of victory dance.

There was only one thing for me to do. Run away. As fast

as possible. I left my oversize boots in the end zone and took off under the goalposts, hoping to reach the fence that separated the track from the adjacent soccer fields. From there, it was a short distance to the bushes that outlined the campus, where I could ditch the Viking head and hide until the coast was clear.

I sprinted as fast as I could while trying to keep the polyfoam head from falling off and revealing my identity. All I heard was the blare of a referee's whistle, and the announcer screaming "Oh the humanity!" over and over again, like some looped sample by a DJ in training. I didn't hear any cleats pounding the Astroturf behind me. Hopefully, there was enough time in the fourth quarter to keep the players focused on repeating the play I had just interrupted.

I reached the bushes and dove in. Before removing the head, I turned back and saw that I was alone for now. The cheerleaders, football players, parents, and coaches were still focused on scoring. I ditched the head in the bushes, climbed through the other side, and ran as fast as I could away from the school.

About a block into my escape, I realized that without the heavy boots and Viking head, I was now a guy running in what looked like a miniskirt from the Jurassic era. If Stone or Tortelli found me after the game, I would be strung up like a piñata in the quad and hit with a sharp stick until my organs spilled out like candy. I decided the best thing to do was to re-enter the bushes and hide until nightfall. When it was dark, I could make it back to my car and my regular school clothes and return home safely.

TWELVE

I'm secure enough in my masculinity to admit that I wept openly for much of the three hours I lay hidden in the foliage that surrounded the school. One month into my new "healthy choices" lifestyle and I was camping like a cross-dressing homeless person, staging gladiator tournaments with the insects I found in my hovel. If this is what sobriety looked like, I was not a fan.

Stone was probably drawing up the exit papers now. What am I saying? He'd probably had those papers ready to go ever since he kicked Alex out of school. All he needed was Coach Harkness's testimony that I was the one who borrowed the suit to know who sabotaged the game. My dad wouldn't even argue when Stone punished me this time. He'd just sign on the dotted line and ship me off to Langdon Military Academy.

The only glimmer of hope I had was the fact that only

Eddie knew it was me who performed during the game. If I could come up with a clever alibi to give Coach Harkness, I might stand a chance of staying at Meridian and not having my limbs torn off by every player on the football team.

I brainstormed in the dirt for hours, but the best idea I came up with was that my evil twin, the one we keep locked in our basement, had framed me. This was actually a storyline from *Secretos Subterráneos*, which I was pretty sure Harkness hadn't seen. After careful consideration, I decided the plan was unworkable. It would require a whole new wardrobe and a convincing British accent, so I kept thinking.

"Stay hidden," my squirrel spirit guide advised from a nearby telephone pole. "Burrow deep and emerge in time for the spring harvest." After dispensing his words of wisdom, the squirrel scrambled up the pole and tightroped along the line, until it was picked off by an owl.

"Don't listen to the squirrels," the owl said with his mouth full. "They're all idiots."

I hoped that was the end of my spirit guide and/or detox hallucinations. But who was going to help me now? If only I could get in touch with Spencer, but my cell phone was in my pants, and my pants were in my BMW, and the BMW was parked in the student lot, and the student lot was under video surveillance from dusk to dawn. If I wanted to find Spencer, I'd have to go on foot. It was dark now, so I could walk without being seen. Just to be safe, I stayed close to the bushes that lined the campus. If a car or a torch-bearing mob approached from the opposite direction, I was fully prepared to launch myself back into the foliage.

Lunley had told me that Spencer lived two blocks away from school, in an apartment complex near the fire station. Lucky for me, there was only one apartment building near the fire station. Unlucky for me, there were twenty units, most with their curtains closed, making it impossible to peer inside. I walked up to the rows of mailboxes, hoping to see the last name "Knudsen" printed on a label somewhere, but they were all blank. The only way I was going to find him was if I started knocking on doors. But who would open their door to a dirty teenage boy dressed as a barbarian?

Turns out, no one. Apartment after apartment, I had conversations with frightened occupants through locked doors. "I'm looking for Spencer Knudsen," I'd say, to which they would reply, "We don't want any!" Judging by the voices, I'd guess the average age in this complex was 110.

It wasn't until I had worked my way around back that I spotted a tiny figure standing on the back lawn, eye glued to a telescope. "Spencer?" I said.

He looked over, and if he was surprised to see me in his backyard dressed in a tattered Viking garment, he didn't show it. He fitted his glasses to his face and walked over to where I was standing. "Hello, Lawrence," he said.

"Hey, Spencer." I did my best to explain my situation. Perhaps my rendition of a near-death catastrophe lacked the necessary dramatic flourishes to elicit the kind of shock and awe I would expect from a listener. Instead of gasping, Spencer regarded me more like a Boy Scout receiving instructions for how to tie a simple knot. When I finished, he stared at me for a few minutes and said, "The boomerang effect."

"Excuse me?"

"It's a term used by social psychologists to describe how a persuasive message can sometimes have the opposite effect of what's intended."

"And this applies to me how?"

"You tried to persuade Dawn that the Viking was a dashing romantic figure, like Cyrano, only to have her despise the mascot for making her fall and ruining her perfect pyramid."

"Her fall wasn't that bad," I said, hoping it were true. "Still, I'm sorry I didn't listen to your concerns."

"Cyrano's story does not end happily."

"It did for Steve Martin," I said. "Can you help me? I can't go back to my car wearing this dress."

"Brynja," Spencer corrected.

"What?"

"What you're wearing. It's called a brynja. And it's supposed to be made from iron rings, not polyester. During the

Viking age, warriors—"

"Spencer, I'm kind of in a panic here."

A woman from one of the apartment windows yelled something in a foreign language. It sounded like German on a pogo stick. Spencer closed his eyes, sighed, and then responded in the same nonsensical way. I suppose it's culturally inappropriate for me to say it was nonsensical just because I couldn't understand it. What I mean to say is that Spencer yammered in Norwegian before speaking normal again.

"It's my mother," he said. "She worries about me being outside alone."

This seemed odd considering he was in his backyard. "Tell her you're with me."

"That wouldn't help."

"Where's your dad?"

"He works most nights in the lab."

"Mad scientist?"

"He's thorough, not deranged."

I tried to steer the conversation back to my problem. "So, can I borrow some of your dad's clothes?"

"My father's clothes won't fit you. He's smaller than I am."

I didn't see how this was possible unless Spencer's dad was a gnome. "Then I'm screwed."

"If you will allow me to make a suggestion."

"Please."

"Not only do you need to get back to your car, but you need an alibi for the time of the football game."

"Right."

"I would advise you to join the LARPers in Arroyo Park."

"Is that a term I'm supposed to know?"

"LARP stands for live action role play. A group of people physically act out their characters' actions in improvisational theater on public grounds."

"You mean those weirdoes I see jousting in medieval costumes every Friday night?"

"Exactly. As it is currently Friday night, you'll find them in Arroyo Park. If you can insert yourself among their ranks and convince them to escort you to campus, you'll have an excuse for why your car was parked so long in the student lot and a cover to hide the fact that you're wearing what remains of the mascot's uniform."

"Spencer, you are brilliant!" I said, happy for any way out of my current predicament. "Can you come with me?"

"Unfortunately, I need to stay here and track a previously unidentified comet."

"Is that bad? For us, I mean."

"You're thinking of a meteor. Comets orbit the sun."

"Well, that's good news. Although I'd welcome being vaporized by a crashing meteor at this point."

"I can lend you some items that will help you disguise your disguise."

Spencer went inside and returned a few moments later carrying a plastic sword, shield, and phony beard. "Where did you get this stuff?" I asked.

"I'm going to dress as the Duke of Cornwall for Halloween."

"Of course you are."

A piercing scream shattered the quiet of the evening. I heard a door slam in the distance, followed by the slap of feet against pavement. Suddenly, a frantic woman was standing between me and Spencer, shielding my little mentee with her body. The woman was what most would call stout, like she had once wrestled professionally. Even if she never opened her mouth, you could tell she wasn't from this country. Her hair was gray, which is not something you see on most women in their early forties. She dressed like an Amish person, with an apron tied around a plain dress. In her hand was some long utensil that looked like a combination of a strainer and a spork. Even in the dark, I could tell she was freaking out. She looked at me like I was some serial killer trying to lure her son into a van with the promise of candy.

Spencer attempted to calm her down, but she wasn't buying his explanation. She grabbed him by the shoulders and marched him back inside the house, leaving his telescope standing alone on the apartment building's shared lawn. It wasn't until I heard the door slam that I realized my Viking attire might have made me seem a little strange. If I had looked out my kitchen window to see my son talking to a teenage boy in a dress and brynja, I might have been a little overprotective too.

I picked up Spencer's costume accessories and made my way toward Arroyo Park.

THIRTEEN

The lights near the tennis courts illuminated the patch of lawn reserved, I assumed, for LARPing. A group of men and women stood around two guys in the middle of a spirited bit of swordplay. Their armor and weapons looked much more authentic than what I was wearing and I suddenly felt self-conscious about my plastic shield and sword, like I was showing up at a polo tournament riding a hobby horse.

"What ho!" a voice boomed from my left. I turned and saw a buxom Renaissance woman approaching with a ring of flowers resting on her gray hair.

"Oh, I—"

"Methinks I spy a challenger!" She grabbed me by the arm and led me into the crowd.

"Huzzah!" cried a group of merry men. I don't know what I was expecting, but I was surprised by the number of adults in the crowd. Didn't these people have more responsible things to do than prance around the park at night in decorative frocks, silly hats, and knee-high boots? Their long, stringy hair stuck to their sweaty foreheads from their fourteenth-century workout. Some men drank out of heavy cast-iron beer steins, breaking a number of city ordinances, I'm sure, about open containers in public parks.

I scanned the crowd for kids my age but didn't see anyone I recognized. All the teenage LARPers wore some kind of helmet or face mask, which not only protected them from getting stabbed in the face, but also saved them from being recognized by normal people.

"Actually, I was kind of hoping—" I began, but was cut off by a dwarf in full combat gear.

"I challenge thee to duel, thou beef-witted clotpole!"

"Excuse me?"

More cheers of "Huzzah!" accompanied the dwarf's pronouncement. These cries distracted me enough so that I didn't see the little guy rush and strike me squarely in the kneecaps. I don't know what his sword was made of but it was a stronger alloy than my plastic toy. I fell like a clipped toenail. "What the fuck?" I spat.

"Thou utterest a most strange and vexing language," an older woman dressed as the queen said. She looked like my aunt Betty, the one who gave me a spice rack for my last birthday. "Whence comest thou?"

The dwarf looked ready to rush me again. I figured I had better get into character and plead my case.

"Please, kind sirs and wenches," I began, hoping "wenches" was a term of endearment. "I needeth your assistance to protecteth me from a villain who meaneth to doeth me harm."

"Dost thou speak of Sir Watkyn, most dreaded foe of Shadow Lake?" someone cried.

"I do, sir." I had no idea what I was saying but figured I was better off agreeing whenever possible with this merry band of lunatics.

"Oh, he is a knotty-pated pignut if ever there was one," another boy cried.

"He attacketh my army neareth the sacred place of learning," I said, pointing toward the high school. "I am the sole survivor and require safe passage back to my vehicle."

The dwarf raised his sword and silenced the whispered murmuring. "Methinks this reeky miscreant be a spy for Sir Watkyn."

"No!" I said. "He is my sworn enemy!" I began to wonder if this little guy wasn't some friend's younger brother I had tortured in my youth.

"Methinks your quest be honorable," a young maiden said, cozying up to me. I thought I recognized her from first-period history, only in that class she was a rather plain-looking girl whose breasts were usually hidden behind textbooks and bulky sweatshirts. Now they were on full display, pressed together in her tight corset.

"Thank you, my lady," I said. It took every ounce of energy I had to maintain my focus on her bright blue eyes, set at a slight diagonal angle on her face. "I beseech thee, escort me to my awaiting carriage and I shall reward you handsomely with McFlurries!"

"What of the demons that roam the streets like bat-fowling ratsbane?" the dwarf asked.

"They are no match for our noble quest!" my blue-eyed maiden proclaimed. I realized it was Audrey Sieminski. I had gone to school with her since the sixth grade but had never once spoken with her. I hoped she didn't always talk like this.

Audrey, the dwarf, and two other teenage warriors gathered around and promised to accompany me back to the high school. They would provide the perfect camouflage under Stone's video surveillance. Set among these Renaissance warriors, I was no longer the kid wearing the mascot uniform; I was just another in a long list of reasons why Stone called us the "Dumbest Generation."

Before we embarked on our journey, an older man, maybe in his forties, approached and handed me a string of garlic and a heavy metal cross. "Hell is empty and all the demons are here," he said.

I looked at him. "Mr. Franklin?" This guy was my eighth-grade English teacher. The dude was obsessed with Shakespeare and made us reenact scenes from *Romeo and Juliet*, even though at that age most of the guys would rather poison Juliet than kiss her.

"Tis Sir Rodrick of Gloucester," he corrected.

"Okay," I said, accepting his gift. "Thanks, Sir Rodrick."

He bowed and went back to chatting up the buxom gray-haired lady who'd ushered me into their ranks.

We made our way back to campus, sticking to the side streets to avoid the cries to "Go fucketh yourselves" from passing cars. I thought that once we were away from the park we could drop the act, but my compatriots would not hear of it. Every time I said anything normal like "What the dillo? Why they be dissing?" I was met with uncomprehending stares and complaints that my foreign tongue doth baffle the senses. I did my best to chat up Audrey anyway.

"Doth the young maiden wish to grasp my blade?"

She responded by kicking my shins. "Kind gentleman, do not think I can't guard my sacred chastity while fighting our mortal enemy."

"Gotcha," I said, rubbing my leg. "I just meant, doth thou desire protection against said enemy." I handed her Spencer's plastic sword to show her my intentions were honorable, but she just scoffed at my generosity.

"The demons will not fear weapons made of such flimsy material." She crushed the plastic toy between her two fingers and then handed it back to me.

"Halt," the dwarf cried. "Methinks I spy a demonic crusade approaching."

We huddled together on the sidewalk, two in front, two behind, and prepared to do battle with whatever appeared. I was either deep into character or all this talk of demons had messed with my psyche, but I swear the night air grew distinctly colder. The streetlights started to flicker and the chirping crickets went silent. An aroma of hairspray and skunk wafted toward us, making our eyes water.

The black crusade emerged from down a gravelly driveway; their crunching steps sounded like those of warriors marching over the dry and brittle bones of their victims. Instinctively, I dropped Spencer's plastic sword and gripped the iron cross and string of garlic.

"What effrontery is this?" asked the diminutive devil. It wasn't hard to recognize Zoe Cosmos, even in this dim light. She wore a long-sleeved black vinyl dress, which must have required a few intakes of breath to fit into, and lacy, fingerless gloves. She pointed a long, sharp nail covered in black polish in my direction and murmured to her horde. "This one is mine."

"We seek safe passage to the sacred place of learning," I

said in a tone a few octaves higher than I wanted. "Please let us pass."

Zoe removed a short, sharp blade from her knee-high boot and approached. Her vampire brethren encircled us like a black velvet curtain. "We'll let you pass," Zoe said. "But we require recompense."

I didn't know what that meant but it sounded expensive. "What payment do you require?" Audrey asked.

"Nothing of consequence," Zoe purred. "Only your souls!"

The vampire horde surrounding us all hissed in response. One girl, dressed in a long, flowing cape and short shorts, still wore her headgear. You never think about vampires needing orthodontia until you see one whose fangs are encased in metal.

Why weren't these people stoned? I wondered. Why wasn't *I* stoned? This whole experience would make way more sense if we were wasted. But we weren't wasted, and it was still fun, in a vaguely shameful way.

Audrey snatched the cross and string of garlic out of my hand and took a step toward Zoe. "Retreat, thou spleeny crook-pated dewberry!"

Zoe laughed at the weapons Audrey shook in front of her. "Really?" she said. "Garlic? You think you can . . ."

But Zoe didn't get a chance to finish because Audrey swung the rope of garlic above her head and clocked Zoe a good one across the face. "Bitch!" Zoe cried.

"Run!" Audrey screamed, and the four of us did just that. We pushed through the vampire blockade, which fell like the anemic waifs they were, and sprinted down the street in full retreat.

"I will have your soul!" Zoe shouted from behind. "Mark my words. You will be mine!"

I can't say that Zoe's words did not send a chill down my spine. I may have been a curiosity to her before, but now I was a target. Her hunger would not be quenched until she fed on my blood and organs. I repeated this line to Audrey once we had reached the safety of the school parking lot, because it sounded both sincere and Shakespearian.

"You are valiant," Audrey replied, her chest heaving from our run. I watched it rise and fall and fell into a sort of trance. The dwarf snapped me out of it by swatting my bottom with his sword.

"You promised us McFlurries, remember?" he said. I draped my arms around him and Audrey and walked toward my car, making sure our esprit du corps was captured by the video cameras above. I gave a quiet shout-out to Spencer for coming up with the plan that might just save my ass.

The McFlurries vanquished our hunger, and we reunited with our brethren at Arroyo Park. (Sorry, after spending time in the Renaissance, it's difficult to drop the lingo.) I bid them farewell and God speed, et cetera, et cetera, et cetera. "See you in history," I whispered to Audrey, pleased with the literal and figurative meanings of the phrase. If Audrey picked up on my witticism, she did not acknowledge it. She simply nodded her head, did a little curtsy, and bounced back to the battlefields.

I called Eddie right away to apologize. "Good friend, I do beseech your forgiveness for my royal fuckup."

"Are you high?" Eddie asked, and rightly so. I had to explain to him what had happened to me since the debacle on the football field.

"Are you sure you're not high?" Eddie asked again.

"I swear. Can you ever forgive me?"

"I guess. I realize you didn't shatter my dreams on purpose."

"Thank you."

Eddie explained all that had happened after I ran away. Dawn, with a twisted ankle, hobbled off the field, supported by her cheerleading squad and Brett Bridges, editor in chief of our school paper, *The Beacon Signal*, or *The BS* as most students call it. "Who did this to you?" he kept asking her, despite the fact that she was sobbing in pain. Lucky for me, Dawn had no idea who was under the suit. Most of the girls still thought it was Phyllis Larouche, a junior who had been cut from the squad last year when she tweeted about Dawn's thigh dimples.

"And the game?" I asked.

"We lost."

"Shit."

"Coach Harkness saved your ass by keeping our secret from the team. They're ready to kill the person who cost them their win. I don't know if he'll be so generous with Stone, though. I saw them talking after the game."

"Shit."

"Harkness came up to me after and said he wanted the suit back first thing Monday."

"I ditched the head in the bushes by school," I said. "I'll go retrieve it now."

"Good idea."

"Eddie, once again, I'm really very sorry."

"It's okay. Hopefully Dawn's injury is bad enough to bench her for the season. Then we can commiserate in the stands. If not, I plan on making a speedy recovery."

I hung up and drove back to the bushes where I ditched the mascot's head. In the darkness, it was hard to see anything, but I figured a yoga ball–size Viking head would stand out, even in this dim light. After searching for twenty minutes, I couldn't find it anywhere. I even sneaked back onto the football field and retraced my frantic steps. It wasn't here. Sometime while I was battling midgets and vampires, someone had snatched the mascot's head from my hiding place.

"Diablerie," I murmured, dredging up the only French word I remembered from my cultural-exchange experience in Dijon. My French parents used this term repeatedly to address my behavior when I lived with them two summers ago. It's not a term of endearment, which is why I switched to Spanish when I started high school.

The whole way home, I tried to convince myself that the missing Viking head was no big deal. Most likely, an inno-cent bystander discovered the costume on an evening stroll and took it home to scare the wife and kids. But what if it was Stone? I pictured him going all CSI on the thing, dust-ing it for fingerprints or swabbing it for DNA evidence. There was probably a gallon of my sweat and saliva soaked into that polyfoam mask. Why didn't I bury or burn it when I had the chance? There was nothing I could do now but wait until Monday morning to learn my fate.

I pulled into our garage around eleven o'clock and instantly got pinged by Mom. These alerts sound every time she posts something new to our family website. I logged on to the site and watched the video she posted. Mom looked like a sad clown. My two little cousins had clearly used her face for a game of "let's have fun with makeup." Her lips and cheeks were the same shade of bright red. Dark, uneven lines had been drawn on her eyebrows, making them look like black licorice Twizzlers. One of the girls had used the pencil to add a teardrop tattoo near Mom's right eye. Looking at Mom's face, it was hard to tell if my cousins lacked fine motor skills or they had moved from worshiping princesses to gangbangers.

"Hey, honey," Mom said. "Don't I look pretty?"

Juniper poked her face into the frame and squealed, "We're not finished!"

"Yes you are, dear," Mom said, pushing her aside. "Aunt Gloria needs a rest."

Aunt Lucy's voice off camera screamed, "Juniper and Violet, get off your aunt right now!"

Mom smiled wanly into the camera, which was a bit unnerving with all her makeup. Like FaceTiming with the Joker.

"Just wanted to check in and see how you were doing." Mom brought the camera closer and whispered. "It's a bit exhausting here. I forget what it's like to be around so many kids. My sister's great, but she doesn't set any kind of boundaries for the little ones. Probably because she's too busy screaming at Dashiel." Dashiel was my age and supposedly an amazing baseball player. Dad loved to talk about how colleges started recruiting him as a sophomore. "We have it so easy with just the three of us, right? I can't remember the last time we had the kind of screaming matches they have here.

Anyway, I just wanted to say how much I miss you and hope we can Skype soon. Kiss kiss."

I clicked the Like button instead of responding with my own video. It had been a long day and I didn't have the energy to recount the strange events that had led to me nearly getting killed by a mob of angry football fans and a horde of vampires. Thank God I'd had Spencer and Audrey to protect me. I wished I didn't have to wait through the weekend to thank them. I figured I should keep a low profile for the next couple of days. I didn't know who had the Viking head now, but I needed to come up with a quick escape plan in case they could trace it back to me.

FOURTEEN

That night I dreamed a one-eyed Viking was chasing me and my merry band of Renaissance warriors through a maze of cannabis plants. We ran through the tall stalks, getting lost and high along the way. Every few seconds, a giant hand would reach down, snatch up one of the LARPers, and eat him. From the ground, I could hear the bones being crushed like pretzel sticks between the giant's teeth. Eventually, it was just me and Audrey, darting through the leafy plants, trying to find a way out of the labyrinth. "Save me!" Audrey implored. I could feel the hot breath of the Cyclops Viking on the back of my neck. "I can't!" I screamed. "I'm nobody." Just then the Viking's hand grabbed me by the neck and lifted me toward his mouth. As I moved skyward, I tried to grab as many of the oily buds from the plants as I could. Better to face the jaws of death with a nice buzz, was the way I saw it.

Just as I was approaching the Viking's cinder-block teeth, a horn blared and pulled me out of the nightmare.

"Jesus Christ, what the fuck!" I jumped up to see Estrella standing there, smiling and holding a horn. "I don't need you to do that on Saturday, Estrella," I said, covering my ears with my pillow.

"*Lo siento,*" Estrella said with an embarrassed laugh. Part of me thinks she enjoys scaring the shit out of me every morning.

Since I was up now, with no hope of going back to sleep, I logged on to our family site and posted a short summary of my night terror on the "Troubling Dreams" page (being careful to change the cannabis plants to eucalyptus trees). That should give Mom something to think about, I thought, smiling. Good luck interpreting that one.

I closed my laptop and went downstairs. I found my dad sitting at the kitchen table with his *New York Times* and coffee. "Shit," he mumbled. I think it was in response to something he read, but you never know with him.

"You got home late last night," he said as I sat down.

"I was at Eddie's house."

"Eddie the cheerleader?"

"Yeah."

"Hmm." Dad shook his head and went back to the paper.

"What?"

"Nothing," Dad said. "I didn't think you guys were still friends."

"We are."

"Doesn't he get made fun of a lot?"

"No, not really."

"That's surprising."

"You said my other friends were idiots."

"They are. Isn't there someone on the football team you could hang out with?"

Not anymore, I thought.

My dad looked at his watch, swore again, and then gulped the remains of his coffee. "I'm teeing off at nine. Want to be my caddy?"

"I'm kinda busy today."

"Doing what?"

Packing a suitcase and preparing my escape route, I thought. "I've got homework and stuff."

"You know, there are a lot of kids your age at the golf club."

"Really?"

"Want me to sign you up for some lessons?"

"Golf's boring."

"You could work at the pro shop or restaurant."

"I'll think about it."

"It's a good place to make connections. It's not just *what* you know . . ."

"It's *who* you know," I said, finishing Dad's favorite piece of advice. "I know."

"How will the people you're spending time with now help you accomplish your goals?"

Two of them saved me from getting killed last night, I wanted to say, but stayed quiet. "Aren't you going to be late?" I said, indicating the clock.

Dad sighed. "Fine. I'll see you later today."

Dad left and I poured myself a large bowl of Frosted Flakes. After I finished slurping down my breakfast, I joined Estrella on the couch for an episode of *Secretos Subterráneos.*

I spent the rest of the weekend in hiding, scanning social media to see what evidence existed of my involvement in the "Mascot Mayhem," as the *BS* website had termed the catastrophe. "Sources say the perpetrator is a Meridian student bent on destroying the team's chances at a win this season," Brett Bridges wrote in his news summary. "That Viking's dead," Jerry was quoted as saying. I prayed Coach Harkness would keep his mouth shut until I saw him on Monday.

Rumors circulated. Most suspected Phyllis Larouche, based on the photos Crystal posted of me in the mascot costume. "I wasn't even there!" Phyllis asserted, sharing her own pictures of a weekend trip to Napa. I zoomed in on one of Phyllis in a tank top and compared our biceps. They were depressingly similar in both muscle and tone. I spent the rest of the weekend curling bags of flour.

While I was following the various trending hashtags of the event (#murderourmascot, #killingvikingsisjustified, and #thevikinghasnopenis), I couldn't help but notice how much fun people were having without me. Facebook and Instagram were loaded with images of people at Saturday-night parties. Will and the guys were dancing shirtless at a beach bonfire. Chester and his crew were crammed in someone's apartment, red Solo cups held aloft like trophies. There were selfies of people at concerts, in parks, modeling swimwear. I had traded all this for what? My sobriety suddenly seemed incredibly stupid. All it had done was lose me friends and get me into trouble. Everyone was having fun and I was hiding out in an empty house, binge watching *Secretos Subterráneos* with my family's cook.

I liked a few Facebook photos and favorited a few tweets, hoping someone would acknowledge my existence. Maybe invite me over. I frantically refreshed the page, but heard nothing. What would I do if someone did ask me to join them? I couldn't go to these events and expect to stay sober. I waited, hoping for some mystical counsel from my squirrel, but he was gone, eaten by the wiser owl, who had better things to do than talk to a bored and lonely teenager.

I needed to be strong, like Odysseus. Have Estrella tie me

to a chair, blindfold me, and stuff beeswax in my ears so that I wouldn't be tempted by these Internet sirens. Or I could just turn off my phone and shut my laptop. Great, now I no longer had to stay away from pot, but social media as well. If I kept this up, I'd be a monk by Christmas.

I went to my closet and took out my old sketch pad where I drew my origami designs. Maybe I could lose myself in a complicated fold the way I used to. I opened the drawing pad on my desk and found a rolled joint stuck between its pages. I must have hidden this here knowing my parents would never look in my sketch pad for drugs. They never understood my enthusiasm for origami and were visibly disturbed whenever I spent a weekend holed up in my room only to come out holding a small grasshopper.

I held the joint in my hands and debated lighting up.

This was like a sign, right? Some benevolent god was taking pity on me and providing this much-needed release from my suffering. It wasn't even a big joint. Just enough to help me relax. I could smoke it in my room with the window open and no one would know. Both Dad and Estrella were asleep, dreaming of missed putts and mining collapses, respectively.

I looked at my open sketchbook and saw the diagram I had done for an origami lily. This would make a nice gift for Audrey, to repay her for saving me from Zoe's clutches. I'd make it small, so I could pass it to her in class, like a note. She'd understand the meaning, after the adventure we shared Friday night.

I took the joint and placed it in my shoebox of origami figures and grabbed a leftover sheet of paper. I didn't have any purple, so the lily would have to be red. Maybe I'd make it a rose instead. It required more complex folding and would distract me from that joint in my shoebox for the rest of the weekend. If I finished early, I could make a bouquet. I sat down at my desk and got to work.

FIFTEEN

On Monday, I ran into the cafeteria and told Spencer I had to talk with Coach Harkness and that I'd be right back. He simply nodded his head and went back to reading *The Brothers Karamazov*, his free reading choice for freshman English. I found Harkness on the football field, cradling a cup of coffee while the few students whose counselors hated them enough to enroll them in zero period P.E. sleepwalked around the track.

I began by thanking him for not telling the players about me borrowing the mascot costume. "You may have lost the game, but you saved a life," I said. "I am forever in your debt."

"I told Principal Stone you have the uniform. He wants it returned today."

"Well, here's the thing," I said. "The uniform was stolen on Thursday. *Before* the game." This is what's known as a half-truth. The uniform was stolen, just not when I needed it to be. Moving the date of the crime up a few days gave me my alibi for the game.

"Who would steal a Viking costume?" Harkness asked suspiciously.

"My thoughts exactly," I said. "That's why I didn't lock my car door."

"You're telling me that wasn't you dancing around at the game Friday?"

"I wasn't even at the game," I said. "Just ask Eddie."

"I did. He didn't know where you were."

"I was LARPing."

"What the hell is LARPing?"

"It's live action role play. We dress up in medieval costumes and fight in Arroyo Park."

"See anyone in a Viking costume?"

"No, it's strictly Renaissance era."

"So, we don't know who sabotaged our game?"

"It seems so. Although I wouldn't put anything past those Cupertino Crayfish. They're real bottom-feeders."

Harkness grunted.

"I would appreciate it if you didn't mention my involvement with the uniform to anyone on the team. I do feel responsible since the costume was stolen from my car. And of course, I'm willing to pay to replace the uniform."

"I'm glad to be rid of the thing," Harkness said. "That costume was cursed. I pity whoever has it now."

I left Harkness and headed toward the cafeteria to confer with Spencer.

When I reached my usual table, I found my ward nibbling on his dried fruit and yogurt. I wanted to talk with him about the missing Viking head but was interrupted by Brett Bridges, thrusting what looked like dirt clods onto our table. "Hey, Lawrence!" he said. "Enjoy some homemade bran muffins for breakfast."

"Thanks," I said, picking up the mini stool softener. "What are these for?"

"I'm running for homecoming king."

"You're *running* for homecoming king?" I asked, incredulous. I had never seen someone compete so blatantly in a popularity contest. Brett was the editor in chief of our school newspaper, a position he won, now that I think of it, by buying the staff an espresso machine.

"Becoming homecoming king is like winning any other public office," Brett said. "It requires some campaigning. I've already locked in the votes from the Latino Movement Club."

"You're Latino?"

"You don't have to be Latino to be interested in their culture," Brett said, continuing to hand out his culturally inappropriate muffins. Why not churros? Everybody loves a good churro in the morning. "Who's this?" he said, motioning to Spencer.

"He's my . . ." Once again, I got tripped up on an appropriate title for Spencer. "He's a freshman I'm helping."

"Nice to meet you," Brett said, extending his hand for Spencer to shake. In addition to trolling for homecoming votes, he was likely looking to recruit new members to the Young Republican Club. Spencer's formal attire made him an ideal candidate. Brett eyed Spencer's starched open collar, probably fighting the urge to clamp it shut with a bow tie.

"Did you hear about what happened?" Brett asked, his eyes sparkling behind his tortoise-shell glasses. "The school was vandalized last night."

"Vandalized? How?"

"Someone stenciled 'Reserved for Idiot' in white paint on Stone's parking space. He's furious."

"That's . . ." I was about to say "hilarious," but was cut off by an eagle landing on my shoulder. That's what it felt like anyway. When I turned to dislodge the talons, I saw Stone's iron fist attached to the soft flesh above my collarbone.

"Come with me, Lawrence," Stone said, lifting me from my chair. The last things I saw before Stone dragged me away were Brett's widening eyes and broad smile. It was like some stranger had just dropped a file marked "Confidential" into his lap.

* * *

Stone hauled me into his office and threw me into the vacant chair opposite his desk. "Have a seat," he said, closing the door.

"How are you this morning, sir?" I asked.

"Peachy, Lawrence. Thanks for asking. Do you know what this is?" He swung his computer monitor in my direction. His screen was divided into nine smaller screens, each with a different view of the school campus. There was the library. The quad. The cafeteria (where I caught a glimpse of Brett grilling Spencer for information). On the top right was a view of the parking lot.

"Is it a breach of our civil rights?"

"Shut up, Lawrence."

"Oo-kay."

"Look what the cameras caught last night." Stone pressed a button on his keyboard and started turning back time. The morning sun set, darkening the area for a brief moment until the overhead lights came on. Then a dancing Viking moonwalked into the lot and lifted white paint off Stone's parking space with a set of cardboard stencils. Stone paused there and ran the tape forward so I could watch the vandal in real time. There was the Meridian mascot painting the words "Reserved for Idiot" on the dark concrete. I couldn't help but chuckle.

"Think that's funny, do you?" Stone asked, his bushy eyebrows furrowing. "Want to see something really hilarious?"

Stone rewound the recording some more until we reached the moment I entered the lot on Friday with my LARPing buddies. I leaned forward, nearly pressing my nose against the monitor; I looked just like the other LARPers around me. I breathed a huge sigh of relief and leaned back in my chair. "This isn't the most exciting video."

"I think it's very interesting," Stone said.

"You don't spend much time on YouTube, do you?"

"Care to explain what you were doing in the parking lot at eleven o'clock at night?" Stone said, now glaring at me like I was the last hash brown on a warming tray.

"It's embarrassing, actually. I-I'm a LARPer," I stammered. I explained LARPing to Stone, trying to sound like a seasoned practitioner of the art.

"Sounds suspicious. You guys on ecstasy or something?"

I sighed. "Why do you assume that every time a teenager engages in creative play that it's the result of taking drugs?" I figured it was time to turn the tables on this interrogation. Put Stone's suspicious nature on trial, the way my dad does when incriminating photos are entered into evidence.

"I assume it because it's usually true."

"Well, this time it's not. Actually, my involvement in the group was inspired by my eighth-grade English teacher, Mr.

Franklin, who's a member of the group and can attest to my presence last Friday." I was amazed at how quickly my brain was coming up with all this bullshit. This must be one of the more positive side effects of clean living.

"That still doesn't explain why you parked your car in the school's lot, rather than on the streets near Arroyo Park."

"LARPing rules do not allow us to use modern transportation to and from events. It helps us get into character. The parking lot is close enough to the park so that my driving wouldn't be noticed by the other Vikings."

"Did you say Vikings?"

"I meant knights. I failed World History and still get the two confused. Did you know that a meteor is different from a comet?" I asked, hoping to change the subject.

"Here's what I know," Stone said, ignoring me. "I know you borrowed the mascot uniform from Coach Harkness. I know you were at the football game. I know someone dressed as the mascot sabotaged our team's only chance for a win this season. I know that when you returned to your car, you were dressed in a costume that looks suspiciously like Viking attire. I know that someone dressed as our mascot defaced school property. I know that if I can get a confession out of Mr. Salgado then I'll be able to transfer you to Quiet Haven where you'll no longer be my problem. I know that colleges do not like to see expulsions on a student's permanent record. I know that McDonald's is always hiring. That's what I know."

I gulped. Stone was never going to believe I had nothing to do with this prank. He was like Odysseus's nemesis, Poseidon, an angry god who uses his powers to transform an easy trip home into a ten-year epic journey.

The bell rang, announcing the start of first period and the end of Stone's interrogation. "Well, I better be going. Don't want to be late for class."

"The bell tolls for thee, Mr. Barry. The bell tolls for thee."

I left Stone's office and rushed to the nearest bathroom. I was shaking all over and needed to take a few deep breaths to calm myself down. The boys' bathroom isn't the ideal place to take deep breaths, but it was the only space on campus that provided some privacy. Once safely protected by the four walls of the stall, I put my head between my knees and considered Stone's case against me.

It didn't look good. All Stone had to do was prove it was me performing at the game and I would be blamed for everything. Eddie wouldn't talk. Everyone underestimates his strength because he's a cheerleader, but that guy is as tough as nails. I once saw him stare down a two-hundred-pound wrestler who criticized one of Dawn's brownies at a fund-raiser. The guy ended up buying a dozen. But there were probably loads of other ways Stone could place me at the scene of the crime. Crystal's photographs, for one. They could probably zoom in on one of her shots and match the scar on my elbow. I lit myself on fire playing with matches and rubber cement when I was a kid (okay, it was last year) and now I have a scar that looks like Abraham Lincoln. What about my fingerprints? I'm sure they were all over the cheerleaders. That's what I get for trying to lift them out of the dog pile created by their collapsed pyramid. Stone could even go and talk with my former teacher Mr. Franklin, threatening to expose him as a LARPer unless he testified the exact time of my arrival and departure from Arroyo Park. My story had so many holes, and Stone would be happy to see me buried in any of them. He would blame me for sabotaging the game (rightly so) and defacing school property (wrongly so), and my future, the one I was hoping would never meet my past, would run into it like a comet crashing to earth.

And what's with the mystery vandal using the mascot head to spray-paint "Reserved for Idiot" on Stone's parking space? Was he trying to frame me? But why? I didn't have any enemies. Until yesterday, that is. Now I could count every football player and cheerleader as my mortal enemy. But they couldn't work that fast to destroy me. Besides, no one other than Eddie and Spencer knew it was me in that costume. Maybe the mystery tagger just stumbled upon the mascot head and used it to disguise himself while in front of the camera. Maybe it had nothing to do with me, and everything to do with Stone.

I left my protective stall and walked to first-period history. To discourage tardies to her first-period class, Ms. Atkins allows students to sit wherever they like; first come, first served. This means that all the seats in the back row are taken by the punctual and prepared, leaving the front row for the slackers like me. I sat down and took out my notebook and started copying the notes on the board. When Ms. Atkins paused in her lecture on Manifest Destiny, I turned around and scanned the room for Audrey. I didn't see her anywhere. I was beginning to think I had mistaken the LARPer I met last Friday for someone else when I saw her in the back corner, looking like she had just tumbled out of bed. Her brown hair, so carefully pulled back and adorned with daisies on Friday, fell in front of her face in a mass of frizzy curls. She wore large, unflattering glasses that sat crooked on her nose. Her bulky sweatshirt had a bad case of acne, sprinkled as it was with tea and food stains. I tried to keep the shock of disappointment from registering, but it must have flashed across my face long enough for her to notice. When I smiled and nodded my head in her direction, she ignored me and went back to scribbling in her notebook. As soon as the bell rang, she raced out of the classroom before I had a chance to call out to her. I reached into my backpack and pulled out the rose I had so carefully worked on over the weekend and threw it in the trash on my way out the door.

SIXTEEN

Stone called Eddie in to see him at brunch and ruined any possibility of conferring in person. Luckily, we both had vision-poor second-period teachers and were able to sync our stories before the bell rang. I told Eddie what I confessed to Stone (which was a long text message—good thing my English teacher decided to show a movie today), and his smiley-face emoticon indicated that he understood and would corroborate my version of events. When we finally met in fourth-period Yearbook, he was able to tell me everything that happened.

"First he played good cop and offered me candy. Then he played bad cop and threatened to suspend me. Then he played Robocop and quoted California Education Code Section 32261 on school crime and violence. Then he sounded like Kindergarten Cop and told me how even principals have feelings and that his were hurt by the vandal's act."

"Thanks for not bowing to that kind of pressure."

"He knew that the mascot sat with me for part of the game. Obviously, he's spoken to other witnesses. I told him I thought it was Phyllis Larouche. I hope she's got a good alibi."

"You guys talking about the Viking Vandal?" Crystal asked, sneaking up on us as usual.

"The what?" we asked in unison.

"That's what Brett's calling it on the *BS* website. Check it out." Crystal flipped her iPad around and showed us the headline, "Viking Vandal Vexes VIPs!"

"That's some awful alliteration," Eddie said.

"Brett thinks it's some kind of conspiracy," Crystal said. "Listen to this. 'Both Stone and Harkness refuse to comment on the ongoing investigation but have offered a twenty-five-dollar Starbucks gift card to anyone coming forward with information on the person's identity.'"

I breathed a sigh of relief over Stone's cheapness. A couple of lattes would hardly be reason enough for someone to snitch.

Crystal continued reading. "'Tortelli and the rest of the offensive line have offered to provide security detail for anyone with information related to the case.' That incentive should inspire every nerd at Meridian."

Eddie and I both looked at each other and gulped simultaneously. Those nerds were smart. And sneaky.

"What?" Crystal said, leaning in closer. "You guys know something?"

Eddie explained how we'd both been interrogated by Stone this morning. Crystal nodded. "I thought it was you too, Eddie," she confessed. "Until I saw you in the stands. But why would Stone think it was Lawrence? He never goes to games."

"Exactly!" I said. "Why indeed?"

"Unless you two were up to something. Where's your sling, anyway, Eddie?"

"Oh, that," Eddie said, looking down at his right arm, now sling-free. "My doctor said I don't have to wear it as long as I don't carry any heavy objects."

Crystal eyed him suspiciously.

"He's not a very good doctor," he added.

"Did you take any pictures of the mascot?" Eddie asked.

"I got tons."

"Can we see them?" I asked, as nonchalantly as I could, which apparently wasn't very nonchalant because Eddie kicked my shins from underneath the table and glared at me in warning.

"Sure," Crystal said, bringing up the album on her tablet. She scrolled through the pictures, pausing every now and then to show us a particularly good action shot of Jerry

Tortelli. There was Jerry throwing a pass. There was Jerry running with the ball. There was Jerry in the shower, his privates only slightly covered with an oversize bar of soap. "I Photoshopped that one," Crystal said proudly.

She scrolled forward until she got to the pictures she had taken of me as the Viking. We examined them closely, the way the detectives on *CSI: Miami* scour a crime scene for evidence.

"Whoever it was, they were a horrible dancer," Crystal said.

"It's probably hard to move in that suit," I said.

"And they smelled really bad," Crystal said.

"Can you imagine how hot that costume must be, though?" I said.

Eddie glared at me from behind Crystal's right shoulder and I shut up.

"The slender arms look feminine," Crystal said, zooming in on the image. "But I think our smelly dancer is male. What we're looking for is a hairless white guy with no muscle tone."

"There's got to be thousands of guys who fit that description," I said, rubbing my arms.

"I bet I could identify him at the homecoming dance," Crystal said.

"You want to help Stone?" I asked.

"I want to help Jerry," Crystal said dreamily. "He'd be so grateful. I'm going to show these to Harkness. Maybe he'll let me be the official team photographer."

"You better keep those guns under long sleeves for the next couple of weeks," Eddie said after Crystal had left us.

I looked at my pale forearms, still flabby after two days of lifting. "We need to find out who stole the mascot head," I said. "Whoever it is could get me in a lot more trouble. Stone's ready to transfer me to Quiet Haven as it is."

"Any leads?"

"I have no idea. It could be anyone with a grudge against Stone."

"So . . . anyone."

"Right."

"Wanna go to lunch and make a list of suspects?" Eddie asked.

"Can't today," I said. "I got this thing."

Eddie waited for me to elaborate, but the truth was I didn't have any details to give him. I was hoping to go to lunch with Adam and my crew but I hadn't texted them yet. A look of disappointment flashed across Eddie's face before he excused himself to go upload some candids from the Back to School Dance. I felt bad for blowing him off, but I needed to hang out with the guys before they banished me for good. While Eddie was occupied at the computer, I took out my phone and sent a message to Adam. *Chipotle?* he texted back a few minutes later. *See you in ten.*

As soon as the bell rang, I ran out to the parking lot and found the guys clustered around my car. "Dudes!" I yelled, high-fiving them.

"Wassup, dude?" Adam said. "Mind driving?"

I unlocked my car, and the five of us crammed in. The day was sunny and I wanted to be seen, so I opened the convertible top and entered the line of cars waiting to exit the parking lot. At lunch, there's always a bottleneck of vehicles trying to make a quick getaway. We inched forward slowly and shouted greetings to the girls passing us on foot. It felt good to be back with my crew. There was power in numbers, no doubt about it. For the first time in weeks, I felt safe and protected from Jerry and the football team and Zoe and the walking dead. Even Stone seemed like less of a threat.

I kept waiting for one of the guys to ask me where I'd been or what I'd been up to, but all they talked about was how hungry they were.

"So, my house arrest is nearly over," I said, making up an excuse for my absence these past few weeks.

"You've been grounded?" Adam asked.

"Yeah, that's why I haven't been around much," I said.

"I thought it was because you were helping the needy," Will said, lighting up the vape pen.

"Dude," I said. "Can't you wait until we exit the parking lot?"

"Relax," Adam said, sucking in the vapor. "Wanna hit?"

I shook my head. "I'm cool."

Adam passed the pencil-shaped inhaler to the guys in the backseat. I debated putting the top back on but didn't want to appear like more of a tool to my friends. They seemed to like having an audience anyway. One of the Nates waved a sophomore girl over to our idling car and exhaled into her face. "Gross," she said, waving the smoke away. Then she asked for a puff, which Nate gave her.

I focused on getting out of the parking lot. There were at least ten cars in front of me waiting to exit. Some responsible driver was letting all the pedestrian underclassmen have the right of way on the sidewalk. Didn't they know drivers had priority in this mass exodus? Freshmen and sophomores were supposed to yield to those who could run them over.

I honked my horn in frustration, which only prompted every other car in the lot to chime in. Before I knew it, the cacophony had drawn the attention of Riddel, our campus security guard. I looked in my rearview mirror and saw him approaching in his golf cart. The cart we had adorned with the Student Driver sticker only a few weeks ago.

"Seriously, guys," I said. "Put that thing out. If Riddel catches us, I'm getting sent to Quiet Haven."

I heard the guys in the backseat whisper something and laugh.

"What?" I said.

"Nothing."

"You guys said something. What was it?"

"He called you a pussy," Adam said, laughing.

"All I'm asking is that you guys light up after we've left the lot. Is that so hard? Are you *that* desperate to get high that you can't wait two minutes?"

Riddel pulled up alongside my car and looked in. "Gentlemen," he said. He was wearing his Oakley sunglasses, trying to affect the look of the LAPD cyborg who kills everyone in *Terminator 2*.

"Afternoon, Mr. Riddel," I said. "Lovely day, huh?"

The guys in the backseat burst out laughing, probably at my strained cheerfulness. Riddel, of course, took this as mockery against his person.

"You mind pulling over?" he said.

"We're kind of in a hurry here," Adam said.

"Pull over," Riddel said. "Now."

I swung out of the exit line and parked my car in the first available space. The guy in the car behind me unrolled his window and shouted, "Sucks to be you, Lawrence!"

Riddel got out of his golf cart and sauntered over to my side of the car. He scanned the interior without saying a word. The guys in the back must have stashed the vape pen somewhere because Riddel only grunted before asking me to breathe in his face.

"Excuse me?" I said.

"Come on," he said. "Let me smell it."

I heard the guys choke back their laughter. I complied with his request, having nothing to hide except the normal halitosis that comes from drinking too much coffee. Riddel stood inches away from my face and didn't twitch a muscle. "You can go," he finally said, uninterested in using his personal breathalyzer on the other occupants in my vehicle. I pulled into the line of traffic waiting to exit the parking lot. As soon as we hit the road, the guys erupted in laughter and lit up again.

"You guys are dicks," I said, and drove to Chipotle.

But maybe I was the dick. I should've stayed with Eddie.

SEVENTEEN

The Viking struck twice more that week. Tuesday night, he superglued the locks and hinges on the doors to the administration building so no one could enter. Thursday night, he dumped some chemical into the pool that turned the water bright pink. Each prank was captured by video surveillance, according to Brett Bridges on the *BS* website. The footage didn't reveal the Viking's identity, and the administration was still issuing no comments to our reporter's many questions. By Friday, thanks to Brett's coverage, people were talking about the Viking as if he were some superhero avenging the administration's disciplinary actions against our most delinquent students.

I, of course, remained high on Stone's Most Wanted list. He called me in after each prank and grilled me about my whereabouts. Unfortunately, I didn't have an alibi for either night, as both my parents were out of town. Dad was in Phoenix all week, helping a client get out of a complicated prenup. Mom was still laid up at Aunt Lucy's house, suffering from preadolescent overexposure. In her last video, she complained about how the family crowded into her bedroom for dinner so they could all be together. "My comforter might as well be a picnic blanket," she complained.

That left me under the care of Estrella, who passed out every night in front of the television. The only evidence I had that I wasn't at the scene of the crimes were the timestamps of my online activity, but I couldn't show those to Stone because most of my tweets talked about how much I hated school and/or sobriety.

Without any hard evidence, all Stone could do was threaten me with expulsion and arrest if and when I was finally caught in the act of vandalizing the school. "No one's going to save you this time, Barry," he said at the end of each meeting. "I don't care how good a lawyer your dad is."

I turned to the only person I knew who had the brainpower to help me out of this situation: Spencer. It was weird how important our mentoring sessions were becoming for me. I learned more valuable information in my thirty minutes with Spencer than I did in any of my classes. The other day, he'd explained why zombies wouldn't be able to attack us without a functioning circulatory system, which was an enormous relief.

We met at our usual morning session to discuss the case against me. "The Viking only strikes at night when the surveillance cameras are on," Spencer deduced. "Clearly, he wants these acts of vandalism to be seen by Stone."

"But why?"

"Maybe he isn't out to destroy the school," Spencer said. "Maybe he's out to destroy you."

"What do you mean?"

"You were the person last seen in possession of the Viking costume."

"Right."

"So, any acts of vandalism performed in the Viking costume will naturally be blamed on you. Are you committing these acts, Lawrence?"

"No!"

"Well, then. I would look to your enemies."

"But I don't have any enemies." Did I? Everyone loved Lawrence Barry. I was the life of most parties. How many times had I swallowed spoonfuls of cinnamon just because someone thought it would be hilarious? I always obliged any request to serve as taxi driver, pot dispenser, or cleanup crew. When I thought about it, most of my friends were kind of leeches, but none of them would turn on me like this after sucking me dry. Besides, they didn't have the creativity or initiative for the pranks the Viking pulled.

But who else did that leave? Who could hate me enough to try to get me kicked out of school?

And then it dawned on me. "It's Zoe Cosmos," I said to Spencer.

Spencer looked at me with interest, which involved the slight raising of his right eyebrow.

"Last time I saw her, she swore she would have my soul."

"You two have a complicated relationship."

"If I tell you something, do you swear to keep it to yourself?"

This was kind of a stupid question. As far as I could tell, I was the only person, besides teachers, that Spencer spoke to. Still, I waited for him to nod before I continued.

"Zoe and I hooked up at a party last year."

"By 'hooked up' do you mean you engaged in intercourse?"

"What? Ew! Gross, Spencer. No." I shook my head, trying to rid it of the image Spencer had conjured. Why would Spencer go there? I didn't think he knew anything about sex. That was going to be the focus of one of our future sessions, but I was saving it for spring because I didn't think he was ready for my porn collection. "We just messed around."

"Were you inebriated?"

"Of course," I said. "I woke up the next morning with my neck covered in purple hickies. It was awful. I had to wear turtlenecks for a week. Anyway, she kind of stalked me for a while after I stopped responding to her texts."

"Hell hath no fury like a woman scorned."

"Exactly. I'm sure she's the one framing me. She was out the night I ditched the Viking head in the bushes. She saw me in the mascot uniform."

"She seems the most likely suspect then."

"So how do I catch her?"

"Your best chance of catching her in the act is to wait for her at school. But if Stone sees you on campus at night, he will promptly arrest you."

"Right. That might be her plan anyway. To lure me into her web and trap me like a fly."

Spencer stared at me blankly. I pushed on.

"What I need is someone who can give me an alibi and is brave enough to stand up to Zoe's dark forces."

"I'm not allowed out after eight o'clock except for stargazing."

"Yeah, what's up with your mom anyway?" I hadn't had a chance yet to ask him about her insane behavior last Friday.

"She did not want to leave Norway."

I waited for Spencer to continue, but he stopped talking. I pressed for details. "Why did she freak out, though? Was it the Viking costume?"

"She would have reacted the same if you were dressed in your normal attire. Her impressions of the United States have been formed by excessive viewing of *Law & Order*. Are you familiar with the show?"

"Which one?"

"My mother watches all of them. It has given her a distorted view of life here. She thinks that if you step outside, you will be murdered."

"Has she seen our town?" I asked.

"It is illogical, and thus pointless to argue with her."

"But you have to. Otherwise, you'll never leave your back lawn."

"She lets me go to the library."

"And the park, right? How did you know about the LARPers?"

"My mother and I saw them performing on our way home from the supermarket. She thought it was a turf war."

"Spencer, we have to fix this. There's more to life than school and the library."

"You're forgetting I have my telescope."

"Oh right. My bad. You've got everything you need."

"I sense you're being sarcastic."

"I am. Let me talk with your mom. As your mentor, I feel it is my duty."

"I assure you, that would only make things worse."

"Well, we've got to do something."

"Let's solve your problem first. You need a witness who

can help you catch the saboteur."

"I was actually thinking about the girl I met at LARPing last week."

"They're congregating tonight if you want to see her again."

"I do want to see her again," I said. "And I need her to be in battle gear."

I arrived at Arroyo Park at the same time as last week. I wasn't in costume this time, so I stayed in my parked car and observed the LARPers from the curb. The crowd was spotlit in the dark by the streetlights, which were positioned twenty feet from each other along a cement bike path that snaked through the park's lawn. It didn't take me long to spot Audrey in the crowd. She was the only maiden carrying a sword and picking fights with the menfolk. The gray-haired women kept trying to lure her away with gossip or dancing, but she took little interest in these traditional gender roles. She was an anachronism within an anachronism.

When I sensed the crowd breaking up, I got out of my car and pretended to walk casually along the bike path, as if on an evening stroll.

"Hey, Audrey," I said, approaching her.

She spun around and squinted. Where were her glasses? Maybe corrective lenses didn't exist during the Renaissance.

Or maybe she only wore them at school to prevent people from seeing how hot she was, the way Clark Kent hides behind his dorky attire to protect his Superman identity.

She looked even more beautiful tonight than last week. She was dressed again in her Renaissance costume, which turned her breasts into a giant billboard that screamed, *Check these out!* Moving upward, my eyes drank in her pale, slender neck leading to her full, red lips, delicate nose, and slightly crooked eyes. Her forehead was sprinkled with perspiration, making her glow in the light of the streetlamp. A thin ringlet of light brown hair curled down from the mass of curls held back by a decorative hat.

"Lawrence," she said. "What brings you out in such strange costume?"

"I was just passing by and thought I'd say huzzah!"

Audrey smiled. She had a small gap between her two front teeth, which was weirdly sexy.

"Wither goest thou?"

"Me? Nowhere, really. How about you?"

"I am to bed. It has been a tiring evening. I am aweary of these revels."

"I can give you a ride. If you like."

"Good sir, I thank ye." She did a slight curtsy and followed me to my car. I worried she might carry the act too far and exclaim, "What strange carriage is this?" when she saw my BMW, but she got in without comment.

We settled in our seats and buckled up. Before starting the car, I turned to her and said, "Actually, I have a favor to ask you."

Audrey shifted uncomfortably in her seat. "I hardly know you, sir," she said softly.

"It's nothing weird," I said. "I was just hoping you could help me catch a vampire posing as a Viking."

I explained the situation as best I could, telling her everything from my disastrous mascot performance at the football game to my most recent meeting with Stone.

"That villainous harpy!" Audrey exclaimed after I told her my story, which was like the perfect thing to say. I would have leaned over and kissed her right then if I didn't think it would drive her out of my car and into oncoming traffic.

"How can I assist you?" she asked.

"How would you like to go on a stakeout?"

"Hold you the watch tonight?"

"Aye, m'lady," I said, and turned on the car.

EIGHTEEN

We parked across the street from the school and waited in the darkness. After about fifteen minutes, I realized this was an awful plan. Who knew when or if Zoe would make an appearance? Still, I didn't say anything because I liked being next to Audrey. Despite spending the last few hours sword fighting, she smelled of honey and lavender, and her fake English accent sounded like Hermione Granger.

"You sure you don't have to be home?" I asked when my digital clock clicked over to eleven o'clock. As much as I enjoyed sharing this confined space with Audrey, I could tell our stakeout was getting a little boring for her. She was used to swordplay and axe-throwing, not modern-day detective work.

"My grandmother is in deep slumber until the cock crows."

"What about your parents?"

"Alas, they have shuffled off this mortal coil."

"Meaning?"

"I am an orphan."

"Like, literally?"

Audrey nodded. I had never met a real orphan before. To be honest, I sort of thought orphans only existed in children's stories. Practically every book I read when I was little was about a young boy or girl who went off on great adventures after their parents died. It seemed kind of awesome, but I could tell by Audrey's expression that that had not been her experience.

"I'm sorry," I said. "That must . . . suck." I'm sure there was a better way to express my condolences, but at this moment words failed me. If only I had some ready-to-quote lines from Shakespeare like Audrey had memorized, I might be able to console her better.

Audrey shrugged. "They passed away when I was a wee thing. I struggle now to recall their faces, which makes me sad."

"Sometimes I feel like an orphan," I said. "My dad works all the time and my mom is never home. Want to see how we communicate?" I pulled up our family website on my phone and showed Audrey the chat session Mom and I had about my choice of vegetable for dinner.

"'Tis the modern age," she said.

"And it's only going to get worse. She met with some executives at VirtueTech this week who loved her site and want to scale it big."

"Do you miss them?"

"I did. Especially when I was younger. Then I got used to it. It's weird. Sometimes I wonder why my parents even had me in the first place. They've always worked hella long hours. I've pretty much been raised by nannies, cooks, and therapists."

I didn't like the way my driver's seat was starting to feel like a psychologist's couch. This kind of confession was not a great way to impress the ladies, especially on a first date. I should save the vulnerability for later. Right now, I needed to impress her with my rugged manliness. "Wanna see some origami?"

"Pardon?"

I reached into my backseat and grabbed the *Golf Digest* magazine Dad had conveniently "forgotten" when I gave him a lift to the airport. After carefully tearing out a page, I did some quick folds on the hard surface of my dashboard and presented Audrey with an adequate swan. Not my best work, but given the paper and workspace, it wasn't bad.

"'Tis a thing of beauty," she said, turning the creature around in her hands.

"I can do better," I assured her. "When I was thirteen, I won a silver medal in a national origami design contest."

"You're an artist," Audrey said. Did I detect a note of surprise in her voice? It was hard to tell through the fake British accent.

"Not really," I said. "I don't make much anymore."

"Why not?"

I shrugged. "Origami isn't cool like graffiti or even cartooning. It's closer to doing tricks with a yo-yo."

"Not true. Your work is like sculpture. You create winged creatures out of nothing."

"That's what I always loved about it. The purity. It's just you and the paper."

"Few men can see a swan in a plain piece of parchment." Audrey placed her fingertips against my thigh. "Do not trouble yourself with the opinions of others. To thine own self be true."

"Tell that to my dad. He was so happy when I gave up origami and started smoking pot."

"You lie."

"It's true. I mean, he wouldn't admit it, but he likes me better now that I have friends."

Audrey pulled her hand back and used it to cover her mouth. I didn't know if she was shocked by Dad's behavior or my own. Did she not know I smoked pot? I assumed everyone knew that, given my history of fuckups.

"But I'm done with that now. The pot smoking, I mean. I gave it up. Cold turkey."

Where do we come up with phrases like "cold turkey" and "on the wagon" to describe sobriety? Seems like we should update these to better convey the agony of deprivation. Something like "I'm off the grid" or "I'm flying coach" would work better.

"Anyway," I continued, "what sucks about Zoe framing me is the timing. It's like, I finally start to get my shit together and then I get in trouble for something I didn't do. Maybe it's karma."

"Our wills and our fates do so contrary run."

"How do you pull phrases like that out so easily?" I asked.

"I read a lot of Shakespeare."

"Because . . . ?"

"It's beautiful. His language makes sense to me. Even when I don't understand it."

"I feel the same way about Homer."

Audrey's mouth dropped open a few millimeters in surprise. I had to fight the urge to lean over and kiss her parted lips.

"You speak of the poet, not the cartoon character?"

"The poet. I've been reading *The Odyssey*."

Audrey closed her eyes and spoke in the soft voice of the Muse.

Many cities did he visit, and many were the nations with whose manners and customs he was acquainted; moreover he suffered much by sea while trying to save his own life and bring his men safely home; but do what he might he could not save his men, for they perished through their own sheer folly.

I stared at Audrey in wonder. This was the opening of *The Odyssey*. The girl must have a photographic memory. Either that or she heard the music in these classic texts that helped her memorize the lines. What I could do with Led Zeppelin lyrics, she could do with Shakespeare and Homer.

"Those are the lines that hooked me," I said. "Especially that last part."

Audrey nodded. "Odysseus's recklessness kills his crew."

"What? No, you have it backward. It's the crew that almost ruins him."

"The hardships they face arise from Odysseus's irresponsibility."

"Odysseus is the only smart one on board. His shipmates are the idiots."

"Kind sir, when your only route home is by sea, is it

intelligent to anger the ocean god by blinding his son?"

"The Cyclops was going to eat him!"

"Only because Odysseus broke into his home and stole his property!"

"I don't think it's cool to eat someone just for crashing at your pad."

"Odysseus slaughters all the suitors in his home for doing the same thing."

"That was different. They were trying to steal his woman."

Audrey groaned in exasperation. The sexual tension was definitely rising between us. Either that or Audrey was about to punch me. Sometimes I confuse the signals.

I wanted Audrey to lean a little closer, but she clung to the passenger door as if still undecided about her exit strategy. She probably thought I was that same dumbass stoner from last year. The one who might be pursuing her as part of some bet about who could hook up with the biggest weirdo on campus. I decided to allay her fears.

"This outfit really accentuates your"—don't say breasts, don't say breasts—"breasts."

"What?"

"Eyes! I meant eyes. You've got really pretty eyes."

Even in the dark I could feel Audrey's blush. Her face warmed the interior of my car like fast-food takeout.

"You know," I said with all the tenderness I could muster. "I could help you with your look."

"Help me?"

"Yeah. I've recently started mentoring this freshman who was a total mess. He had no clue how to fit in. He carried his viola case everywhere, wore cuff links to school, corrected people's grammar. Stuff like that. I've been working with him and now he's like a normal person. Well, not totally normal. He still cuffs his pants and doesn't look you in the eye when he's talking to you, but he doesn't stand out as much as he did before."

"And this is how you'd help me?" Audrey said, her tone about twenty degrees cooler than when she'd last spoken. "You'd make me normal?"

"Yeah. And you've got way less work to do than Spencer."

"Prithee. What is normal?"

"Normal is . . . normal."

Audrey looked at me strangely. Clearly, she was looking for a better definition of the word than the word itself.

"Normal is, well, you don't really see normal, because it's everywhere. It's invisible."

"So, you want me to be invisible?"

"Well, when you put it like that it doesn't sound very good."

"I think I'd like to go home now."

"Don't be mad. I'm not explaining myself very well. By normal, I mean normal. Shit, I did it again. What I mean to say is, you're smart, nice, and super hot when you dress in these Renaissance costumes. I want people to see that but not make fun of you. I want you to stand out but not in a weird way. You should stand out and simultaneously blend in. Does that make sense?"

She nodded but I could tell we were done for tonight. Maybe forever.

I dropped her off in front of a modest single-story home a few blocks away from school. Given Audrey's love of dress-up and make-believe, I half expected her residence to have turrets and be surrounded by a moat, but it was a normal house, as far as I could tell in the dark. A dim porch light illuminated a front door with peeling yellow paint. The lawn near the sidewalk was mostly dirt and weeds. I would have offered to loan her our gardener to spruce the place up, but Audrey didn't seem open to this kind of constructive criticism.

"See you at school Monday," I said as she exited the vehicle. She left the passenger door open and stormed up her walkway. About halfway to the front door, she paused, spun around, and marched back to me.

"My tongue will tell the anger of my heart, or else my heart concealing it will break," she said. She thrust the origami swan I had given her in my face. "Did you make this creature for me because it is what you think I am or what you want me to become?"

"What? No, I—"

"I know you mean well in wishing me normal, but I have no desire to be common."

"That's not what I meant."

"Might I remind you that *you* are the one dueling vampires and Vikings. That's hardly normal behavior. But it is precisely why I have grown fond of your company."

"I'm sorry. Forget I said anything."

Audrey nodded curtly and walked back to her home. Fixing her was going to be harder than I thought. At least with Spencer, he listened to my advice (and sometimes grudgingly accepted it). Audrey didn't even realize there was a problem that needed correcting. Still, the bigger the challenge, the bigger the reward. If I could fix Audrey, it wouldn't be so embarrassing to claim her as my girlfriend. I'm sure she'd see this as a win-win.

I did the gentlemanly thing and waited for Audrey to enter her home, but she just stood at the entrance and waved like someone on a stalled float. Eventually, it felt kinda weird to just sit there parked outside her house, so I drove off. I saw her shrink in my rearview mirror, but she didn't make any move to go inside.

I was exhausted when I got home so I went straight to

bed. As soon as my head hit the pillow though, my cell phone buzzed with an incoming text. My first thought was that it was Mom asking me to log in my sleep time (a new feature she was beta testing), but the text came from Eddie. *Did u do this?* he asked. Underneath his message was a photo of a pile of rubble. Two-by-four boards lay scattered in someone's driveway beside mounds of tissue paper and chicken wire.

What's this? I typed back.

The sophomore class homecoming float. It's been destroyed.

WTF? I texted back. Why would Eddie think I would do something like this? He texted me back another picture that was apparently being sent to every Facebook friend of Lindsey Spector, the sophomore class president. Spray-painted in bright red on her driveway was the message:

Better luck next time Lawrence.

NINETEEN

"There should have been a comma!" I said to Stone on Monday, after he summoned me from first-period U.S. History. "The message should have read, 'Better luck next time—comma—Lawrence.'" Whoever did this was sending me a message. With lousy punctuation."

"That's not the way it reads," Stone said.

"Why would I sign my name to an act of vandalism? I'm not that stupid."

Stone let that one hang in the air for a good thirty seconds before responding. He thrust a grainy black-and-white photo in my direction. I picked it up and saw a familiar Viking staring back at me. Whoever was wearing the mascot head was scaling a wooden fence, holding a crowbar.

"When was this taken?"

"Neighbors of the Spectors have a surveillance camera.

They said they saw some kid matching your description sneak into their yard around ten o'clock Friday night."

"How does this picture match my description?"

"You were the last one seen in possession of this Viking costume."

"But I already told you, it was stolen from my car."

"Yes, that's what you *told* me." He let that one linger too, hoping his stress of the word would persuade me to confess. It didn't.

"Can I go now?" I asked, after we sat in silence for what seemed like hours. "I'd like to get back to Ms. Atkins and the League of Nations."

"Fine," Stone barked. "But know this. You are not going to ruin homecoming for this school. It's the one week in the goddamn year that everyone looks forward to. No matter what it takes, I'm going to stop you. The terrorists will not win!"

I backed up slowly until I was out the door. Stone had just begun his rant against the Eighth Amendment to the U.S. Constitution when I exited the building.

I plodded back to class feeling like a warty ogre in Fairyland. Over the weekend, the more spirited members of our student body had beautified the campus with homecoming decorations. A giant banner hung at the entrance of the quad with the words "Once Upon a Time" written in large golden

Old English script. Posters depicting scenes of various fairy tales were taped up on walls, like pages ripped out of a giant's children book. Colorful paper streamers hung from the hallway overhangs and snaked up every post. The cafeteria had been transformed into the gingerbread house from Hansel and Gretel, a rather ominous metaphor for all the students who ate there regularly.

The decorations did nothing to lift my spirits. This was turning out to be the worst day of my life and it was only 8:30 a.m. Estrella had the week off, so I'd woken up late and missed my meeting with Spencer. He probably could have found a way out of this mess in the time it takes him to eat his yogurt. Then I got to U.S. History to find Audrey had transformed back into her homeless attire and wouldn't even say hello to me. When the summons came from Stone, a chorus of "oohs" and "ahhs" filled the class as if my history teacher had just turned the slip of paper she was holding into a dove and launched it in the room.

I debated going home, but that would just make me look even guiltier. Besides, I wanted to see Audrey before class ended and apologize for being such an ass last night. Maybe make plans to do another stakeout. Now more than ever, I needed a crime-fighting partner.

Just before I reached my classroom, Jerry Tortelli grabbed me by my shoulders and slammed me up against the wall. "Where you off to, Larry?" I hated it when people called me Larry, only because it invited the unfortunate coupling with my last name. That's right. When my parents named me after some favorite great uncle, they didn't consider that my name might one day be Larry Barry. Jerry had yet to make this connection. "Back to class," I said with what little breath I had left in my lungs.

Jerry stared at me. He had a ferret face that just asked to be punched. It's probably how he turned out so mean.

"Let me see something first," he said. He grabbed my left arm with both hands and examined my flesh as if looking for the meatiest section to take a bite. His thin lips twisted into the kind of snarl you see on animals in the middle of the food chain. "You've got girly arms," he said.

I yanked my girly arm out of his grip. "I'm not going to prom with you, if that's what you're asking," I said, and tried to scoot sideways into my classroom. Jerry pushed me up against the wall again and thrust his meaty arm up against my throat.

"Feel that, Larry?" His breath smelled of partially digested bacon. Or it could be the fried flesh of a younger sibling. Jerry's crushing of my windpipe made it impossible for me to speak, so I simply nodded.

"That's the last thing you're going to feel if I find out it was you in that mascot costume. We would have won that game if it wasn't for you."

"It wasn't me," I squeaked. A fitting epitaph for my tombstone, I figured.

"Pictures don't lie. Crystal showed me the photos."

"So?"

"Your arms are as skinny and weak as the mascot's. I'd say they were a perfect match."

The bell rang and I assumed our boxing match would end with Jerry releasing me from the ropes and returning to his corner. But he didn't. He kept me pinned to the wall for all the passing students to see. Boys and girls paused on their way to class and admired the scene, as if I were some squirming piece of art hanging in a museum. "His face is a nice shade of purple," one commented. "I like how he appears to be floating, his feet just inches above the ground." I pleaded with my eyes for someone to intervene, but no one dared come near and ruin our tableau. Brett, his scandal senses tingling, ran up with his camera and snapped our picture. "Any comment on your current predicament?" he asked.

I thought I'd be stuck smelling Jerry's bacon breath for the entire passing period, but then something struck him on the back of the head, causing him to drop me to the ground. I looked at the floor and saw an apple roll away. Jerry picked it up and looked around for the wayward Madison Bumgarner but found no one matching that description. I did my own visual scan and saw Audrey at the end of the hall, smiling mischievously like she did after swatting Zoe with the strand of garlic. She nodded, then disappeared around the corner. Jerry ran after some poor freshman wearing a Giants baseball hat and I sneaked back into my classroom and collected my things. My mood improved a little knowing at least one person at this school had my back.

Unfortunately, the feeling of security that my alliance with Audrey produced only lasted till brunch. When I went looking for Spencer in the cafeteria, an angry sophomore flung a carton of chocolate milk at me, missing my head by inches. Its contents exploded on the wall behind me, splattering a tile mosaic of Cesar Chavez and nearly starting a race riot.

Pretty much everyone else shunned me both in and out of class. Apparently, you can vandalize the school all you want, but touch a class's homecoming float and you're suddenly America's Most Wanted. Even Eddie wanted nothing to do with me. "Dude, I can't be seen with you right now," he said when I approached him in Yearbook. "No offense."

"*Et tu*, Eddie?" I muttered, repeating the only line I remembered from my eighth-grade reading of *Julius Caesar*. I was only in this mess because of him and his stupid crush on Dawn Bronson.

At lunch, I went searching for Spencer in the library, but

he was nowhere to be found. Was he avoiding me too? On my way out, I overheard a group of tenth-grade girls talking about making me the sole participant in a dunk tank fundraiser, which sounded like a spirited way to waterboard someone.

The only person who would talk with me was Brett Bridges, and that was only because he needed a confession for his "School Under Attack" series on the *BS* website. He had already posted his story about the morning altercation I had with Jerry. "Tortelli Corners Suspect" was the headline that ran over a picture of Jerry pinning me to the wall. "Stone doesn't summon you to his office unless you've done something wrong," Tortelli said in the article. "I know that dude's guilty." Brett talked with students in my first-period class who confirmed my summons to Stone's office and with students who knew me in my younger, wilder days. "That guy threw up on my pony," Samantha Fitzsimmons said, dredging up an incident I had hoped had faded from memory.

After school, he tracked me down on my way out to the parking lot and hounded me for a quote. "Why do you hate homecoming?" he asked, thrusting his iPhone in my face.

"I don't hate homecoming. I'm innocent."

"Where were you at the time of the float attack?"

"I was studying."

"Any witnesses?"

I thought about Audrey. The one girl who could rise to my defense wouldn't speak unless dressed in her Renaissance Faire costume, and even then most people wouldn't understand her. "No. Do you usually have people witnessing your studying?"

"Yes. I work in study groups. Is it just homecoming you hate, or the whole school?"

"I don't hate either."

"Because you were kind of a derelict last year. Didn't your friend get sent to Quiet Haven?"

"So?"

"So, is your plot to destroy homecoming some kind of revenge?"

"This interview is over, Brett."

"Vote for me for homecoming king!" he said, and slapped one of his stickers on my chest. When Brett saw his neon sticker on my polo shirt, he paused, then ripped it off like a Band-Aid. "Actually, you're not the best billboard for me right now. No offense."

I needed Spencer's help to find a way out of this mess. I drove to his apartment but no one was there. Either that or his mom saw me standing outside and locked her son in a panic room until the intruder disappeared. I ran through the list of places Spencer was allowed to visit. Luckily, it was a short list. If he wasn't at home or school, he was probably at the public library. I got in my car and drove there, *Fast & Furious* style.

TWENTY

The library was only a few blocks away, sandwiched between the police department and an old folks' home. I could see why Spencer's mom okayed the venue. Having never been inside before, I was surprised how bright and bustling the place was. There were parents reading to their kids, middle schoolers playing games on computers, and a cluster of teens hanging out in the manga section, devouring the comics with a concentration I normally associate with secret agents dismantling a bomb.

I spotted Spencer sitting alone at a table in the back corner and made my way toward him. I don't know why I had such faith that he could help me win back my reputation. It's not like his previous plans had worked in my favor, although it wasn't fair to blame him when I was the one who bungled his brilliant tactics. Maybe I just liked talking to him. He,

Eddie, and Audrey were the only ones who didn't judge me for being such a screwup. They listened to my problems and sincerely wanted to help me solve them. No one else in my life showed that kind of interest, except maybe Estrella, but all her advice was in Spanish and usually involved an excessive number of Hail Marys.

"Hey, Spencer," I said.

"Lawrence," he said, positioning his finger on the magazine page to keep his place. "I didn't expect to see you here."

"Watcha reading?"

Spencer held up the magazine, which was titled *The Journal of American Folklore*. "I'm trying to familiarize myself with the American fairy tales on display for homecoming."

"I think you'd have better luck in the children's section."

"Yes, you're probably right," he said, closing the magazine. "But the rules governing the children's behavior in that section of the library are fairly lax."

"Listen, I was hoping you could help me." I sat down across from him and explained my predicament. Spencer nodded, acknowledging that he was aware of the growing animosity toward me on campus. "I overheard a group of sophomore boys talking about deflating your car tires this morning."

"I have to prove to everyone it wasn't me. How can I do that?"

"You still believe the person wearing the Viking mask is Miss Cosmos?"

"I'm sure of it."

Spencer cocked his head and thought for a moment. "Our strategy must be twofold."

I liked how he referred to this as "our" strategy. Spencer and I were in this together.

"First, we must warn the other class presidents that their floats are in danger."

"I can do that," I said. "Dawn is the senior class president. Eddie can give me her phone number. I'm Facebook friends with Susie Durango, our class president. I can post something on her wall."

"If Miss Cosmos is trying to frame you, she'll probably leave the junior class float alone."

"Right. That leaves the freshman class. Unfortunately, I don't know any freshmen."

"I am a freshman."

"Oh, that's right. I keep forgetting you're not a graduate student. Who's your class president?"

"Heidi Schwam. I know her. We can warn her now if you have a car."

"You're allowed to leave the library? What about your mom?"

"She's running errands. She said she'd return in one hour,

which gives us thirty-two minutes to alert Miss Schwam if we leave now."

Spencer didn't wait for my answer. He packed up his things and ran a hand over his hair, which was already as flat and neatly divided as the magazine he left open on the table. It suddenly struck me that Spencer may have actual feelings for this Heidi Schwam. This meant that he wasn't an android after all. Of course, deep down I'd always known Spencer was human, but still it was nice to see this confirmed. I escorted him to my car and within minutes we were driving to Miss Schwam's house.

"So what's the other fold in our twofold plan?"

"After we warn the presidents, you must follow Miss Cosmos."

"What do you mean?"

"Now that she is targeting sites beyond the school grounds, her actions are less predictable. You must follow her to discover the next site of attack."

"A preemptive strike. I like it. I'm like a military drone."

"I'm not advocating you eliminate her."

"Right. Understood."

"Just follow and stop her before she destroys another float. Perhaps Miss Sieminski can assist you?"

"I was thinking the same thing," I said. In my mind I pictured Audrey in a tight corset taking Zoe down in a shallow mud puddle, the two of them splashing about, getting all wet and dirty, bodies intertwined . . .

"Lawrence, stop, we're here," Spencer said, snapping me out of my fantasy. I shook my head clear and parked in front of Heidi's house, which was decorated with political ad signage for the upcoming election. If I recognized any of the candidates or understood any of the initiatives, I would be able to tell you her family's political leanings. But unfortunately, I did not. The *This House Is Protected by Smith & Wesson* sign made me think they leaned Republican.

I looked over at Spencer and saw him anxiously running his hands down his pant legs, like they were twin irons pressing out creases. What fantasies were running through his overdeveloped brain right now? Probably something involving him and Heidi in front of a giant whiteboard covered with a complicated math equation. I had to help him win her over. He might be an expert in all things that required thinking, but when it came to matters of the heart, no one could incite strong feelings like Lawrence Barry.

We rang the doorbell. Before anyone answered, I quickly untucked Spencer and ruffled his hair. "Trust me, dude," I said, when he grunted something. "Girls like to see something they can fix."

Heidi opened the door and smiled like she didn't know her teeth were covered in braces. Her sandy blond hair was in pigtails and she held a clarinet in her hands.

"Hey, Spence!" she said.

"Hello." Spencer's voice cracked just a little. "Heidi, this is Lawrence Barry."

"'S'up," I said, nodding my head.

Heidi nodded back, but something in her response seemed a little apprehensive. I figured it was because she wasn't used to having cool upperclassmen dropping by her house uninvited. This could be useful in helping her see Spencer as a dangerous bad boy. Another thing the ladies seemed to like.

"We've come to talk with you about some concerns we have about the freshman homecoming float's safety," Spencer said.

"What do you mean?" Heidi looked a little confused, so I clarified.

"We think someone's going to trash it."

Heidi opened the door and led us inside. Any questions about her family's political leanings were cleared up when I glanced around at the walls and mantels of her living room. A framed copy of the Constitution hung under a spotlight above their fireplace. Next to it was a picture of a man in full military garb I assumed to be Heidi's father shaking the hand of President Bush. There were other framed photos of military vessels as well as model replicas of fighter planes, battleships, and tanks. Medals of valor and a neatly folded flag were encased in what looked like a glass coffin.

Heidi must have noticed my mouth hanging open because she said, "My dad's a Marine."

"That's cool. Where does he keep his weapons?" I asked, trying to lighten the mood.

"In the bedroom," Heidi said. "I'm not allowed in there." An orange tabby cat sauntered into the room. "C'mere, Patches," she said, scooping him up and cradling the squirming animal in her arms.

We walked to the backyard, where the float was being assembled. My first thought in seeing it was that we were too late; the vandal had already struck. When I saw Heidi standing before the structure proudly, I realized that this was what it was supposed to look like, but for the life of me I could not figure out what fairy tale it was modeled after, unless there's some Brothers Grimm story about a massive piece of chicken wire and tissue paper that I hadn't read. "*The Little Mermaid*?" I guessed, just to be polite.

"Thank you!" Heidi beamed, finally losing some of her apprehension toward me. "No one else seems to get it."

I looked at Spencer to gauge his reaction, but as usual he was about as easy to read as my trigonometry textbook. At most, I detected a forlorn expression as he looked at the pile of rubbish that sat on the truck bed on Heidi's lawn. It was a disaster, but most freshman floats are. The biggest question I had was how our Viking vandal was going to sabotage something that already looked like a pile of junk.

"I heard about the sophomores' float getting destroyed," Heidi said. "Everyone thinks you did it."

"That's not true," I said. "Someone is trying to frame me."

Heidi turned to Spencer for confirmation. "The person committing these acts of vandalism is using the Viking mascot uniform to hide his or her identity. Since Lawrence was the last one seen in possession of the uniform, suspicion has fallen on him."

"You don't think he's doing it?" Heidi asked.

"I do not," Spencer said.

"We just came to warn you," I said.

Heidi looked over at her float. "I can get my dad to do some recon," she said, thinking aloud. "We've got some netting we can use to booby-trap the backyard."

"No land mines?" I said, again trying to lighten the mood.

"I don't think the situation calls for that," Heidi said in total seriousness. "Yet."

"Okay," I said, backing away. "Looks like you've got things covered here."

"Hey, Spence," Heidi said, touching Spencer on the shoulder. "Since you're here, wanna work on Ariel's tail with me?"

"I, uh . . ." For the first time since I met him, I saw Spencer struggle for an answer. The poor guy must be doing furious mental calculations trying to figure out how much time remained before his mother returned from her errands. Heidi's hand on his shoulder probably wasn't helping his concentration.

"Spencer and I are going to a concert," I said, to help the guy out.

"You going to hear the youth symphony perform that Tchaikovsky piece?" Heidi said, bouncing from heel to toe.

"Nah. We're going to the Japandroids concert at the Fillmore. See ya!"

Spencer opened his mouth to speak. Not trusting his ability to improvise, I hastily escorted him out the door and back to my car. Spencer was strangely quiet during the ride back. I figured he was trying to find a way to thank me, but when I parked the car, he left without saying a word. Most likely he was worried that his mother was scouring the stacks looking for him. I followed him inside in case he needed any help with her.

I watched Spencer do a quick visual scan of the area and then walk into the boys' bathroom. After waiting outside for a few minutes, I walked in to find out what was wrong. Glancing under the stall door, I saw his polished dress shoes furiously tapping the linoleum floor.

"Spencer?" I said. "You okay?"

"I wish you hadn't done that."

"Done what? Made you look cool?"

"Lied to Heidi. It was unnecessary."

"I was just trying to help."

"The story you told is not something I can continue. What do I say when Heidi asks me about the concert tomorrow?"

"Tell her it was awesome. I've seen them before. I can give you details."

"I can't invent things like that, Lawrence. You have put me in a very uncomfortable situation."

"Spencer, I'm sorry. I was only trying to help."

"I don't know why you think you have to lie to have people like you."

"What? I don't do that. It was just a story. You're making way too big a deal about it."

"If you don't mind, I'd like to be left alone now."

"Seriously?" When he didn't respond, I left. That's what you get for trying to help people. It's like what Spencer said earlier about the boomerang effect. You try to do something nice for people and all it does is bite you in the ass. Well, fuck it. If Spencer didn't want to look cool in front of the girl he liked, he could sit and cry in that bathroom stall all day for all I cared.

I drove home and ignored my phone alerts telling me there was a new message on our family website. All I could think of was that I wanted to get wasted. I texted Will and the two Nates, but none of them wrote back. They probably wanted nothing to do with me after I flipped out on them during our Chipotle run. The only way I'd be invited back into the fold was if I opened my house for a keg party, but I'd seen what happened to places when they were filled with a bunch of drunk teenagers and it wasn't pretty. I wasn't ready to make that kind of sacrifice to restore my popularity. Not yet.

I went up to my room and took out the joint I had hidden in the origami shoebox in my closet. The rainbow zoo of animals and insects I had created over the years stared back at me like neglected pets. Maybe Spencer was right. Maybe I did lie to make people like me. My whole persona was like a wobbly house of cards that threatened to collapse at any moment. The first two beams of this foundation were created when I lied to Eddie in eighth grade about going to Hawaii. I didn't want to look pathetic for being left behind by my parents for Dad's "no kids allowed" fiftieth birthday party. Eddie always took these cool vacations with his family and I didn't want him to think that my family was any different. But of course Eddie wanted to hear about the trip, which required making up a bunch of stories, and supporting them with photographic evidence, which required learning Photoshop. The harder part was keeping Eddie away from my parents, which meant never inviting him over to my house, which required a whole new set of lies to explain, until eventually it all got so complicated it just became easier to drop Eddie as a friend and take up smoking pot.

At least pot let me forget about the unstable architecture of my personality, if only for a moment. Maybe that was why it was such a relief to hang out with Spencer, Eddie, and Audrey. They were already so weird, I didn't feel the need to impress them. In the two evenings I had spent with Audrey, I told her things I hadn't admitted to the guys I'd hung out with for the past two years.

I dropped the joint back in the shoebox and dug my student directory from the depths of my desk drawer. I wrote down Zoe Cosmos's address, then dialed Audrey's phone number. A woman answered on the first ring. "Who is calling?" she asked.

"My name's Lawrence," I said. "Is Audrey there?"

"What is it you want with Audrey?" She sounded Russian. There was a hint of KGB in her interrogative style.

I need her help to fight a demon, I wanted to say, but instead I claimed to need help with homework. The woman dropped the receiver onto what sounded like a hard Formica surface and clomped away.

I heard Audrey pick up the phone a few minutes later. "I got it, Grandma!" she yelled. I waited for Grandma to hang up the phone but I didn't hear any clicks. In fact, her heavy breathing on the other line was quite audible. "Grandma!"

Audrey yelled again. "Hang up the phone!"

Grandma refused to oblige so I started peppering Audrey with largely made-up questions about our U.S. History homework. Throughout our discussion I could hear Grandma's Darth Vader rasps on the other end. Finally, Audrey hung up the phone on her end and stomped downstairs, where Grandma was probably seated at her listening station at the kitchen table. After some struggle, Audrey wrestled the receiver away from Granny. "Sorry about that," she said, breathing heavily.

"No problem. I just wanted to thank you for nailing Jerry with that apple," I said. "You should really be playing softball with that arm."

"Would that make me more normal?" Audrey said in a barely audible voice.

Ugh. This wasn't starting off well. "No, that's not what I meant at all. I just wanted to thank you for rescuing me. Again."

"It was my pleasure."

"Listen, are you free tonight?" I asked. "I could use your help with something."

"I think so."

"Good. Meet me at Arroyo Park at seven. And come dressed for battle."

TWENTY-ONE

I waited for Audrey on a bench by the illuminated tennis courts. Two old dudes swatted a ball back and forth, a bit wobbly on their failing knees. I must have fallen into a kind of trance watching the ball move in its slow, plunking rhythm, because I didn't hear Audrey right away.

"Good evening, Lawrence."

I turned and saw her standing about ten feet back near a cluster of trees. She seemed reluctant to enter the glare of the overhead lights. I left the middle-aged dads with their terrible backhands and moved toward the Renaissance maiden waiting for me under the canopy of redwoods.

Audrey, as usual, was beautifully made up with her tight corset, billowy dress, and lace-up boots. Her hair was pulled back with a headband and decorated with tiny daisies. In her left hand she held a sword that, in the glow of the nearby tennis court lights, looked almost real.

"Where is your weapon?" she asked.

I pointed to my forehead. "My weapon is intelligence."

"Oh." Audrey sighed. "I thought we would be sword fighting."

"No, we're battling vampires."

I explained the situation as best I could in Shakespearian English, peppering my speech with many "thous" and "whatnots" and "forsooths." Audrey looked confused.

"Your speech lacks clarity," Audrey said. "Am I to understand that we are protecting a mermaid from a bloodsucking hellion?"

"Basically, yes."

"But Lawrence, surely these are figments of your overactive imagination. Such things do not exist in this world."

"Oh, they exist," I said. "As sure as wizards and dragons."

She couldn't argue with this logic. We walked back to my car and drove to Zoe Cosmos's house.

Zoe lived in a modest two-story house with a porch swing and a nicely manicured lawn bordered by daisies. Something my history teacher said about the banality of evil floated into my head as I parked the car across the street and turned off the engine.

"Think Zoe is adopted?" I asked.

Audrey shrugged.

"Probably switched at birth by a Satanist nurse," I went on. "I bet the Dark Lord wanted his daughter to grow up in a typical suburban home."

Audrey clearly wasn't interested in talking about Zoe's upbringing, so we sat in uncomfortable silence for what felt like hours. There was no visible movement, either in the house or outside. From the front window we could see the dim, flickering light of a television in some back room, but beyond that both the house and the street were quiet. "Maybe we already missed her," I said. "Think we should drive to Heidi's?"

Audrey, all dressed for battle with no one to slay, looked at me with a bored and annoyed expression. "I would prefer if you just took me home."

"I need you, Audrey," I said. "I can't fight Zoe on my own."

"Methinks you have feelings for this girl and for some reason you brought me along to rub my face in your amorous quest."

"What? No! Gross! How could you think that?"

"The border between love and hate is unmarked territory, Lawrence. I believe you are in no-man's-land."

"No, I'm firmly planted on the side of hate, believe me." Now it was my turn to be offended. "You must think I'm an incredible asshole to bring you along to help me score with Zoe Cosmos."

"It is my humble opinion that you do not know what you want."

This would have stung more if it hadn't come from a girl living simultaneously in two different centuries.

"I can see why you like her," Audrey went on. "She is unafraid to present herself to the world, unlike me."

"She's evil," I said. "I like *you*, Audrey. Okay? I like spending time with you, even though I can't understand what you say half the time. I like your bravery, your imagination, your independence. I especially like this lace-up thing you wear, and think it suits you much better than those bulky sweatshirts you're always dressed in at school. If I'm going to face my death at the hands of the devil, then I want you by my side because I have confidence that you will help me, and even if you can't, yours is the face I would like to see before I have the lifeblood sucked out of me."

I was prepared to go on, inspired as I was by the sweet and sad expression on Audrey's face, but she leaned across the seat and stopped my lips moving with a kiss that tasted of maple syrup. "Did you have pancakes for dinner?" I asked, pulling away and staring at her face.

She nodded.

"I thought I was the only one who refused to pigeonhole pancakes as breakfast food." I smiled, and then, to use a Renaissance phrase, I ravished her. We made out, maneuvering our bodies around seatbelt buckles and emergency parking brakes, not to mention Audrey's sword, which kept jabbing me in the ribs.

A passing car spotlit us with its high beams and we broke apart for a moment. I looked at Audrey's dreamy expression in the soft light of the streetlamp and thought I'd never seen something so lovely. "Can I ask you a question?"

"Of course."

"Promise you won't get mad?"

"I make no such promise," she said, straightening up. "Choose your words wisely, sir."

"Why do you dress the way you do at school? Your plain-Jane attire is, like, on purpose, right?"

Audrey turned her head and stared out the window at the darkened suburban street. After a few minutes of silence, she turned to me and spoke in a soft voice. "In middle school, I had one friend. Chloe. We were as close as twin sisters. One day, a group of girls decided they didn't like Chloe and tormented her until she transferred schools. Their foul play was heinous, but what made it worse was how random it was. The girls could have just as easily persecuted me, but giddy Fortune's furious fickle wheel selected my friend for their abuse. After Chloe left, I decided that the safest way to survive was to become invisible. So that's what I did."

"That's awful."

"Now it's my turn to ask a question."

"Fair enough."

"Why do you care so much about catching the Viking?"

That was easy. "I don't like people thinking I'm an ass-hole."

"But aren't there easier ways to clear your name?"

"I guess. Maybe I'm tired of people thinking I'm an idiot."

"You want to be the hero," Audrey said, smiling. "You want people to like you."

I shrugged. "Is that so bad?"

"It can be if the people you want to impress aren't worthy."

"I happen to think there are more good people at our school than bad."

Audrey's smile faded. "I'm afraid we disagree on this point."

As if on cue, Zoe walked out of her house.

"There she is," I whispered. Strangely, I didn't feel any of the coldness I normally experience when Zoe is within a few city blocks of me. Audrey must act as some kind of shield of goodness, protecting me from Zoe's dark arts. We watched our suspect glance up and down the block and then head off in the direction of the school.

"Come on," Audrey said, opening the door. "This may be our only chance."

I joined Audrey on the sidewalk, unsure if it was proper detective etiquette to trail our suspect holding hands. I felt like some gesture of appreciation for the makeout session was required, so I squeezed her elbow.

We followed Zoe from a distance of about half a block. It was hard at times to see her, given that she was dressed all in black. At one point, she turned around and her pale face looked like it was floating in space. Both Audrey and I ducked behind a parked car and held our breath, hoping she hadn't spotted us. When she started moving again, she walked slowly, like someone taking a stroll on the beach, or in Zoe's case, the burning lake of hellfire.

When she finally reached the block where Heidi lived, she slowed her pace even more and we had to hide behind a tree to avoid being seen.

"I knew it," I said when she finally stopped a few feet from the gate that led to the backyard of Heidi's house. "She's the one."

"Where's the Viking head?" Audrey asked. "Why isn't she disguising herself?"

"She's probably doing some preliminary scouting."

Zoe paused before entering Heidi's backyard and looked around the bushes that bordered the side gate. When she reached for the gate's handle, she must have triggered some motion sensor, because she was immediately illuminated by a beam coming from under the eave of Heidi's house. Zoe quickly jumped back in the bushes and hid until the light switched off. When it did, she emerged slowly and seemed to take stock of the situation. A few minutes later, we saw her move over to the neighbor's house, open the gate, and disappear behind the wooden door.

"Let's alert the family," Audrey said. "She's going to try to enter from the back."

"We need to catch her in the act," I said. "I'm going to follow her."

"I'll go to the other side of the house and block her exit," Audrey said, and disappeared.

Zoe had left the neighbor's side gate slightly ajar, so it was easy to peer in and see if she was waiting for us. She wasn't. The door opened up on a narrow corridor sandwiched between the neighbor's house and the gate. I saw Zoe at the back, climbing up a tree with boughs that hung over into Heidi's backyard. She was going to drop into Heidi's yard from above and then do her dirty work. I guessed she wasn't going to worry about disguising herself this time, maybe because entering and exiting Heidi's house was more complicated than at the other houses she had broken into. She probably didn't want anything impeding her escape plan.

I waited for her to drop from the tree branch she clung to, but she just sat there. Maybe Heidi's dad was doing recon in the backyard, but when I peeked through the slats of the wooden fence, I just saw the mess of a float where it had been earlier that day. No sign of Heidi's dad. I checked my watch. 11:30 p.m.

I sneaked a little closer, keeping close to the gate, trying to get a better look at what Zoe was up to. While balanced on the tree limb, she pulled her cell phone from her pocket. For a brief second, the screen illuminated her face before she called someone and whispered something I couldn't hear from my distance. A few seconds later, I saw the Viking's head pop up from the other fence, the one that bordered the neighbor opposite us. The one Audrey was supposed to be guarding.

"Zoe must be the advance lookout," I muttered aloud. It made perfect sense. Even with Satan's help, dismantling floats was a two-person job.

I watched our Viking jump down into Heidi's yard and cautiously approach the float. He was wearing a backpack and when he got up close to the structure, he unzipped it and pulled out a crowbar and what looked like wire cutters. He walked around the structure, probably trying to figure out how he could make this thing look any worse.

I held off raising the alarm because I wanted Zoe busted. If the family caught the Viking now, she could scamper down the tree and escape into the night with me powerless, as usual, to stop her. No, I had worked too hard to let her off that easy. This devil was going down, and she was going down tonight.

I ran over to the tree and grabbed hold of the branch where Zoe was perched. Zoe gave a yelp of surprise as the bough dipped dramatically, causing her to drop her phone onto Heidi's lawn below. I started shaking the tree branch, trying to loosen her grip and make her drop to the ground. Zoe hung on like a cat trapped above water, but our combined weight was too great for this limb and the thing creaked and snapped, sending her plummeting onto Heidi's lawn. I heard Zoe land with a thud and an oomph.

I jumped up and peered over the fence. "I got her!" I called out to Audrey.

The lights in Heidi's house suddenly came on, freezing the Viking in his tracks. He dropped his crowbar and took off running toward the opposite fence. With a leap worthy of a parkour enthusiast, he was up and over the barrier and out of sight. At least we still had one half of the crime syndicate. I vaulted over the fence myself, though not as gracefully as our bandit, landing on Zoe's leg, which made her scream bloody murder.

"Gotcha!" I screamed, wishing I had thought up a better catchphrase.

Zoe stared at me, her face full of rage and pain. "You idiot!" she screamed back. "We nearly had him."

"Yeah, but now we have you," I said, more pleased with this witty retort than my "Gotcha" comment earlier.

Seconds later, Heidi and her dad were standing behind me. Heidi was in flannel pajamas decorated with what looked like tiny Republican elephants. Her father was in boxers and a T-shirt, his bulging muscles filled with steroids and adrenaline.

"Zoe, what happened?" Heidi asked. She was holding a cell phone. I looked down at the phone that Zoe had dropped. It lay about a foot away from where she fell. I started to make some connections that didn't bode well for me.

"You two know each other?"

"She's my mentor in the Buddy Club," Heidi said. "She was helping me catch the Viking."

"Lawrence ruined everything," Zoe groaned.

"But . . . how?"

"Zoe was guarding the float," Heidi explained. "She just texted me to call the police when you came along."

I don't know which information stunned me more: the fact that I had just let the Viking escape or that Zoe was in the Buddy Club. When my counselor suggested I join the program, I thought he saw potential in me to help someone in need. If Zoe was a mentor too, it could only mean one thing: the Buddy Club was a cult that sold the souls of freshmen to Satan.

"At least your float is safe," I offered weakly. Heidi's dad grabbed me by the shirt collar and dragged me inside.

I was held captive in Heidi's kitchen while they examined the video Zoe had made of the Viking's appearance. Zoe had just started zooming in on the shadowy figure when my shaking of the tree made it impossible for her to hold the camera steady. All the footage showed was Zoe experiencing a magnitude 7.0 earthquake until my face appeared saying, "Gotcha."

Heidi's dad, clearly trained in the art of breaking down terrorist suspects, interrogated me for thirty minutes, trying to extract a confession that I was in league with the Viking. I did my best to explain what happened but he kept accusing me of "playing dumb."

"I don't think he's playing," Zoe said at one point.

"Maybe we should use the enhanced interrogation techniques," Heidi suggested. Her cold, hard stare matched her father's, and suddenly I realized why she'd run unopposed for freshman class president.

"Baby, you know we can't do that," Heidi's dad said.

"Because of the Geneva Convention," I said.

"No, Dad's inversion table is broken."

"The neighbors complain about the screaming," he added.

They kept me for another twenty minutes before letting me go. Heidi's dad drove Zoe home but left me stranded at

the curb. I looked around for Audrey but didn't see her anywhere as I walked back and picked up my car. I expected to
find a note stuck to the windshield from Audrey, maybe apol-
ogizing for not coming to my rescue, but there was nothing.
Maybe she ran out of ink and parchment. Or maybe I had
totally made a fool of myself and now Audrey wanted nothing to do with me.

TWENTY-TWO

I drove to school the next morning full of anxiety and dread. I half expected Stone to be waiting for me in the student parking lot with my exit papers. As soon as Zoe and Heidi offered their eyewitness accounts of me helping the Viking Vandal, he would have all the evidence he needed to transfer me to Quiet Haven. He couldn't prove I was the Viking, but he wouldn't need to. It was enough that I aided and abetted the vandal in his crimes. Perps went to Rikers on flimsier evidence, or so *Law & Order* would have you believe. It was over. Better to accept it now than to cling to false hope.

I stepped out of my car, and who should be there to greet me but Zoe, looking like an oil spill on the Mediterranean Sea. Today, she'd accentuated her black attire with a black beret, which sat on her thick, bristly hair like an upended cereal bowl. Her powers must have been set to low because the sun and birds didn't drop lifeless from the sky.

"I've been waiting for you, Lawrence," she said. Her lips looked stained with the blood of the innocent.

"What do you want?" I fell back against my car and tried to control my bowels.

"You," she said in the quiet, sinister voice usually adopted by deranged hypnotists, "are taking me to homecoming."

"What?" I rasped.

"You. Are. Taking. Me. To. Homecoming," she repeated.

Unable to breathe, I shook my head as if she were trying to spoon-feed me a puree of brussels sprouts and gasoline. I saw students exit their cars and walk toward the campus, completely unaware that the world was coming to an end. I wanted to scream for help, but some deeply embedded survival instinct cautioned me that the story of Lawrence Barry being bullied by a four-foot-eight-inch girl would be repeated as campus folklore well beyond my graduation date.

Despite my heart beating in what felt like triple time, my body seemed suddenly deprived of blood. I would have fainted if Zoe wasn't sandwiching me between her body and the side of my car.

"Why?" I managed to squeak.

"I like you. Is that so hard to believe?"

"Yes."

Zoe ran a long, crimson-painted nail along my forearm.

It felt like someone dragging a burning match against my skin. "You're cute, in a dumb puppy kind of way," she said. "Which reminds me, you'll be wearing a studded collar and leash to the dance."

"What? Why?"

"Revenge, mostly. Plus it will go with my outfit. You shouldn't have ignored me the way you did last year after we got together."

I couldn't breathe. My fingers clawed at my throat, trying to get my windpipe to open. All I managed was a few choked gasps. "Never," I managed to say.

"Then I show Stone the little movie Heidi made of you foiling our attempt to capture the Viking. I think you know what conclusion he'll draw from seeing that."

"You wouldn't."

"I think you know I would."

"I have an alibi," I said. Audrey could testify on my behalf, provided they had a translator who spoke Shakespeare.

"You say alibi, I say accomplice. Who do you think Stone will believe?"

Zoe had me trapped in her web. Both she and I had seen the Viking make his getaway last night. If I used Audrey as my alibi, Zoe would claim she was the Viking and then we'd both get in trouble. It did look kind of suspicious that Audrey disappeared after I was caught. I'm sure she had her reasons for running away, but Stone wouldn't listen to them.

"You're evil," I said. "Why are you even in the Buddy Club?"

"I feel like I have something to offer," Zoe said, examining her bloodstained nails. "Plus, I enjoy virgin sacrifices. Tell you what. I'll convince Heidi to ask your little friend to the dance and we can double date. Would you like that?"

"Does Heidi like him?"

"She does. She's pretty conservative and thinks Spencer's formality is refined. She has no idea he's on the spectrum."

"What do you mean?"

"You don't know either?" Zoe cackled and four crows alighted on the roofs of cars surrounding us. "That's hilarious. Your buddy is autistic."

"No, he's not." I'd seen autistic kids before. At least I thought I had. They're the ones that pass out from too much emotion. Or was that narcolepsy?

"You're so adorably dumb," Zoe said, and walked away. "The dance is this Friday. Get me a black corsage and I won't muzzle you."

I stumbled onto campus, my mind reeling with the revelation that Spencer's brain wasn't superhuman. What if I did something that damaged him permanently? The image of him locked in the bathroom stall at the library suddenly appeared in my mind with horrifying clarity. I needed to talk with Lunley, pronto.

I sneaked around the back of the cafeteria to avoid Spencer and made my way toward the counselor offices. Lunley's door was open, so I stormed in and demanded some answers.

"Is Spencer autistic?" I asked.

Lunley was dipping a tea bag in a steaming cup of water.

"Good morning, Lawrence," he said, ignoring my question. He carefully lifted the tea bag with a spoon and squeezed it like a sponge over his mug. Then he deposited the soggy remains in the mini compost bin he kept next to his wastepaper basket.

I repeated my question.

"We don't know," Lunley said. "He's never been tested."

"Why don't we test him?"

"His mother doesn't want to. She's worried he might be unfairly labeled."

"Do *you* think he's autistic?"

Lunley held his teacup to his nose and breathed in. The aroma seemed to calm him, which was odd because to me it smelled like wet dog hair. He set the cup down and indicated for me to sit on the yoga ball in front of his desk. "I think he may be on the spectrum."

"That's what Zoe said. What does that mean?"

"It means there's a wide range of autism, from severe to

high functioning. Severe autistic kids need special schools, whereas high-functioning ones can be mainstreamed. We have several high-functioning kids here at Meridian."

"Can't you force his parents to test him?"

"Why should we do that? Have you observed him struggling?"

"He's not normal, if that's what you mean."

"That's a pretty subjective term, don't you think?"

"No, I don't think it is."

"Am I normal?" Lunley asked, taking a sip of his tea.

This seemed like a trick question. "You're on the spectrum," I said.

Lunley choked down his tea and then burst out laughing. "Nice one," he said.

"What I mean," I continued, "is that you can look around the campus and see immediately who fits in and who doesn't."

"Fitting in is easy though, right? You just have to *act* normal. Most people can learn to do that. People on the autism spectrum can't."

"So that's it. Spencer's problem is that he can't *act* normal?"

"He can't pretend to be something he's not."

"You make it sound like it's a good thing."

"I'm not saying people like Spencer don't struggle. People with autism often suffer from intense anxiety and depression.

That's why I thought you'd be such a good mentor for him. You're friendly and warm and generous."

Lunley seemed sincere, but part of me wondered if he was just sucking up to keep me in the program. "You should have warned me," I said.

"What would I have told you? That Spencer may be on the autism spectrum? I don't know that he is. He's been at this school for only a few months. And I didn't want you treating him different."

"So you're like his mother in that way."

"I guess you're right. On some level, I can understand her concern."

Once again, I felt the urge to take Lunley's yoga ball and bounce it against his head. I wondered if any of his more belligerent students had done that to him. Instead, I took a deep breath and told him I thought he should take me out of the Buddy Club. "I just don't think I'm helping him," I said. "I may be making his life worse."

I'd dragged a disabled kid into a plot to save my own ass. That was like hitching a ride on someone's wheelchair.

"The fact that this concerns you shows me that you belong in the club," Lunley said. When I didn't respond, he continued. "Why don't you try a new approach with Spencer. Instead of trying to help him, just be his friend. If you're still unhappy by the end of the quarter, I'll see about getting Spencer reassigned."

I agreed to Lunley's terms, even though I knew he was wrong. Being Spencer's friend would be way harder than being his mentor. I left his office and walked directly back to my car in the student parking lot. Crawling inside, I reclined the seat and curled into a fetal position. No way I was going to first-period history today. I couldn't look Audrey in the eye and tell her I was taking Zoe to the dance. (Or to put it more accurately, she was taking me—in a leash and dog collar.) She already suspected I liked Zoe. I'm sure I could trust her enough to tell her the truth, but would she trust me enough to believe me? I wasn't ready to find out, so I texted Dad and told him I was going home with a stomachache. Honestly, I had felt like throwing up ever since I woke up this morning.

I stayed in bed all day watching cartoons. It felt good to revisit my childhood, when a tummy ache was treated with Estrella's blankets, ginger ale, and SpongeBob marathons. I realized why Audrey liked traveling back in time so much through LARPing. Things were so much easier in the past; it was a place of refuge from our shitty present and even shittier future.

Eddie texted me just before lunch.

Dude. Where r u?

Sick

Sick sick or fake sick?

Sick sick

Drink fluids

OK

And no medicinal marijuana

Thx doc

Dawn brought me a brownie today

Fur reelz?

Well, she brought them for the whole squad. But she gave me the biggest one

Our conversation was interrupted by a FaceTime request from Mom. I congratulated Eddie on his accomplishment, happy to be done with his crazy, and answered Mom's call.

"Hey, Mom," I said, impersonating a sick person.

"How are you feeling?"

"Better. Thanks. I think I just needed some rest."

"You got me thinking that our website needs a physical ailment page. Someplace where you could log in comments about headaches, stomachaches, fevers. Maybe we could link it with our Fitbit data."

"Sounds great, Mom." I hadn't worn my Fitbit in a year. The thing felt like the kind of tracking devices scientists place on animals they're studying. Plus, Dad kept taunting me with messages about my lack of physical activity. So I flushed it down the toilet.

"I'm going stir crazy lying in bed all day."

"How are things with Aunt Lucy?"

"It's like living in a reality show. So much drama."

"Really?" *Anyone going to the homecoming dance in a dog collar?* I almost asked.

"Dashiel went to a friend's beach house for the weekend and I guess there were no parents there. Lucy flipped out and grounded him for a month."

"Harsh," I said. If Mom took the same tactics with me, I wouldn't leave the house until I was eighty.

"Everything is so explosive around here. All they do is yell at each other. It's so unhealthy. Lucy clearly doesn't know what's going on in her son's life. I told her our website might help her communicate better with Dashiel, and you know what she did? She laughed at me!"

"Laughed?"

"She said their communication was just fine and that the problem with Dashiel was he was a sneaky little shit, like all teenagers. You're not like that, are you, honey?"

"Not at all," I said.

"That's what I told her. The thing I can't figure out is why Dashiel isn't more defiant. The day after he got grounded, he and Lucy went out for a jog together in nearly matching outfits. Go figure."

"Yeah. Weird." I tried to think of the last time Mom and I did anything together. We made a gingerbread house one

Christmas when I was seven or eight. We snacked on all the gumdrop candies so the final product looked like it was made out of cardboard and Elmer's glue.

"I gotta go now," Mom said. "The guys at VirtueTech want to show me some redesigns they've made to the site. I'll check in with you later, okay?"

"Okay, Mom. See ya."

I signed off and entered our conversation start and end time on the communication log. Seven minutes. A new high. We were trending upward.

At four o'clock, I decided to drive over to Audrey's house and see how she was doing. She came to the door wearing clothes that actually fit. Her jeans were tight enough to show off her curves and butt. In a strange coincidence, or maybe soul-mate signage, she was wearing a SpongeBob T-shirt that clung nicely to her chest and revealed toned, freckled arms. Her wild, frizzy curls were pulled back with a bandana. She must have been doing something artistic because she had a smear of gold paint on her left cheek. "Lawrence!" she said. "Where were you today?"

"I stayed home sick."

"What ails you?"

"Zoe. I have to take her to the dance this Friday."

"What?"

"She's blackmailing me. If I don't take her then she'll tell

Stone I helped the Viking escape."

"But you didn't. I was there."

"Were you?" I mumbled as I stared at the splatter of gold on her cheek. I knew that color. It was the same shade painted on the beard of a certain Viking that had gone missing. Zoe's words about Audrey being my accomplice slithered into my ears like Parseltongue. Audrey *was* there. Just as she was there the night the costume disappeared. Just as she was out the night the sophomore float got destroyed.

"What is it, Lawrence?" she asked. "You're looking at me strangely."

"You don't like school very much, do you?"

She shrugged. "It's tolerable," she said, gripping the doorframe a little tighter.

"Homecoming must suck for you, right? All that enthusiasm for something you hate?"

"I do not grasp your meaning," Audrey said. She closed the door and positioned her body so I couldn't see inside her house. The paint smudge on her cheek stood out in contrast with her reddening blush.

"What are you painting?" I asked.

Audrey's eyes widened. Her mouth dropped open, but the only thing she said was "Eek." I pushed the door open with my right shoulder and barged into her house. There was a small entranceway that led into the living room, which was wallpapered with climbing vines and flowers. There were thousands of teacups in the room, a sign of a serious hoarder or caffeine addict. Every surface, from shelf to piano to windowsill, had a series of mini ceramic cups just waiting to be crushed by a bull. I was that bull.

"Where is it?" I asked.

"Good sir," Audrey said. "Prithee, tell me what you seek?"

"You know what I seek. Where's your room? Down this hallway?" I ran down the hall and entered the open door at the end. There, resting on a drop cloth on the floor, was the Viking head. A jar of yellow paint lay next to it, touch-up for the Viking's flowing mane and beard. *"Diablerie!"* I said.

"Audrey?" an old woman's voice called from the adjacent room.

"Yes, Grandma."

"Is that a boy?"

"No, Grandma. Just the TV."

"Turn it down. I'm resting."

Audrey grabbed my arm and pulled me back toward the front of the house. She was surprisingly strong. Maybe not surprisingly. Regular swordplay with adult men probably keeps one in pretty good shape. She swung me outside and closed the door. "Lawrence, let me explain."

I took a few steps back and waited for her to continue, my mind reeling. Audrey struggled for words. Her inability to talk was completely at odds with her bouncer-like ability to throw me out of her house. "Tell me in Old English," I said, desperate for the confession.

"Last night, I was on my way to the other side of the house when I heard you raise the alarm. I was on my way back to you when I bespied a small figure with an enormous head scrambling over the fence. When I heard the commotion in the backyard, I assumed you had alerted the family, and rather than join you, I gave chase. The villain was nimble and knew the terrain, but he was impeded by his mask and must have known I would eventually capture him. In desperation, he withdrew the mask and let it fall at my feet. I stumbled over the obstacle he had thrown in my path, which allowed the bandit to make his escape. Not knowing what to do with the piece of evidence, I brought it to my house. I was going to inform you at school today, but you weren't there."

"Why are you painting it?"

"I'm afraid his countenance suffered some damage when I stepped on it. I was simply trying to make some repairs before I returned it to you. Please. You have to believe me."

"I don't know what to believe," I said, turning to walk back to my car.

"Lawrence," Audrey called from behind. "What should I do with the head?"

"Keep it," I said. "I never want to see that thing again."

I got in my car and drove home.

TWENTY-THREE

That night, I dreamed I was slow dancing with Audrey in our high school gymnasium. We held each other tight and spun in slow circles as the disco ball sprinkled us with multicolored light. I buried my head in Audrey's honey-scented hair and was just about to kiss her full, red lips when I felt someone tap me on the shoulder. I turned around and saw the Viking standing behind me. "May I cut in?" he said, and then he split Audrey right down the middle with his giant sword. "Thou art a puny, sheep-biting giglet!" he roared, swinging his weapon at my head.

I woke up drenched with sweat. It took a long, cold shower to shake off the nightmare. After I collected myself, I logged on to our family website and entered the story on the "Troubling Dreams" page and waited for Mom's response. Given her long history of therapy, I thought she'd be quick to interpret some of the dream's symbolism. All she wrote a few minutes later was *The giant sword is a phallic symbol representing the penis and sexual drive.*

Thanks, Mom, I wrote, ending my session with Mrs. Freud. I made a mental note never to consult my mom on matters of the subconscious ever again. Now our little exchange existed permanently in cyberspace for future generations to mock.

I left for school hungry and unsettled, thinking life had only gotten stranger since I stopped smoking weed.

Walking onto campus, I was in a fouler mood than when I woke up. I looked around at the students milling outside the school. Why had I told Audrey there were more good people than bad at our school? I hated Meridian and its stupid homecoming traditions. Heading toward the cafeteria, I wanted to tear down all the celebratory banners and fairy-tale decorations. Why did we need a week to celebrate the most popular students at school? Don't they get enough attention every day of the year? Wasn't this why we fought a war with the British? So that we wouldn't have to be beholden to a monarchy? Why is it we still long to be ruled by kings and queens?

I reached the entrance to the cafeteria and saw a posted list of homecoming court nominees. I tore the list off the glass door and saw a predictable list of names. Dawn and Jerry topped the list of twelve students most likely to be voted queen and king. Brett Bridges secured a slot too, thanks to his campaigning. Maybe now he'd drop his Viking exposé reporting and focus on smearing his fellow nominees.

I crumpled the list and threw it in the trash. Spencer was seated at our usual table, eating his healthy breakfast of Norwegian foods. For the first time, I felt hesitant to join him. I didn't want to treat him differently, but how could I not now that I knew he might be autistic? Suddenly he was like a chemistry experiment you weren't sure would bubble, freeze, or explode.

"Spencer?" I said softly. "Hey there, buddy. It's me. Lawrence."

Spencer looked in my direction and raised an eyebrow. "Hello, Lawrence."

"How are you feeling?" I said, sitting down.

"Fine. Are you worried I'm still angry about our last conversation?"

"I feel bad about upsetting you."

"You needn't worry. I am fine. In fact, I have some news to share with you."

"Please, tell me."

"Can you speak in your normal voice? I find this tone . . . unsettling."

"Fine," I said, trying to relax. "Wassup?"

"Miss Schwam has asked me to the homecoming dance."

"And how does that make you feel?" I heard my mother's

voice coming out of my mouth but was powerless to stop it. Spencer scowled, showing a clear and appropriate emotional response. Maybe he wasn't autistic after all.

"I am flattered, but unfortunately I cannot go."

"Why not?"

"My mother would never allow it."

"Do you want to go?"

"I think it would be enjoyable, yes."

"Then you should go."

"It is impossible. Miss Schwam told me you were taking Miss Cosmos, which I found curious."

"She's blackmailing me into taking her."

I filled Spencer in on the events of the previous two days, beginning with my botched attempt to thwart the Viking and ending with my discovery of the mask in Audrey's home.

"Her story certainly sounds plausible," he said.

"I know. There are just too many strange coincidences."

"But you were with her prior to the events at Miss Schwam's house. She didn't have the mask with her then."

"She could have stashed it near the house earlier."

"I suppose," Spencer said. "Still, she has no motive."

"She hates the school."

"Has she ever said as much to you?"

"Pretty much. Plus, she doesn't participate in, like, *anything*."

"That shows she's indifferent, not antagonistic."

"Okay. Maybe she hates me."

"Have you told her you're taking Zoe to homecoming?"

"Yesterday."

"*After* these attacks have happened. Why would she want to frame you before then?"

"Maybe she's a psychopath. That would explain the whole LARPing thing, wouldn't it?"

"Psychopaths are characterized by their superficial charm and egocentricity."

"Hey, guys!" Brett said, placing his hands on the backs of our chairs. He was wearing a T-shirt emblazoned with his yearbook picture and the phrase "The Man Who Would Be King." He threw down some chocolate coins on our table. I picked one up and saw Brett's profile embossed on the gold foil. "Did you read the latest story on the *Beacon Signal* website?" he asked.

We shook our heads.

"You should check it out." Then he left to distribute his chocolate wealth to the next table. "And don't forget to vote for me at Friday's assembly," he said over his shoulder.

I pulled up the *BS*'s page on my iPhone and placed it between Spencer and myself. "Editor Thwarts Viking's Attempt to Destroy School," the headline read.

Beacon Signal editor Brett Bridges saved the school from another attack by the vigilante known as the Viking Vandal last night. "I'd been tipped off that an attack was imminent so I stepped up my midnight patrols," Bridges said. "That's when I saw him."

"Is it standard journalistic practice to write about yourself in the third person?" I asked.

"It is not," Spencer answered. We continued reading.

The Viking, armed with two bottles of bleach, approached the school from the south entrance, moving toward the football field. "It was clear that his plan was to destroy the turf using the bleach," Bridges said. "Maybe he wanted to write another disparaging remark about Principal Stone. I wasn't going to let that happen."

Armed with a baseball bat, Bridges crept up behind the Viking as he attempted to scale the chain-link fence that surrounds the field. Years of training on both JV and Varsity baseball teams helped Bridges wield the bat with authority.

"I swung the bat against the fence as a warning," Bridges said. The Viking, however, showed little fear or remorse and continued his break-in attempt. Knowing there was no time to lose, Bridges hit the Viking on the back of the legs, forcing him to drop to the ground.

Disarmed, the cowardly Viking ran away before Bridges could unmask him. The bottles of bleach

are now with the authorities and undergoing finger-
print tests.

"I'm sorry he got away," Bridges said. "Next
time, he won't be so lucky."

Bridges will surely be lauded for his bravery but
his modesty makes him reluctant to accept the title
of hero. "I'm just doing what any other student at
Meridian would do."

My eyes rolled so far back in my head I could see my
amygdala. "What a load of crap," I said.

"It does seem a bit self-aggrandizing."

After Spencer explained what self-aggrandizing was,
I heartily concurred with him. "And worse than that, it's
not even true," I said. "The Viking head was at Audrey's last
night."

"Unless Miss Sieminski went on a midnight patrol, Brett
has fabricated the entire story."

I vowed to check Audrey's calves in class. I didn't know
how I was going to do this, but it was the only way I could
confirm that Brett's story was bullshit.

Audrey wasn't in class when I arrived. Maybe it was her turn
to take a mental health day. Or maybe her calves were recov-
ering from being hit by Brett's baseball bat. No, I couldn't
think like that. Brett had made that whole story up. Spencer
was right. Audrey may have had the means and opportunity,

but she had no motive.

The morning passed uneventfully, except that everyone kept eyeing me suspiciously and pointing at my legs. During lunch, Jerry and his football buddies held me upside down by my sneakers and rolled down my pants legs (or rolled up, given my inverted position) to inspect my calves. "Those are the palest, weakest pair of legs I have ever seen," Jerry yelled, confirming my innocence and my wussiness for the crowd, who walked away disappointed.

When I got to Yearbook, I found Eddie in a jovial mood, which only made me more depressed.

"I'm going to ask Dawn to the dance today," he said. "It's my last shot. What have I got to lose, right?"

I nodded weakly, all the while mentally listing the things Eddie could lose by following this course of action: his dignity, his reputation, his joie de vivre, his optimism, his faith in humanity, his belief in a kind and loving God. The list went on and on.

Seeing Eddie look at me with his puppy-dog eyes, I couldn't help but recall my tenth-grade reading of *The Catcher in the Rye*. There's a moment in that book when Holden tells his sister of his dream of being the catcher in the rye and stopping the innocent children from running off a cliff or something. We discussed that metaphor for two days, but it didn't hit me until now what Holden was talking about.

Eddie was about to run off a cliff and I should find a way to save him.

"Dude, the dance is two days away. Don't you think Dawn's lined up a date by now?"

"Why do you always have to be so negative?" Eddie said. His puppy-dog eyes suddenly turned Doberman on me. "Can't you just support me this one time?"

"I'm just saying," I said. "Homecoming is a stupid tradition."

"Homecoming is *not* a stupid tradition," Eddie said, his voice drawing the attention of others in the class.

"Really? What's so great about it?"

"It's about coming together as a school. Everyone participates to celebrate our community."

"Community?" I spat. "Is that what you call it?"

"Yes," Eddie said.

"Then why the social hierarchy? Why even have a homecoming court?"

"Because it's a tradition!"

"Because it's tyranny!"

"I agree with Lawrence," Crystal said, sneaking up next to me. I didn't know how I felt about this alliance. Eddie and I had always sided against our editor in chief. Just standing next to her made me feel traitorous.

"It's *so* not a tyranny," Eddie said. "The homecoming court is nominated and elected by the student body."

"Those people are preordained from birth," I said.

"Exactly!" Crystal said.

"What are you two talking about?" Eddie said, shaking his head.

"Homecoming isn't about celebrating community," I said.

"It's about celebrating the king of kings!" Crystal said.

"Right," I said. "Wait, what?"

"Jerry Tortelli represents the highest ideals of this school: strength, courage, and washboard abs. He is the living embodiment of all that we strive to be. It is honorable and just that we bow down to him and honor the sacrifices he has made for our great nation!" Crystal's voice boomed, her eyes bulged, her whole body started to tremble. It suddenly became apparent that we weren't on the same side, which was kind of a relief. We both believed homecoming honored the popular, but Crystal clearly saw this as a good thing.

The room got real quiet after Crystal's pronouncement. She must have realized she had said too much, because she started handing out page assignments to the assistant editors.

"Dude, she's totally lost it," Eddie said after Crystal had dispersed the crowd.

"Yeah, it's weird how a person can become obsessed with someone they have no hope of ever dating."

"I know, right?"

There was a slight pause in which Eddie failed to catch the clue I had lobbed in his direction.

"So, you think I should ask Dawn before or after practice?"

"After," I said through a clenched smile. I wasn't the catcher in the rye. I was the air traffic controller telling all the little children they are clear for takeoff. Have a nice trip! Mind that first step. It's a doozy.

I told Mr. Koran I thought my pancreas had burst and excused myself from class. The situation was a mess. Spencer wanted to go to the dance but couldn't because his mom thought an American dance involved kids having sex on the gymnasium floor with assault rifles. Eddie wanted to go to the dance too but had set his hopes on taking the most unavailable girl on campus. Meanwhile, I had no interest in going to the dance but would be dragged there in a dog collar by a bloodsucking vampire. If I refused Zoe, I would be kicked out of school on Friday and shipped to Langdon Military Academy on the first plane leaving for North Dakota.

I wandered the halls trying to find a way out of my predicament. Eventually, I found myself walking across the student parking lot, where I found a couple of freshmen writing RESOL in shaving cream on the rear window of my car.

"What the fuck do you think you're doing?" I screamed.

They took off running in opposite directions, making it impossible to slam their puny heads together. I reached my car and started wiping off the foamy letters, which just smeared shaving cream all over my hands and window.

"Goddamnit!" I screamed, pounding the trunk of my car with my fists. Would I be forever branded with this tattoo? I should just save everyone the time and get T-shirts made. I could wear RESOL as my logo, like the Izod alligator or Polo pony.

"You okay?" a voice to my left asked. I looked up and saw the smiling face of Dawn Bronson staring down at me. She reached out to touch my shoulder but then hesitated as if I were a baking pan that was too hot to handle without an oven mitt.

"You're Lawrence, right? Eddie's friend?" Dawn smiled at me with her pearly white teeth. As my grandfather used to say, you couldn't assemble a more perfect mouth with glue and a hacksaw. He wasn't known for his folksy wisdom.

My mouth dropped open. Like Eddie, I had known Dawn since freshman year, when she was my campus guide during orientation. Unlike Eddie, I did not follow her into every activity hoping she might notice me nipping at her slender ankles. The fact that she knew my name shocked me. I think the right word is "stupefied," if that isn't one of the three unforgiveable curses from Harry Potter. I tried to form a reply—all I needed to do was nod my head to indicate I understood her—but I couldn't do anything but smile awkwardly and cough something that sounded like a distressed chicken.

"Did someone vandalize your car?" Dawn asked.

I nodded. I needed to regain the power of speech soon or risk complete social annihilation.

"A lot of people think you're the one destroying the floats," she said.

"But I'm not," I choked out. "I swear."

"I believe you."

"You do?"

"The person who's behind these attacks is obviously smart. And creative. And strong."

Dawn must have registered the hurt look on my face because she added, almost as an afterthought, "And evil. I can tell you're not evil."

"Or smart, creative, and strong."

"Well, you do have a reputation as kind of a burnout."

"That's true, I guess." It was sad that this was the thing that exonerated me in Dawn's eyes.

"You know, you don't have to turn to drugs if you're feeling depressed. I can help you."

"Help me? How?"

"Wanna get some coffee?" Dawn asked.

I was too shocked to speak, so I simply nodded again. Dawn motioned for me to follow her to her car, a gleaming red Mercedes convertible. How was this happening? I asked myself as I opened the passenger door. Minutes ago I was getting bullied by a couple of ninth graders and now I was about to go for a ride with the most popular girl on campus. Life could be a fairy tale, just like our homecoming theme promised.

"You work for the animal shelter?" I asked, picking up a stack of pet adoption flyers from the floor.

"Just part time," she said. "My mom demanded I cut back my hours because I brought home a stray after every shift. You should see our house. It's like a zoo."

"I love animals," I said with as much enthusiasm as I could muster. Really, domesticated animals kind of annoyed me. And don't get me started on chickens.

"I've got the cutest dog for you. His name's Waffles and he needs a good home. Pets can really help if you're feeling depressed."

"I'm not feeling depressed."

"Oh. Sorry. I just thought, you know, with the drugs and all."

We buckled up and drove out of the student parking lot. I only wished there were more people milling about to see me with Dawn Bronson. People might be less suspicious of me if they saw me in the company of the senior class president/cheerleading captain/future benevolent overlord. Maybe I'd get lucky and Michelle Sharkley would see us at Starbucks and broadcast our coffee connection to the entire student body through her blog, *I'm Just Sayin'*.

We drove to the nearest Starbucks. On our way I texted Eddie and told him to be at the student parking lot at the end of lunch. I didn't know how I was going to do it, but somehow I was going to prep Dawn for his homecoming proposal. At the very least, I could find out if she was already planning on going with Jerry and save him from any potential humiliation.

After getting our respective drinks (for Dawn, a vanilla latte; for me, a mocha Frappuccino), I directed us toward one of the more visible tables in the store. This place got a lot of traffic at lunch and I wanted as many people as possible to see me with the most popular girl on campus.

Dawn spent most of the time counseling me on alternatives to drugs and alcohol. I didn't tell her I'd been sober for nearly a month for fear that she would lose interest in me and cut our meeting short. Instead, I nodded through her lectures on the healing power of exercise ("It's all about the endorphins!"), the benefits of a regular sleep pattern ("Science has shown that teens need at least nine hours a night!"), and how

to make avocado brownies ("Loaded with antioxidants!").
Maybe this was how she made such a speedy recovery from
the pyramid fall at the game. Either that or she was a robot.
But a robot's skin wouldn't be so tan and smooth and soft,
unless scientists have gotten really good at disguising their
robots.

On the way back to school, I tried to work our conversation around to her plans for the homecoming dance.

"So, you looking forward to Friday?" I asked.

"The game? Heck yeah. We're totally going to KICK
BUTT." The caffeine and sugar had amped up Dawn's natural
enthusiasm for all things school spirited.

"And the dance?"

"It's going to be AWESOME. The decorations are AMAZ-
ING. You're going, right?"

"I think so."

"You have to go! It's HOMECOMING."

"Who are you going with?"

"Oh, other people on the homecoming court. It's kind of
a requirement. We're renting a limo."

Before I could press her for details, we pulled into the
student lot. Dawn parked her car near the football field
and grabbed her backpack from the backseat. I scanned the
lot for Eddie and found him waiting at the entrance to the
main quad. I steered Dawn in that direction, trying my best

to casually interrogate her.

"Is Jerry going with you?"

"He's supposed to, but he's being weird about the whole thing. He says it will depend how he feels after the game. I think he's taking this losing season pretty hard."

"But if he wins homecoming king?"

"Well, then he'll have to go."

"Hey, look. There's Eddie," I said, pointing.

Eddie stood with his hands dangling at his sides, staring at us like Dawn and I had switched heads or something. Clearly he was stumped trying to figure out what bend in the space-time continuum had brought us together. I waved to him but his body seemed to have entered a state of rigor mortis.

"Hey, Eddie," I said, hoping to snap him back to reality. "I was just talking with Dawn about her plans for homecoming."

"You going, Eddie?" Dawn asked.

Eddie stared at Dawn like a heavily sedated kid in front of a giant TV screen.

"Eddie's weighing his options," I answered for him.

"Ooh," Dawn cooed. "Got a lot of dates lined up?" She nudged him in the shoulder and sent him wobbling like a toy punching bag.

I waited for Eddie to respond, but apparently he had lost

the ability to speak or manage his saliva production.

"Dawn's going with other court members," I said. "With or without Jerry."

I intended this information to kick-start Eddie's brain functions, but he only responded by burping out something that sounded like "chowder." We both waited for him to clarify, but he showed no compulsion to elaborate.

"Anyway," Dawn said, turning to me. "I'm having some friends over to my house tonight to play some board games. Wanna come?"

"Sure," I said. "Sounds fun."

"You can come too if you want, Eddie."

Eddie had now completed his zombie transition and moaned something neither of us could understand.

"Okay, some other time then," Dawn said. "See you at my house at seven." She bounced off to class, leaving me alone with the walking dead.

"What's the matter with you?" I said, shaking my friend. "That was your big opportunity."

"You heard her," Eddie said, scowling. "Dawn didn't want me there."

"What are you talking about?"

"After she invited me. I said I'd love to come and did she want me to bring a snack, like my famous avocado brownies. They're loaded with antioxidants."

"When did you say all that?"

"What are you talking about? You were standing right next to me."

I was beginning to think that my friend experienced reality a little differently from the rest of us. Maybe it was a coping mechanism he had developed to help him deal with three years of embarrassing conversations with the girl of his dreams, although if that were the case, I didn't understand why he didn't just imagine Dawn agreeing to marry him. I mean, if you're going to break from reality, why not go all the way, right? In his imagined scenario, he still got dissed, which didn't say much for his subconscious self-esteem.

"And then she says, 'some other time then.' It's clear she wants you all to herself."

"Don't worry, buddy. I'll make sure to talk you up tonight. She should be primed and ready for you to ask her out tomorrow." Of course, all this depended on Eddie regaining the power of speech.

"Thanks, Lawrence," Eddie said, slumping toward class. "You're a good friend."

TWENTY-FOUR

Many tribes initiate their young into adulthood through formal rites of passage. The Jews have their bar mitzvahs. The Mexicans have their quinceañeras. The Bushmen of Africa do something with face painting and circumcision. We don't have any such formal ceremonies in white suburban culture. Where I come from, all you get is a warning—"You're eighteen years old now and can be formally charged as an adult."

Being invited to the Bronson estate was about as close as I was going to get to becoming a respected member of my community. Those who enter the hallowed grounds (mostly honor roll students and debutantes) are said to be forever changed by the experience. Dawn is one of the most respected and admired students at Meridian; the fact that she invited me to her little get-together proved that I made the right decision to lead a more moderate lifestyle.

When I texted my father the news of my invitation, he called me right away. I'd never heard him sound so happy. He's idolized Dawn's father ever since he managed to quadruple his family's already significant fortune through savvy investing in high-tech start-ups. You know that device that allows your refrigerator to order groceries at the supermarket? He made that happen.

"That's great news, son," Dad said. "Go to Nordstrom and find something nice to wear."

"I was going to wear the clothes you got me for Christmas," I said. Dad had bought me a bunch of golfing attire, hoping the outfits might inspire me to take up the game. They didn't.

"You sure this event is casual?"

"It's not an *event*, Dad. It's a get-together. It's going to be small. Dawn mentioned something about board games."

"Do you know which ones?"

"She didn't say."

"That's too bad. I hope it's not something over your head."

"Thanks."

"I'm just saying. I can see the Bronsons playing baccarat or mah-jongg or some shit like that."

"I'll be fine."

"If you can, ask her father about possible summer internships," Dad suggested.

"I will. Gotta go now."

"I'm proud of you, son," Dad said. I waited for him to ruin the moment. It only took him three seconds. "Don't blow this," he said, and hung up.

Estrella was in Los Angeles visiting relatives so I had to dress myself. I picked out the clothes that came closest to my understanding of church attire and ironed them even though they had never been worn. I polished my one pair of dress shoes and refamiliarized myself with how belts worked. After getting dressed and gelling my hair flat, I looked at myself in the mirror. I had transformed into Spencer. Without realizing it, I had channeled his look. For the first time, I wondered if my mentee might have his shit together more than me.

I could feel my anxiety increase with every passing minute. I might look like Spencer, but I couldn't act like him. What if all Dawn's friends wanted to talk about sports and software and stock options (oh my!). I couldn't fake an interest in those things. What did that leave me with? I knew Dawn loved religion and animals. Maybe I should have a couple of Bible verses ready to quote. I could also ask Dawn to show me her petting zoo, as long as she didn't have any chickens. Those things are evil.

If only this was a house party. At least then I'd know what to expect. You enter the parent-less home, grab a Solo cup, and crowd in with the other teenagers seeking social confidence from the keg. But this was something completely different.

I might have to get high.

I hated to break my sobriety streak, but I didn't see any other way I could manage. Without pot, I wouldn't be as funny or interesting or attractive to these people, most of whom probably went to Saint Anthony's private school and only stepped on our campus to do community service.

I dug out the joint from my origami shoebox, tucked it in my pocket, and headed toward the door. Just as I was about to step outside, I got a FaceTime request from Mom. Against my better judgment, I accepted the call.

"We've never talked about masturbation," Mom said as a way of greeting.

"Excuse me?"

"We should talk about it," Mom said. "Lucy and Dashiel do."

"Mom, I don't have time for this right now. I've been invited to a get-together at the Bronsons' and I'm hella nervous."

"What do you have to be nervous about?"

"I don't know them very well. I just don't want to screw things up."

"Just be yourself, honey. You'll be fine."

I hung up and got in my car. Be myself? That was the

worst advice ever. I had to be like Dad if I wanted these people to accept me, just like I had to be like Alex to have Adam, Will, and the two Nates accept me. The only time I was myself was when I was with Spencer and Audrey and Eddie. I didn't have to impress them. They accepted me for who I was. Or, they were so unpopular their opinion didn't really matter. I hoped it was the former.

I debated lighting up on my way to Dawn's place, but decided against it when the road started taking the kinds of twists and turns you see in a Mario Kart game. The über-rich in my area purposefully build their estates on circuitous lanes in the hills so no one can find and rob them. The street-lights are dim and barely illuminate the signs, which are often nonexistent. I swear, at one point my GPS voice sighed in frustration at my ninth wrong turn.

Eventually I found the place. Her house sat at the end of a two-mile drive that took me past horse stables, an orange grove, and something that looked like an oil rig. I parked my car next to the other BMWs and Mercedes and held the joint to my lips. As much as I'd enjoy smoking on this warm fall evening, I hated to break my one-month sobriety streak. I hadn't gone this long without inhaling since freshman year, and I was finally feeling quasi-good about myself. It wasn't just that my body was rid of toxins (although it was nice to no longer be smelling like sweaty cheese and hocking malt-ball-size loogies), I had never resisted temptation for this long. Before this month, delayed gratification meant not getting high until lunch. Now I was living for the future, instead of the present, and it felt great. Maybe there was a little of Odysseus in me after all.

Besides, it would be rude to get high after Dawn treated me to an hour of free drug counseling at Starbucks. No, I could do this. I was smart, funny, and interesting. Spencer was right. I didn't need to lie or get high to make people like me. I pocketed the joint and walked up to Dawn's house.

In a normal house, finding the front door is as easy as following a brick or stone path through a lawn to a doorway lit by a porch light. At Dawn's house, however, there were five gravel paths that led from her parking lot without any sig-nage or lighting. Even with her three-story mansion looming in front of me, it was hard to tell which of the walkways led to the front and which led to various back doors and servant entrances on the estate. One of them was probably designed to help their rescue dogs find their condos in the back.

I took off down the widest path, which snaked through pink lilies and lavender bushes, their aroma so sweet I wanted to pinch the buds off, pop them into my mouth, and chew them like candy (I wasn't stoned, I swear, just hungry). Halfway down the path, I realized I was headed toward the backyard instead of the front door. Just before turning back,

I heard what sounded like scissors cutting through tinfoil. I spun around and immediately froze. A trio of chickens were standing behind me, their tiny heads twitching in silent communication. They ran their long talons against the gravel, sharpening their claws against the stones. All three fluffed their feathers, readying for a fight. It took every ounce of courage I had not to lay down and die. Instead, I just backed away slowly, never letting them out of my sight.

I should probably explain why I hate chickens so much. It's because they're creepy. If you've ever seen one that's not plucked and wrapped in cellophane, they have the twitchy aggressiveness we've come to associate with meth addicts. Who knows, maybe they're pissed that we grind them into McNuggets. I totally get that. But being justifiably insane doesn't make you any less dangerous. When I was a kid, one attacked me in a petting zoo after I was coaxed into feeding it a blueberry. Since then, I've come to believe that all chickens are out to kill me. I see them communicate this directive to each other through a Morse code of clucking, pecking, and scratching. The three standing before me now were just the latest soldiers sent to do me in.

The chickens saw me backing away and charged. Another thing that freaks me out about chickens is how fast they are. Chubby birds with skinny legs should not be able to stand on their own, let alone scuttle about the ground like crabs that have been tarred and feathered. These chickens launched both a ground and air offensive, pecking at my feet and launching themselves into the air to dive-bomb my head. I screamed in agony and ran blindly down the path, hoping to run into a pack of wolves roaming the Bronson estate.

What I ran into was a two-story-tall tower. The structure looked like it was made out of cut stone, but what I felt when I collided into it was wooden beams and tarp. I bounced off the wall and fell to the ground. Instinctively, I covered my face with my arms and screamed for someone to help me.

"Lawrence?" Dawn said. "Is that you?"

I looked up and saw Dawn standing a few feet away from me. She seemed unsure about approaching, probably because of the man-eating chickens. When I looked around, I didn't see any sign of the fowl creatures (pun definitely intended). They had obviously called off their attack upon seeing Dawn. They were smart, those chickens. They weren't about to risk alienating their food source by tearing me to shreds in front of her. This battle could be continued later.

"Hi, Dawn," I said, trying to recover.

"What's going on?" she asked.

"Your chickens . . ." I was about to explain how they'd attacked me, but I've learned that people always blame the victim when I tell them of the chickens' assassination plot, so instead I just said, "I'm allergic."

"Oh gosh," she said, now rushing to my aid. "I'm so sorry."

I couldn't say for sure, but I swear I heard clucking laughter coming from behind the castle tower.

"Let's get you inside and cleaned up," Dawn said, lifting me up and letting me use her as a soft, sweet-smelling crutch. I exaggerated my injury and leaned into her body, inhaling her perfume, which was like a mixture of fresh strawberries and caramel-coated popcorn.

"Is that your doll house?" I said, pointing back to the castle I had run into. The lighted pool it sat before looked like the cleanest, most inviting moat I had ever seen.

"No, silly, that's our float," Dawn said. "We're doing *Rapunzel*. The homecoming queen will stand on the tower and the king will be below."

"Aren't you worried about it being attacked?" I asked, looking around but not seeing any security, unless that's what the chickens were for.

"I invited you here, didn't I?" Dawn said, smiling. "C'mon, let's go inside. Everyone's already here."

We walked through her backyard toward the house. Dawn showed me her dad's helicopter pad and her mom's Richard Serra sculpture. Strolling with Dawn through her estate, I came up with a theory about why her family was so religious: they had to have someone to thank for the untold riches generations of Bronsons had acquired. It must be easier to think that some deity had bestowed these blessings on them for their goodness rather than contemplate all the people they had to step on to reach these heights in the hills.

We entered the house through the kitchen. Dawn introduced me to Lupe and Esperanza, the family's cooks, who were seated at the table, enjoying a heaping bowl of pasta. "We're all vegetarians in the house," Dawn explained. "When you raise animals, it makes it impossible to eat them."

I could eat them, I thought. After this party, I'm heading straight to KFC and saluting the Colonel.

We walked upstairs to what Dawn called the game room and what I called the happiest place on earth. The open space between hallways was designed around a ginormous flat-screen TV with every game console you could imagine. The bookcases surrounding the media center were filled with thousands of DVDs and game boxes. There were comfy couches loaded with giant pillows, which seemed a little redundant to me. In one corner of the room, there was a bar with a soda machine and popcorn maker. To my right, double doors led out to a small balcony within jumping distance of the backyard pool.

The intensity of love I felt for this place quickly vanished when I saw who was sitting around the coffee table. This was not the crowd I was expecting. Rather than resembling the von Trapps, all healthy and singsongy from years of cycling through the Austrian countryside, the people sitting around the open box of Scattergories looked like the rejects from a *Glee* casting call. There was a heavily made-up boy, a Latina with a neck tattoo, an emaciated Asian girl, and some twitchy dude missing an eyebrow.

"Everyone, this is Lawrence," Dawn said. "Lawrence, this is Dijon, Angela, Jin Jin, and Austin."

"You can call me Scabby," the boy with the missing eyebrow said.

"Really?" I asked.

"Austin, we talked about this, remember?" Dawn said. "Use your Christian name."

"But I'm not Christian," Scabby said.

"You know what I mean," Dawn said. "C'mon, let's play."

In all my years of being a fuckup, this was easily the dumbest I've ever felt. I wasn't being ushered into Dawn's social circle. I was just another one of the misfit toys Dawn wanted to convert. I was nothing to her except a project, someone to mold and shape into a good Christian. I wanted to weep, but that would only make matters worse. At the first opportunity, I was sneaking away and smoking the joint in my pocket down to its nub.

I fell into the space saved for me between Jin Jin and Scabby and stared at my Scattergories answer sheet. If the first letter we rolled was *F*, this piece of paper was going to look like the lyric sheet from a Geto Boys song.

When you play Scattergories with people from different worlds, you quickly realize how little you know about other cultures and lifestyles. We spent most of the game arguing and looking things up on Wikipedia to confirm that people weren't making shit up. Dijon knew a surprising number of Cuban singers, and Angela must be a budding geologist for all the stones and gems she could rattle off. Dawn used the game to preach scripture to us whenever she had the opportunity. At one point, we rolled a *B* and the category was "Things found in a purse," and Dawn wrote "Bible verses." When we challenged her, she actually pulled out a notepad from her purse, flipped open a page "at random" and read, "'Let us behave properly as in the day, not in carousing and drunkenness, not in sexual promiscuity and sensuality,' Romans 13:13."

"Why'd you write that verse down?" Dijon asked. "You need the reminder?"

"I have a whole bunch written here," Dawn said, ignoring the question. "Want to hear more?"

The collective answer to this was "No fucking way," but Dawn still worked in more scripture whenever she had the opportunity. For "U.S. cities" she chose "Saint Paul" and then read to us from the New Testament. For "Things at a football game" she wrote "prayer" and then praised Tim

Tebow for sharing his faith with his fans. For "Things you throw away" she wrote "soul," and then read us a verse from James 1:21 that said "Wherefore lay apart all filthiness and superfluity of naughtiness, and receive with meekness the engrafted word, which is able to save your souls." At this point Dijon started fighting back by naming different (and I think largely made up) sexual positions whenever he got the opportunity.

It was during Dijon's rather detailed description of a Dooly Spring (trust me, you don't want to know, especially if you're a dog lover) that I excused myself to go to the bathroom so that I could get high. As I made my way toward the nearest Bronson lavatory, I happened to pass the double doors leading out to the balcony. Out of the corner of my eye, I saw something moving around in the backyard near the Rapunzel float structure. I moved closer to the window, thinking it might be one of Dawn's architects making some modification to the castle. What I saw next chilled me to the bone. There, down on Dawn's lawn, was our Viking mascot.

I shook my head to clear it of any possible hallucinogenic visions. Maybe this was like those times I thought the squirrels were talking to me. Could I be experiencing some weird kind of contact high just by having a joint in my pocket?

The Viking parried and thrust like an expert swordsman. Or swordswoman.

"Audrey?" I yelled down. "Is that you?"

The Viking stopped performing, waved to me, and then removed a can of hairspray and a cigarette lighter from a shoulder bag on the lawn. "Oh my God," I gasped, just as a streak of fire blazed from the can and licked the edges of Rapunzel's braid. Audrey was going to torch the senior float. I had to stop her before she lit the thing on fire and I got blamed once again for being near the crime scene. I threw open the doors, stepped out on the balcony, and screamed, *"Diablerie!"*

The Viking looked up at me and smiled. I know that's impossible given that the Viking head is made out of polyfoam, but I swear, the mask smirked and shot a line of yellow fire right at me.

"Release the hounds!" I screamed.

That seemed to freak the Nordic prankster out a bit. The Viking looked around and then darted for cover behind the castle.

Just then, Dawn and the others ran out to the balcony to see what all the commotion was about. "What's going on?" Dawn asked.

"The Viking," I said, pointing down to the float. "He's going to set the braid on fire."

We waited for the Viking to reappear, but nothing happened. "He's hiding behind the float," I said. "Let's go get him." I was being extra careful with my pronoun use in case Audrey wasn't hiding behind the mask. I had been wrong about Zoe, after all, and didn't want to accuse a girl I actually liked unless I was 100 percent positive.

I dragged the others downstairs and into the backyard. We were a motley crew, but I felt confident we could take on Thor with his blowtorch if we had to. Angela was tough, and who knew what would happen if we unleashed Scabby on our foe. I ran to where I saw the mascot hide but there was no one there. I circled the structure yelling, "Come out, you spongy onion-eyed popinjay!" Those Shakespearian insults just fly out of you while pursuing Viking trespassers.

Of course, Dawn and her crew looked at me as if I were some lunatic. "I swear. He was right here," I said. "He was going to destroy the float."

"I'm outta here," Dijon said.

"*Yo también*," Angela seconded.

"Drop City!" Scabby thirded.

Dawn approached and stood before me with her arms crossed. "Maybe it's time for you to go too, Lawrence. Give me your keys."

"What?" I didn't understand. These two requests seemed at odds with each other.

"I'm not letting you drive in your condition. You're obviously stoned and hallucinating. Are you even allergic to chickens?"

"Yes, I . . ."

"Give me your keys."

I dug in my pockets and pulled out my keys. In doing so, I also pulled out the joint, which landed on the ground in front of us.

"Really, Lawrence? You have to get high to play a board game? That's pathetic."

"But I didn't smoke it," I said, picking up the joint. "See? It's still intact."

"Whatever," Dawn said, snatching my keys out of my hand. "I'm done. Jin Jin, can you give Lawrence a ride home?"

"But my car . . ."

"You can come back for it tomorrow. When you're sober."

"But I am sober."

"Goodnight, Lawrence."

Jin Jin turned out to be a kind, sympathetic chauffeur. "I believe you," she said just before dropping me off. "What you saw was an oni."

"A what?"

"Oni. A demon with horns. They visit me too. Just before I go to the hospital."

It wasn't an oni. It was the boomerang effect. Dawn's

attempt to make me a better person only made me want to get wasted. I was going inside and getting high. Nothing was going to stop me now.

Except my dad, who was waiting for me at the door, shaking his head.

TWENTY-FIVE

"Where's your car, Lawrence?" Dad asked.

"I left it at Dawn's."

"Why would you do that?"

Think fast, Lawrence. Think fast. "Uh . . ."

"Christ, Lawrence. What did you do?"

"Why do you have to go there, Dad?"

"Because it's a familiar road, son." My dad sighed. "Why is your car at the Bronsons'?"

"Dawn didn't want me driving home."

"Why?"

"I don't know. I got a little lost on my way up, maybe she was worried with it being dark and all . . ."

Dad glared at me.

"Are you drunk?" he asked.

"What? No!"

"High?"

"You want me to do a sobriety test?" I said. I closed my eyes and put my finger to my nose.

"Recite the alphabet backward," Dad said.

"Z, Y, X, uh . . . V? Dad, I'm tired, not wasted. I'll pick up my car tomorrow."

"We're getting your car now," he said, reaching into his front pocket and pulling out his car keys. "I want to find out what happened."

There was no point arguing with Dad when he had made up his mind about something. My only hope was that I could convince him I was sober on the drive up to the Bronsons'. I started by telling him everything I'd learned about Cuban jazz singers from Dijon.

"Who was at this party, exactly?" Dad asked as we snaked our way up to Shangri La.

"Just some of Dawn's friends."

"Dawn's friends with someone named Dijon?"

"What's so weird about that?"

Dad shrugged.

"You know, your prejudices against people who are different are a bit antiquated." Boom! If that sentence didn't convince Dad I was sober, nothing would. He was silent for the rest of the trip, which I considered a major victory.

Dad turned up the Bronsons' long, private road just as

Eddie texted me asking how the night went. I didn't have the heart to tell him I'd blown it once again, so I put my phone away and rubbed my forehead, feeling for the word RESOL still imprinted on my skin.

We reached their circular driveway and parked next to my waiting vehicle.

"Thanks for the ride," I said, opening the door. "I got it from here."

My dad got out of the car and joined me on the driveway.

"What are you doing?" I asked.

"I'm coming with you," he said. "I want to know what happened."

I approached the front door feeling like a prisoner being escorted to his execution. Hopefully, Dawn would be asleep and I could get my keys from one of the housekeepers. I rang the doorbell and waited.

A tanned blond woman in her twenties answered the door. She was dressed in a tight-fitting crew-neck T-shirt and black sweatpants. Was this Dawn's older sister or some second wife Mr. Bronson kept hidden from view? I introduced myself and saw the woman's gracious host mask slip off. "Dawn!" she yelled, her words echoing in the cavernous house. "That guy's here for his keys." She quickly vanished behind the door without saying anything. I glanced over at my dad, who seemed to be standing before a judge who had just ruled against him.

A few seconds later, Dawn appeared. When she saw my dad she jumped back a bit and dialed her expression down from pissed to annoyed.

"Hi, Dawn," I said. "Sorry to bother you so late, but my dad wanted me to get my car."

"Miss Bronson," my dad said, extending a hand. "I'm Lawrence's father. I apologize if my son behaved inappropriately at your get-together."

Dawn stood there with her arms folded. She didn't appear ready to turn the other cheek. I racked my brain for something biblical to say but all I could come up with were the opening lines of *The Odyssey*. "The recklessness of their own ways destroyed them all," I whispered.

"Excuse me?" Dawn said.

"Nothing."

Dawn seemed to finally register the trouble I was in and softened a bit. She held out my car keys like they were some leprous body part that had fallen off me, and spoke to my dad. "I just wanted him to get home safely."

"I appreciate that," Dad said. "You're obviously a good person."

Dawn smiled, accepting the compliment. "You know,

most twelve-step programs recommend submitting yourself to a higher power," she said. "I wanted Lawrence to know that he wasn't alone."

"We'll make sure Lawrence gets the help he needs," Dad said, tightening his grip on the back of my neck. We said our good-byes and he escorted me back to the car. Dad wouldn't scream at me as long as we were on the Bronson estate. Maybe I could set up camp somewhere near the fountain at the center of the Bronson circular driveway. Dawn and her family might take pity on me and offer me a home like the animals from the shelter.

"Dad," I said when we reached my car. "I'm not wasted. You can see that, right?"

"Of course I see that," he said. "I wouldn't bring you up here to get your car if I thought you couldn't drive it home."

I breathed a sigh of relief. Maybe Dad was on my side after all.

"What I don't understand," he said. "Is why Dawn *thinks* you're wasted. You obviously did something to disturb her."

"It was the Viking," I began.

"Lawrence, I'm tired and I want to go to sleep. I told you a recommendation from Dawn's dad could open a lot of doors and you messed everything up. I don't understand how this happened. Frankly, it would make more sense if you were wasted. The fact that you're sober makes me think there really *is* something wrong with you."

Dad got in his car and disappeared into the night, leaving me alone by the gurgling fountain. I stared up at the night sky, so clear from on high, and cursed the gods for making me so weak and pathetic.

TWENTY-SIX

Without Estrella home to wake me, I overslept again and missed another morning meeting with Spencer. When I stumbled down to the kitchen, I found a note from Dad on the counter. *Call Mom* was all it said. He had obviously left early to avoid seeing me, his defective son. I ate a bowl of cereal and got dressed for school. Before leaving, I called Mom on the phone rather than use FaceTime. I had the feeling this conversation would be better without the visual.

Despite her being three hours ahead, Mom sounded as groggy and tired as me. She listened to my explanation of what had happened, occasionally sighing in either exhaustion or disbelief. When I finished, she stayed quiet and serious, then said, "Your dad and I think it's best if we enroll you in Langdon Military Academy."

"Mom, please," I said.

"You need discipline, Lawrence. Structure. You're obviously not getting it with us. Maybe you'll get it from Langdon."

"I'm—" I didn't know what to say. I hung up the phone.

My body started shaking and I couldn't catch my breath. I'd never had a panic attack before but I recognized the signs from repeated viewings of *The Sopranos*. This was really happening. I was going to North Dakota. Say good-bye to rolling hills, bike lanes, and gourmet coffee. Say hello to a dull gray landscape broken only by trailer parks and mini malls. There would be bunk beds, twelve of us sleeping in a giant, unheated room with only a thin cotton blanket to keep us warm. Hazing rituals in which I'd be stripped naked and forced into a crowded pigpen. A drill sergeant forever yelling in my right ear. None of these images were in the school's brochure, of course. Somehow, my imagination had conjured life at Langdon as a montage of scenes from movies about basic training, the Holocaust, and nuclear winter.

At that moment, Eddie texted me. *How was Dawn's?*

I groaned.

Not only had I failed my parents, but I'd also let down my friends. Eddie would be forever tainted in Dawn's eyes through his association with me. If he tried to ask her to homecoming now, she'd probably douse him with a bucket of holy water. Spencer, who had a date, would never know the joy of slow dancing to Aerosmith, because his mother feared his escort wanted to steal his organs. These guys were depending on me to save them but instead I let them sink to the bottom of the ocean. Maybe Audrey was right about Odysseus after all. Maybe he was a selfish prick whose recklessness doomed everyone he came into contact with.

With nothing else to do, I decided to get shitfaced.

I know, that's not the most healthy response to emotional setbacks, but at this point I didn't care. I was failing at everything else. Why succeed at sobriety? Besides, everyone already assumed I was a stoner. Why disappoint them?

Rather than respond to Eddie's text, I sent a message to Adam, Will, and the two Nates. *Party at my house after school?* Within seconds the guys all texted me back with variations of *Fuck yeah!*

I stayed in bed all morning watching all three Hangover movies in a row. After lunch, I drove to a liquor store on El Camino where one of the two Nates's older brother worked. It only took two hundred dollars to convince him to purchase a pony keg for me and transfer it to my car parked down the block. After threatening me repeatedly to return the empty barrel, tap, and ice bucket after hours lest he lose his deposit, he took down my address and said he might swing by later with some friends. I figured I wasn't in a position to disinvite him, so I said, "Sure thing, Brad! Spread the word!" Having a death wish really takes the edge

off catastrophic decisions like this.

First thing I did when I got home was disable the video cameras downstairs. Dad wouldn't check in on me until after seven, and by then the party would be winding down. It was a school night, after all. Most of my guests would have to be functional tomorrow for the homecoming assembly, game, and dance. I for one would rather sit through all that stupid pageantry with a hangover than pretend to be interested in my school and its lame traditions.

I hauled the pony keg out of my car and set it up on our back lawn. Looking at the pool, I debated whether or not to cover it. It was too cool to swim, but kids at house parties were known to treat covered pools like waterbeds. I decided to leave the pool open, as it was easier to fish someone out of the deep end than clean up the mess created by motion sickness.

By three o'clock people started arriving. Will, Adam, and the two Nates were the first to show up. They entered giving me hearty *Welcome back!* slaps on the back. They installed themselves on the back patio after filling bowls with munchies from our dry goods closet. A steady stream of guests pushed their way through my front door for the next hour. Each one greeted me by shouting, "Where you been, Lawman? We missed you!"

I wished I could say the same. I barely knew these people.

Most of them were regulars on the party circuit, the ones who showed up at every get-together, whether or not they were invited or knew the host. All of them were a little fucked up, to be honest. You had to be to rally this fast on a school night. Their presence at my house meant that this was indeed party central for Thursday evening. I guess that should have made me feel good, but all I did was count the number of Solo cups in people's hands and make mental calculations of the cleanup I'd have to do later.

Someone had hooked up their iPod to our music system in the living room and was blasting some lame One Direction song. I winced at both the selection and volume. There was enough distance between our neighbors and us that the noise wouldn't bother them. More likely, they'd be pissed off about the number of cars parking on the sidewalk, filling empty spaces the families surrounding us guarded despite having four-car garages.

The guys had started a game of quarters on our kitchen counter and were busy giving every drink to Stephanie Jenkins, who looked like she was three sips away from barfing. "Shtop picking on me," she said after downing the glass. "I've got a shtatishtics tesht tomorrow."

"Hey, Lawman!" Adam said. "Come join us."

I squeezed in. People around me slapped me on the back, which only made me feel hollow. Adam passed me the quarter

and told me to take a shot. The quarter bounced in the cup, which I passed to Will. "Drink up," I said unenthusiastically.

Will pounded the beer and slammed the cup back on the counter. One of the Nates refilled it from a pitcher I had never seen before. I bounced the quarter off the counter and watched it drop into the cup again. This was weird because I was notoriously bad at quarters and never landed shots like this. I passed the cup to Nate and smiled.

"Asshole," he said.

"Thanks, Lawrence," Stephanie said. "How's it feel, Nate?"

"Awesome!" he shouted, and slammed the cup down. The other Nate refilled it.

"Dude, there's gonna be a killer party tomorrow night," Will said.

My quarter bounced again into the cup. I passed it to Will.

"Really?" I asked.

"Some girl Chester knows is throwing a rager in Santa Cruz," Adam said.

I bounced the quarter into the cup and passed it to Adam.

"Dude, you're on fire," Will said. "You been practicing?"

"I don't know what's happening," I said. "Being sober probably helps."

"Well, let's put a stop to that," Nate said.

I bounced the quarter into the cup and passed it to Nate.

"Fuck, dude, we're moving this cup farther away," Will said.

Nate left to refill the pitchers of beer from outside.

"You should come tomorrow," Adam said.

Nate returned and filled the cup with the overflowing pitcher. Adam positioned the cup a good foot away from where I was shooting. I still landed the shot.

"Shit, dude," Nate said.

I passed the cup to Nate.

"So what do you say?" Adam said. "We could use a driver."

"I may be going to homecoming," I said.

"Me too!" Stephanie said. "'sgonnabeawesome."

I bounced the quarter into the cup and passed it to Adam.

"Okay, now I'm getting bored," Stephanie said, pouting.

"Who you going to homecoming with?" Will asked.

"Zoe Cosmos."

"That freak?" Nate said.

I bounced the quarter into the cup and passed it to Nate.

"Were you high when you asked her?" Adam asked.

I bounced the quarter into the cup and passed it to Adam.

Something was happening. The gods were not going to let me take a drink. I was going to keep landing these shots until everyone around me was passed out in their own vomit.

"She asked me," I said.

"But you said yes?" Nate said.

I bounced the quarter into the cup and passed it to Nate.

"I didn't really have a choice."

Wait a minute. I do have a choice. Now that I'm being shipped off to Langdon, I don't have to worry about Zoe's blackmail anymore. It was the one silver lining in this mushroom cloud. I could go to this party tomorrow with the guys. Or take someone else to the dance. Tomorrow night was my last hurrah before being shipped off to military school. Who did I want to spend it with?

Will moved the cup behind the pitcher of beer, nearly two feet away from me. "If the quarter lands in the pitcher, you have to drink the whole thing."

"Don't fuck up, Lawman," Adam said.

A crowd gathered around the table to watch my shot. They all started chanting, "Lawman, Lawman, Lawman."

I took a deep breath, but I knew I was going to make the shot. It was fate. I'd never felt the gods' presence so strongly before. It was like Dawn said. All I needed to do was submit myself to a higher power.

"We're waiting," Will said.

I bounced the quarter high over the pitcher. There was no way it was going to land in the cup behind it, not unless a sudden gust of wind blew it off its course toward Stephanie's forehead. A more sober person might have ducked to avoid the collision, but Stephanie wasn't sober. She just sat there and let the quarter bounce off her face and back into the waiting cup.

The crowd went berserk.

I passed the cup to Will and left the table amid the wild uproar. Everyone was so busy comparing their videos of the shot that no one noticed me turning on the surveillance cameras as I left the room.

TWENTY-SEVEN

A few minutes later, I pulled up in front of Audrey's dilapidated home and cut the engine. To be honest, I didn't know what I was doing here. All I knew was that when I asked myself who I wanted to spend my last night of freedom with, her face floated into my consciousness.

I grabbed my backpack, which hadn't moved from its resting place in the backseat since my Starbucks date with Dawn, and dug out my copy of *The Odyssey*. I didn't think I'd be able to find the right words to apologize to Audrey, but I was sure Homer had them. I flipped through the pages, and the gods helped me again by showing me the perfect passage. Unfortunately, it came from Odysseus's mistress, Circe, and not his wife, Penelope, but I wasn't going to argue at this point. I dog-eared the page and walked up to Audrey's front door.

Her grandmother answered the door and barred my entrance. She was a short, squat woman who looked like she'd spent her formative years on a farm. I could imagine her breaking the neck of a chicken with a twist of her rough and calloused hands. "Audrey's sick," she said. "No visitors." She slammed the door in my face and bolted it shut.

I stepped across the front lawn to Audrey's bedroom window. The light was on, so I rapped lightly on the glass, hoping Audrey would peel back the lace curtains and allow me to mouth the words "I'm sorry." She didn't come to the window, so I leaned in close to the peeling window frame and spoke the lines as Romeo would to Juliet.

"Wassup, Audrey? You in there?" Okay, this did not have the Shakespearean eloquence I intended. I took a deep breath and began again. "I want to read you something from Homer because he speaks more eloquently than I'll ever be able to. Here goes. 'Come then, put away your sword in its sheath, and let us two go up into my bed so that, lying together in the bed of love, we may then have faith and trust in each other.'"

I waited for a response. Nothing. Shit. I hoped she didn't take that "let us two go up into my bed" part literally.

"I'm not saying we should have sex. Right now, that is. Eventually, that'd be nice. I guess I just wanted you to know that I have faith and trust in you. It doesn't matter to me if you're the Viking or not. Actually, I know you're not behind all these pranks because ever since I met you, you've only wanted to help me. And not help me like I tried to help you. You don't want to turn me into anything I'm not. I know what that feels like now and it's pretty shitty. Last night, someone tried to convert me into a good Christian, and don't get me started on my parents. They've never accepted me for who I am. I'm sorry if I made you feel like you weren't good enough just because you aren't like everyone else. The fact that you're so different is actually what makes you so awesome. Anyway, I just wanted to tell you that. Okay. Goodnight."

I waited for the windows to open and for Audrey to welcome me into a bosomy embrace, but nothing happened. When I pressed my ear to the window, I think I heard a toilet flush.

"You asked me earlier why it was so important for me to catch the Viking," I continued, more to myself than anyone who might be hiding behind the curtain. "To be honest, I don't care if the Viking gets caught. What I liked was spending time with you. The Viking was just an excuse to do that."

I slogged back to my car and watched Audrey's house from a distance, but it was too dark to see anything. At 8:45 my phone pinged with a message from my dad. *Get home now,* it said. I started my car and prepared myself for certain death.

It was nearly nine o'clock when I got home. My street was still crowded with parked cars, but the night was quiet. A gentle breeze rustled the leaves on the maple tree outside my house. Off in the distance, a neighbor's dog barked.

Entering my home, I expected to see the floor littered with Solo cups, surfaces stained with the condensation of cold drinks, shards of potato chips sprinkled on the furniture, but the place was immaculate. It even had the lemony scent of furniture polish. "Estrella?" I said, thinking she had returned early from her trip down south.

"It's me," my dad said. "I'm in the kitchen."

I walked into the spotless kitchen and found my dad sitting at the counter in front of two red Solo cups, an open laptop, and a bowlful of car keys. He motioned for me to sit next to him, which I did. He moved a frothy cup of beer in my direction and then held his aloft for me to toast. "Nice work, son," he said.

I tapped my cup against his and took a long sip. If this was my last meal, I might as well enjoy it.

"You want to tell me what that was before we call your mom?" he said.

"It was a party."

"It was a giant 'fuck you' is what it was."

I shrugged. "You want me to be popular. That's what popular looks like." I was surprisingly calm on the eve of my execution. Maybe because I wasn't high or drunk or anything. I could even look Dad in the eye and for once stare him down. I was completely unashamed in his presence. I was the injured party here. Not him.

Dad finished his beer in one gulp and then upended his cup on the counter.

"How did you get the place so clean?" I asked.

"It's easy to motivate people if you have footage of them doing things most parents and college admission officers would disapprove of." He pushed the bowl full of car keys in my direction. "You'll have to return these to your friends tomorrow."

"They're not my friends," I said.

"Not anymore, that's for sure," he said, laughing. "Why'd you leave your own party?"

I shrugged. "The party didn't need me," I said. "And I didn't need to be at it anymore."

My dad looked at me. I mean, really looked at me. You know when you have a lousy Wi-Fi connection and the images on your screen are slow to load, then suddenly the network improves and everything syncs seamlessly? That's what this moment felt like.

"I think I get the message, son," Dad said. He picked up our Solo cups and placed them in our recycling bin below the sink. "Let's call your mom."

A few seconds later, Mom's face appeared on the laptop monitor. Her bedroom was dark except for the reading lamp on her bedside table. She looked like she was calling from a military bunker. Her glasses reflected the computer monitor, making it hard to see her eyes.

"Hi, honey," she said, bringing her face close to the camera. She didn't sound pissed, but of course Mom wasn't the one who yelled. She counseled. "Your dad and I have been talking and we think that maybe we're not ready for Langdon."

"Seriously?" I looked over at Dad, and he nodded.

"I've been thinking a lot about our family while I've been confined here at Aunt Lucy's," Mom went on. "It's crazy here, you know. But the craziness, I don't know, it seems healthy, certainly healthier than our family dynamic. I think we've tried to make things easier by eliminating conflict, but now we never talk about anything important. We're like people having a long-distance relationship in the same house. If we send you to Langdon, it will only get worse. And your father and I want things to get better."

"Me too, Mom," I said. "Only without the chats on masturbation."

My dad started coughing violently.

"Deal," Mom said. "But I want everything else on the table. Including your drinking habits."

"Deal," I said.

"You're still getting punished for tonight's party," Dad said.

"What's that going to be?" I asked.

"For the next five months, you'll be working at my office every afternoon after school."

"Work?"

"Yes, work. After you finish your schoolwork, you'll help my assistant with some of her office duties. It will teach you some responsibility and I'll be able to monitor you more effectively in person."

This was my father's way of saying he wanted to spend more time with me. As with everything, he communicated this as if he were giving a managerial lecture to his employees.

"We'll talk more about the specifics when Mom gets home."

"Which should be next week!" Mom said, raising her arms in victory. "God, I can't wait to be vertical again. When I'm better, we should take a yoga class together, Lawrence. Wouldn't that be fun? It would get us off our screens and help us be more present in each other's lives. Actually, this might be something that would appeal to a lot of families, don't you think? There are so few activities parents can do with their teens these days. Yoga would be a great way to combine exercise, mindfulness, and family bonding. It could be part of a whole line of family wellness centers . . ."

"Why don't you work on standing upright first, dear," Dad said, rolling his eyes off camera. He knew where Mom was going with this, probably already pictured the cover of her next book, *Bonding with Buddha*.

Mom took a deep, cleansing breath. "Okay, we'll talk more when I get back. I can't wait to see you two."

Mom kissed the monitor and signed off.

"She's drafting her business plan right now, isn't she?" I said.

"Most likely," Dad said. "Better start practicing your downward dog."

"Will do." Dad and I stood up then and faced each other, not used to hugging it out. After a few seconds of awkward silence, I shook his hand and went to my room.

TWENTY-EIGHT

I woke up the next morning feeling surprisingly pleased with myself. I wasn't hungover, which I was starting to realize was a great way to start the day. When the first feeling you experience upon waking is pain, you know the day is going to be a long one. But I felt great. Part of me was even looking forward to starting my punishment, which is not something you hear people say very often.

I went to my closet and grabbed a hoodie. As I was zipping up, my eyes caught sight of my origami shoebox, tucked away safely on a shelf above my dresser drawers. I pulled the box down and brought it to my desk. Inside, the insects and animals looked tossed about like the cargo in Noah's ark. I picked each one out gently and arranged them on my windowsill, where they could be seen by me and anyone else who came to my room. Staring at them, I realized that I had gone about this mentoring business all wrong. With Spencer and Audrey, I thought I was taking a boring piece of paper and making it look cool, when in fact, I was taking something cool and making it flat and generic. It was the complicated and imperfect folds that made people interesting. The last thing we should be doing is trying to iron them out.

On my drive to school, I kept thinking about the heart-to-heart I had with Mom and Dad. Suddenly, my parents, and maybe parents in general, didn't seem like the gatekeepers to fun I had imagined. They could be allies and actually help us accomplish things too difficult to do on our own. The point, I guess, was not to piss them off. If Odysseus hadn't been such an asshole to Poseidon, he might have experienced much smoother sailing back to Ithaca.

This revelation helped me think of a way I could help Spencer. I mean *really* help him. It would require some subterfuge on my part, but I felt ready for the challenge. I owed it to the little guy for treating him like a project instead of treating him like a friend.

I went to school early to see my counselor. I waited by the entrance until his biodiesel VW Bug pulled into the staff parking lot. "Lawrence," Lunley said, exiting the vehicle. "What brings you by so early?"

"I want to do something for Spencer, but I need your help."

"Wonderful," he said, clasping his palms together and shaking them in what I assumed was an approving gesture.

"It will require that you be a little sneaky."

After securing Lunley's commitment to help, I ran to the cafeteria to meet Spencer for breakfast. I couldn't wait to see if my plan had worked. Spencer was sitting at our usual table with Heidi, working on some mathematical proof and ignoring the crowds around them having normal conversations.

"Hey, Spencer," I said. "Heidi."

"Good morning, Lawrence," Spencer said. Heidi nodded in my direction. Clearly, she was still angry about me foiling her plan to catch the Viking.

"Spencer, can I speak to you for a second?"

Spencer gave some last-minute instruction to Heidi on how to solve the problem and then followed me to the corner of the room. "I apologize for not being available for our scheduled meeting," he began, "but Heidi needed some help with her geometry homework."

"Don't worry about it," I said. "Listen, I need you to call your mom." I held out my cell phone for him to take.

Spencer raised an eyebrow.

"Just do it," I said, and explained my plan. It had occurred to me this morning. The only obstacle to Spencer going to the dance with Heidi was his mother's intense concern for his welfare. If I could find a way to use this for good, I might help her son lead a normal life. Then it struck me. If his mom had to chaperone the dance, she would have to take him with her—not the best way to attend a dance, but maybe not the worst either. (Escorting a vampire in a studded dog collar won the prize for that category.) All it took was a phone call from the school to ask for her help, which Lunley agreed to do as long as I tried to end this semester with a 3.5 GPA. I readily agreed to his terms, feeling confident I could improve my grades now that every afternoon was going to be spent in my dad's office, surrounded by Ivy League lawyers.

He took my phone and dialed his number. Seconds later, he started speaking Norwegian. I waited for some emotion to creep into his voice, as it was the only indication I would have if my plan was working, but his tone was flat throughout the conversation. When he was done, he passed the phone back to me.

"My mother has agreed to chaperone the dance tonight," he said.

I wanted to run back to Lunley's office and kiss him on his patchouli-scented forehead. Spencer was now on his way to his first American high school dance. I saw the corners of my mentee's mouth curve upward slightly. This was a smile. I was sure of it.

"That means you can go, right?" I said.

"Yes, my mother is not comfortable with me staying home alone, so I will be accompanying her."

"And Heidi?" I wanted to make sure he understood the point to all this. He was taking Heidi to the dance.

"If she hasn't already found another escort."

"Well, go and ask her," I said, pushing him in the direction of the table.

I stayed in the corner to give Spencer some privacy. He sat down next to Heidi and told her the news. I assumed things went well because Heidi squealed, bounced on her seat, and threw her arms around Spencer, who stiffened. His upper body stiffened, I should say. I have no idea what was happening below, nor do I wish to know.

The bell rang and the cafeteria spewed out its occupants to their first-period classes. Spencer and Heidi were caught up in the sea of bodies, but I was able to make eye contact, actual eye contact, with Spencer before he left the building. He waved good-bye to me and I gave him a thumbs-up. It felt great to help the little guy in a way he needed to be helped.

Just as I was feeling good about my future, a black cloud descended, obliterating the light and warmth of the morning sunrise. Zoe blocked my exit out of the cafeteria. She was wearing a black T-shirt that was patched together Frankenstein-style with mesh and corset lacing. In her right hand, she dangled a studded dog collar. "I need you to try this on," she said.

My throat muscles constricted. "No way," I choked.

"You are my slave, Lawrence. You do as I say."

Unfortunately, I was still at the mercy of the devil's minion. I had narrowly escaped being sent off to Langdon, but the threat of being transferred to Quiet Haven still loomed large. Unless I did what Zoe asked, she would show her video to Stone and make a convincing case for why I was a menace to Meridian. Of course, she wouldn't have to say much to convince Stone to kick me out of school. He would accept any excuse to get rid of me.

"I'm late for class," I choked, and pushed past her. "Let's do this later."

"Find me at the homecoming game," she yelled. "Or Stone will find you!"

I tried to shake off the feeling of dread, but Zoe's presence tracked me like a shadow. I was doomed to a life of indentured servitude unless I got control of that video. Hopefully, Zoe hadn't already loaded it onto YouTube. As much as I loved the Internet, sometimes it really complicated things.

I wasn't the only one freaking out about leaked surveillance footage. Walking to first period, I was repeatedly stopped by people who wanted their car keys back. Nobody asked me how I was doing or if I got in trouble for hosting the party. Either they didn't care or they were too freaked out about the possibility of my dad sharing the video with their parents and college admissions officers. I was pretty sure Dad would delete the footage, but I didn't want to let these assholes off the hook that easily. "He says it's evidence of a crime scene," I said, causing a greenish Stephanie Jenkins to slump into Will's arms and start sobbing.

I checked my history class for Audrey, but she was a no-show. I hoped she was still sick and not just desperate to avoid me. When the bell rang, Ms. Atkins herded us to the gymnasium, where the homecoming assembly would be taking place. The school ran a minimum day schedule today so students could save their energy for the homecoming parade, game, and dance. To make the day even less strenuous, we got to spend first period watching the members of the homecoming court compete against one another in trials designed to test their intellectual and athletic skills. At the end of the event, we voted on who we wanted to represent us as our king and queen.

I walked to the gymnasium with my class, stopping at the entrance when I saw Eddie sulking in his cheer attire.

"What's up?" I asked, blocking the crowds of students flowing into the gymnasium. The wave of bodies pushed against me, forcing me to the side. I stood next to Eddie and watched him scowl at passersby.

"Dawn's going to the homecoming dance with Jerry. She told the girls at practice yesterday."

"Sorry, buddy," I said.

"I just don't get what she sees in the guy," Eddie said. He shoved an incoming senior and told him, "Sit with your fucking class." The dude walked toward the senior section of bleachers looking as if he had just received a death threat from Santa.

"She's probably only going because it's expected of her, you know?" I said.

"I hate homecoming. It's a stupid tradition."

I gave him a consoling pat on the back. "If I can get out of my date with Zoe, we can hang out at my house if you want."

"Good luck with that," Eddie said.

I left Eddie at the door and joined my class at the far end of the gymnasium. On my way, I passed Stone, who was managing the flow of traffic with his bullhorn and steely gaze. "I'm watching you, Lawrence," he said. "Don't ruin this assembly like you did the last one." I picked up my pace and sat down in one of the few remaining seats in the front row.

The cheerleaders got the homecoming assembly going with some class cheers. Dawn was noticeably absent from the crew and stood off to the side with the other homecoming court members, awaiting their first competition. She bounced on her heels, not used to being sidelined like this during a cheer routine, and whispered to Jerry, who was smiling and pointing to his football buddies in the stands.

"Yell louder, you sad fucks!" Eddie screamed at the section of freshmen he was in charge of motivating, sounding more like a drill sergeant than a cheerleader. One of the teachers pulled him aside and spoke to him with a kind but stern expression. Maybe Eddie was going for a suspension. At least then he could claim Principal Stone rather than Jerry had prevented him from taking Dawn to the dance.

When the stands were sufficiently riled up, Ms. Morgan, the assistant principal in charge of student activities, took the mic and welcomed us all to the forty-seventh annual "tournament of champions!" She was wearing her usual attire of clothes purchased at the student store. Everything from her polo shirt to her socks was stamped with the school's logo.

"These homecoming court members have been chosen by you because of their unique contributions to the school," she began, working the auditorium like the closet motivational speaker she was. "While these individuals have been singled out, they are by no means unique. Everyone here plays an important role in making our school the amazing place it is. As part of homecoming tradition, we must elect a king and queen, but remember, everyone sitting in this gymnasium right now is royalty, and don't you forget that."

Ms. Morgan didn't like competition. She felt it was unfair

to the stupid and weak, which is why she started every high school event, be it basketball game, dodgeball tournament, or orchestra performance, by undermining the achievement of those who were about to perform.

"There's nothing special about the ten people on the court," she went on to say. Her six-foot-two frame allowed her to take long strides and get down court in less than a minute. "You could just as easily be one of them. But fortune has favored them at this particular time and place. Now they will compete for your votes. You decide which couple you want representing your school at today's homecoming game and dance. But no matter what happens, remember that we're all winners."

Despite Morgan's pep talk, or maybe because of it, everyone in the stands slumped a little and grumbled, as if suddenly reminded of their own mortality.

"So that we don't favor the athletes over the scholars, we asked each department at the school to create an activity for the court to compete in. We begin with the English department. Their challenge"—and here Morgan read a piece of paper on her clipboard—"is to create a haiku about our mascot, the Viking."

Each couple quickly huddled together and got to work, tossing out lines and counting syllables on their fingers, while someone pumped "Let's Get It Started" over the loudspeakers.

English teachers suck. Who remembers haiku rules? Not Lawrence Barry.

After a few minutes passed, Brett, wearing a T-shirt with the Facebook "Like" logo next to his face, ran up to the mic. The music stopped while he performed his composition. "The Viking's evil. He will destroy our great school. Kill him, kill him now."

Now, I've never been to a poetry reading before, but I'm assuming it's rare for an audience to boo a poet off the stage. I don't know if the people objected to Brett's poetry or his decidedly antagonistic approach to his subject. Either way, he just stared in disbelief, as if he had focused an entire political campaign on euthanizing puppies only to discover the voting public largely disagreed with his stance on said issue. He looked at Ms. Morgan, who was conferring with Seamus O'Leary, the English department chair and a noted alcoholic. Ms. Morgan turned to Brett and shook her head. "The haiku must contain some reference to nature," she said. The review punched Brett in the stomach. A few seconds later, Dawn pushed him aside and shared her poem into the mic. "The Viking is strong. Like the free and soaring birds, he is majestic." The crowd liked this one way better. Had Brett's "reporting" turned the Viking into a folk legend, like Robin Hood or *V for Vendetta*? Rather than see him as a destroyer of floats (or a float, I should say, since he'd only demolished one), perhaps they thought of him as a rebel who had made homecoming interesting this year. It was the boomerang effect. The thing bent on destroying the school was actually bringing us all together.

Mr. O'Leary gave Dawn the thumbs-up, and she and Jerry were awarded one point.

"The next event comes to us from the world language department," Ms. Morgan said. Señora Valenza waddled up to Morgan and grabbed the mic. She wore her usual funeral attire—black sweater, gray wool skirt; the woman was in perpetual mourning for something that happened in her native Chile. *"Buenos dias, chicos,"* she said. Somehow she made all Spanish words sound evil. *"Te gusta el flan?"* A wave of horror ran through the stands as every student shuddered at the sound of the gelatinous dessert. Plates of flan were set on five tables, placed in front of the court members, who all looked suddenly green and sweaty.

It was the worst pie-eating contest in the history of the school and perhaps in the history of pie-eating contests. Three of the five court members couldn't finish, their gag reflexes kicking into overdrive. Lacey Tomatillo got through half her portion before vomiting all over the floor, which triggered two other couples to run to the nearest bathroom. Throughout the mayhem, Señora Valenza looked on smiling, and for the first time I wondered if she wasn't a war criminal of some sort.

Brett shoved his face in the dish and tried to smear as much as he could on his skin so he wouldn't have to ingest it. Jerry, on the other hand, had no problem inhaling the spongy filling, and even licked his plate clean before Brett got close to finishing. He stood up, knocking his folding table over, and raised his fists in the air. Señora Valenza gave a lackluster *"Muy bien"* and marched back to her chair. The cleanup crew swooped in and quickly wiped the floors.

In hindsight, it was probably a mistake to run the P.E. department's obstacle course after the flan-eating contest. More people hurled when they had to spin in a circle with their foreheads stuck to a baseball bat. Jerry and Dawn easily won that competition as well. They also kicked ass in the science department's Diet Coke and Mentos kiss competition, keeping their lips locked longer than any of the other couples (many of whom had the added challenge of vomit breath to contend with). I looked over at Eddie during that competition and saw him take no joy in watching soda shoot out of the nose of his one true love.

No one's misery competed with Brett's, though. Susie Detterline, his partner, wanted desperately to break their embrace, but he held on to her tight until she kicked him hard in the shins. "You're a monster!" she screamed, and ran away crying, leaving him without a partner for the math department's challenge to rearrange a set of yardsticks to create three squares instead of four. As the couples worked furiously on the scratch paper provided, I watched Brett grow more and more frustrated until he blatantly peeked at Andrei Bilinski's work. This caused Ms. Morgan to blow her whistle and kick Brett out of the games. He made a big display of wadding up his paper and throwing it on the ground. "This isn't fair!" he screamed. "The competition's been rigged from the beginning!" At this point, Stone grabbed our editor in chief and pulled him off the court and toward the door. "You're all going to wish homecoming never happened!" Brett screamed as he left. "Mark my words. The worst is yet to come!"

And so the homecoming assembly had a chilling effect on the school, filled as it was with vomit and Brett's ominous warning. Despite winning the competition, Dawn looked miserable as she watched her subjects file out of the gymnasium with the stunned expressions of people who have just witnessed a terrorist attack. The only one oblivious to the dark mood was Jerry, who held his medal up high, posing for Crystal and her camera.

In Yearbook, Crystal showed the class all seventy-seven pictures she'd taken of Jerry as part of her impromptu lecture, "How to Rewrite History."

"By creating a timeline of Jerry's victories, I'm shaping people's memory of the event," she said. I looked over and saw Eddie gripping the sides of his desk as if the class were suddenly experiencing a bad case of airplane turbulence. "Years from now, when people look at our annual, we want them to remember the triumphant smile on Jerry's face, not Brett's suspension."

"Or the vomit," someone yelled from the front row.

"Brett got suspended?" I asked.

Crystal nodded, smiling. "Turns out you can't threaten people in a gymnasium without some repercussions. Stone takes a pretty hard line on that ever since the badminton tournament with the fembots." By "fembots" Crystal meant the students who attended Victory Prep, an all-girl private school who routinely destroyed us in athletic and academic competitions. When their badminton team beat us in league finals, one of our players threw his racket at the referee and chipped his tooth.

"People are now saying he's the Viking," Eddie whispered, his grip on the desk loosening somewhat.

"What?" I asked. "How?"

"He needed to look heroic for the school," Crystal said, her batlike ears picking up on our conversation from across the room. "Brett isn't Jerry." And here she pointed to a picture of Jerry, his face full of flan. "So he created the Viking to make himself appear strong and resolute against an 'enemy.' It's a classic political strategy."

"Only problem is, people ended up liking the Viking more than they liked Brett," Eddie said.

"That's why he lost it today," Crystal said, turning off the projector with a wave of the remote. We were suddenly immersed in darkness. "All that work for nothing."

Just then Dawn and Jerry stormed through the door, reminding us what the human body can look like with good genes, a strong exercise regimen, and liberal application of spray tan. Eddie took in a deep breath, as if readying himself for the beauty assault about to take place. I, on the other hand, detected a glimmer of malice in their shiny appearance. Something in the way Jerry's lip curled when he saw me told me that something was up. This suspicion was confirmed when Jerry pointed in my direction and hollered, "Larry, you fucker."

Eddie shrank away from me as if I had suddenly been identified as patient zero in a global pandemic. Crystal straightened her glasses and smiled shyly in Jerry's direction.

"Hi, Jerry," I choked, digging around for any writing implement that could be used for a weapon. My hand landed on a tape dispenser.

"You know anything about this?" Jerry's muscular arm heaved a crumpled piece of paper in my direction, which hit me squarely in the forehead. It's a wonder our football team is doing so poorly with that kind of accuracy and precision.

I opened up the letter and read the message printed in Times New Roman.

Your float won't make it to halftime.
Sincerely,
Lawrence Barry

"What?" I said. Eddie and Crystal crowded around, their curiosity winning over their desire to maintain some distance from the social pariah. I could feel them read over my shoulder. "I didn't write this."

"It's got your name on it," Dawn said.

"I see that," I said. "But I didn't write it. Do I need to point out the obvious, again, that threatening messages and ransom notes are typically not signed by their authors?"

"Are you sure you didn't type this out when you were high or something?" Dawn offered. "Maybe as some kind of joke?"

I tried to exaggerate my look of hurt in response to this, but really, this is the kind of bonehead maneuver I would typically make while high. One time, I called the attendance office and impersonated my father in order to excuse my seven cuts to fifth-period European History. I had completely fooled the attendance lady until I said, "Thanks, Mrs. Rosenberg. See you tomorrow," and blew my cover.

"I promise, I had nothing to do with this." I looked to

Eddie and Crystal for support, but they were entranced by the shimmering blonds in front of them.

"Why would someone write your name on this letter then?" Jerry asked, astutely.

"Obviously someone is trying to frame me."

"The same person you saw at my house on Wednesday?" Dawn scoffed.

"I think so. Oh God, you haven't shown this to Stone, have you?"

Jerry snorted. "That dude can't do shit."

"I'm afraid for the person standing on Rapunzel's tower," Dawn said, doing her best to keep a straight face. We all knew it would be her standing on Rapunzel's tower, waving to her subjects as the float was dragged around the football field at halftime. "She could be in danger."

"I'll protect her," Eddie blurted. "I'll guard the float."

Dawn placed her hand on Eddie's shoulder. "That's sweet," she said. "But we'll need you cheering. Besides, we don't want someone walking alongside Rapunzel's castle like a secret service agent. It would totally spoil the effect."

"Lawrence can do it then," Eddie said, putting an arm around my shoulder.

"What?" I said. "No way."

"He's got a costume that he uses for LARPing. He'll blend right in."

"What the fuck is LARPing?" Jerry asked.

"Live action role play," Eddie said. "He pretends he's a knight from the Renaissance."

Jerry and Crystal snorted in unison.

I glared at Eddie, silently communicating my displeasure at being thrown under the bus. But then I remembered all the times I screwed things up for him. This was a fitting punishment.

"Isn't that like asking the fox to guard the henhouse?" Dawn asked. "How do we know Lawrence won't sabotage the float?"

I would sabotage the float if it were a henhouse, I thought, shuddering at the thought of a house full of chickens.

"I'll be there with my camera," Crystal said. "Any funny business and I'll show the photos to Stone."

"For the last time, I'm not the vandal!" I said.

"Will you do it, Lawrence?" Eddie asked.

Believe me when I say that this was the last thing I wanted to do. My social standing had taken enough of a hit when I stopped partying. It didn't help my reputation that I was now seen in the company of a freshman nerd, male cheerleader, and Renaissance woman. If I were to put on a Viking dress and march alongside Rapunzel's castle, it would be the last nail in my coolness coffin.

But then I looked at Eddie, his pleading eyes begging

me to do this one thing for him. The fact that he trusted me to protect the love of his life, after I had screwed up so many times, made me almost grateful for the opportunity to humiliate myself in front of the entire student body.

"Sure," I said. "What time should I be there?"

TWENTY-NINE

After school, I drove home and changed into my costume. With the sword, shield, and beard Spencer loaned me, the Stone Age cocktail dress was sufficiently unrecognizable. Besides, I doubted if Harkness or Stone would recognize the outfit without the mascot head and boots that usually accompanied it.

Before I left, I called Audrey to see if she wanted to join me on this guard detail. Her Renaissance hotness might distract people from hurling things in my direction. Unfortunately, no one answered, so I had to leave a message, which no doubt her grandmother would delete after hearing.

I drove to the far end of the student lot, where the floats were parked, awaiting their first and last appearance on the football field. The freshman float was still a mess of tangled two-by-fours and tissue paper. It had been saved from destruction but bore as much resemblance to the story of the Little Mermaid as my kindergarten scribbles did to the Sistine Chapel.

The sophomores had done their best to recover from the act of vandalism perpetrated against their float, but whoever thought it would be a good idea to position an actual goat in a tableau for *The Three Billy Goats Gruff* did not understand that the animal would ingest practically anything you place in front of it, including tissue paper and cardboard. Their float would be half eaten by halftime.

My class had chosen *Jack and the Beanstalk* as its float theme and constructed a green, leafy tower with a G.I. Joe on top. I doubted anyone in the stands would see the tiny action figure though, which made our entry look like a giant stalk of asparagus.

The senior class float was even more spectacular than when I saw it at Dawn's house on Wednesday. The tower that imprisons Rapunzel was a good sixteen feet high and seven feet in diameter, like a gas tank trailer standing on its end. Black lines were painted on the gray cover to mimic granite stones. Knowing she would most likely be elected homecoming queen, Dawn had designed the structure to allow only her to stand atop the giant tower. Jerry, or whoever was voted king, would stand below, and hold on to the rope of blond hair attached to the cylindrical structure. Along the perimeter of the flatbed ran a two-foot-high border made out of chicken wire and gray tissue paper and designed to look like a castle turret.

When Dawn saw me in full costume, she beamed. "You look great," she said. She was dressed in her cheerleading outfit, but I'm sure she had her gown and slippers ready for when they announced the homecoming king and queen at halftime.

"How do you get to the top?" I asked Dawn. From our vantage point, it looked like the only way up the tower was to scale it using the fake hair as a rope.

"Whoever is elected homecoming queen," Dawn said, smiling, "will enter the tower here." She pointed to a tiny door, about twice the height of most swinging doggy doors. "There's a ladder inside that you climb to the top. Isn't that the coolest?"

I agreed that it was indeed the coolest.

"We've been working on the float since the end of summer," Dawn continued. "Which is why it's so important the vandal doesn't destroy it before halftime."

"I'm on the job," I said, saluting.

"I have faith that God will protect our float," Dawn said, her expression growing darker, more serious. "But if you so much as sneeze on our tissue paper, I will destroy you."

"Understood."

Dawn transformed back to peppy cheerleader. "Go Vikings!" she squealed, and bounced off toward the field. A few minutes later, I heard the whistle blow and the crowds cheering from the stands.

I kept a tight vigil for the first five minutes of the game but then got bored with marching around the structure. My presence was unnecessary, as there were tons of parents milling about, taking pictures of the floats and chatting up the volunteer drivers. A few adults asked me why I wasn't at the game. I told them I was on guard duty, but really I had no intention of letting people see me in this getup until halftime. As long as I was stationed near the float, I blended in. If I left the castle, I would probably be slain by the opposing team or our own bloodthirsty fans.

I hoisted myself up onto the truck bed. The tower filled the width of it, making a march around it impossible. Instead, I kicked off my flip-flops and lay down in the moat as sentry. The sun emerged from the clouds and warmed my hideout, making it almost cozy, like the forts I used to build out of refrigerator boxes and pillows when I was younger. I passed the time by playing Tetris on my iPhone. There was something soothing about seeing all those geometric shapes fall so nicely into place. It gave me a feeling of control. Normally, the pieces of my life crashed in a jumbled mess, but for once things felt orderly, even predictable. Perhaps this guard duty would clear my name and I could live a normal life without the threat of expulsion hanging over my head. Maybe I'd be seen as the hero who saved the senior float through his steadfast guardianship and keen observational skills. . . .

A gunshot sound woke me from my slumber. I looked up and saw that the sun had moved westward by a few degrees. I quickly stood up on the truck bed and peered over the fence that separated the parking lot from the football field. I could just make out the scoreboard at the opposite end of the field. The clock said 0:00. The score was Home 7, Visitor 14. It was halftime.

Adults were getting into their cars, preparing to pull the floats around the field. I did a quick scan and saw that the senior float was still in one piece. No one had destroyed it while I took my afternoon nap. I leaned up against the tower and breathed a sigh of relief.

And that's when I heard something moving inside the structure.

"Hello? Anyone in there?" I asked, hoping that Dawn had already entered the tower and was in the process of ascending the ladder that led to the top. "Dawn?"

Off in the distance, I heard Assistant Principal Morgan announce that this year's homecoming king and queen were Jerry Tortelli and Dawn Bronson. Cheers and applause erupted from the stands. When the noise died down, I put my head against the structure and heard it again—the distinct sound of someone moving inside the tower.

"Who's there?" I dropped to my hands and knees and poked my head through the tiny door at the bottom of the structure. What I saw there chilled the blood in my veins.

It was a chicken.

Before I could yank my head out of the hole, someone straddled my neck and shoulders with their strong legs. "What the fuck?" I screamed. I was helpless as the person above me threw a large, globular object over my head. In a swift move, my captor attached the casing to my body by encircling my neck with what felt like a spool of duct tape. When the job was complete, the person jumped off my back and beat a hasty retreat to the opposite end of the tower's interior. All I could hear was the villain's heavy breathing. And the frantic pecking of the chicken.

I tried to pull out, but with the large object attached to my head, I was too big to fit through the tiny trapdoor. There was only one way to go and that was in. Maybe if I crawled through the tower's entrance, I could stand up and remove the object that had been forcibly attached to my body.

I crawled inside and stood up with some difficulty. Whatever object had been taped to my head was making it hard for me to get my balance. When I was fully upright, I realized there were two eyeholes for me to see out of. With shaking hands, I reached up and felt my new exterior. There was a large, beak-like nose and bushy mustache where my face used to be. That's when I understood. It was the Viking's head.

I scanned the tiny confines of the area looking for my captor. When I saw her crouching to my left, holding a mangy-looking, red-headed chicken, I gasped in horror.

It was Crystal.

"Hello, Lawrence," she said, stroking the chicken's back.

"Crystal," I said. "What the hell are you doing?"

"You haven't guessed yet?"

"Wait. *You're* the Viking?"

"I *was* the Viking," she said. "Now you are. Have fun in here with Mr. Winkles."

I was trying to make sense of it all when she threw the chicken at my face. All I saw was a flurry of feathers. Luckily, the mascot mask protected my face, but every other part of my body was exposed to the chicken's stabbing beak and claws. I fell back against the opposite wall and covered my privates like a soccer player in front of a penalty kick. Over my heavy breathing I could hear Crystal outside congratulate Dawn on her homecoming election. A few seconds later, Dawn squeezed through the trapdoor in her sequined gown and tiara.

A searing pain in my foot made me double over in pain. The chicken must have pecked my bare foot. I bent down just as Dawn was standing up. Our heads knocked, but as my head was encased in polyfoam, I didn't feel much pain.

"Mother Teresa!" Dawn swore. I looked up and saw her adjusting her tiara. "What are you doing in here? And whose chicken is that?"

"Dawn, you have to help me."

"Lawrence?"

"Yes, it's me. Crystal is setting me up."

Dawn responded by pushing me aside and ascending the ladder. "I don't have time for your games right now, Lawrence. We're about to start moving."

I tilted my head and saw her flaming red dress and heels recede as she ascended to her rightful position of homecoming queen, perched atop her tower like some sparkling trophy out of everyone's reach. Within seconds, she disappeared through the trapdoor at the top and I was trapped inside this cockfighting ring of a tower with Mr. Winkles.

I couldn't do anything until I removed this head. I dug my nails into the duct tape and tried to shred it off my skin. When that didn't work, I tried ripping the mask in two but didn't have the strength to tear the material with my bare hands. Where was the bloodthirsty prospector and his handy pickaxe when you needed him?

I heard a nearby car engine start. We must be getting ready to tour the field. The sudden movement disturbed Mr.

Winkles, who started clucking frantically. I tried to shoo the creature out the swinging door, but every time my foot neared the chicken it pecked at me and darted out of my limited line of vision. When the car started, jerking the truck bed forward, I fell against the tower and felt the whole structure creak and sway. Above me, I heard Dawn give a frightened cry as Rapunzel's tower started to feel more like the Leaning Tower of Pisa. I stretched my arms out and tried to steady the float, but that's hard to do when your body's shaking like a leaf.

The chicken circled me in the ring like a prizefighter, flapping its wings and pecking at my ankles. Every time I moved away, it darted in my direction and tried to pierce my flesh with its beak or talons. I didn't have a lot of room to maneuver, and every time I dodged the chicken's attack, I crashed into the side, making the whole structure shake and teeter. All the while, Dawn's heels tapped out an angry Morse code above me that probably translated to "Stop trying to kill me, you fucking idiot." I imagined Dawn with a painted smile, doing her queenly wave, while the ground beneath her feet shook and became increasingly unstable.

The chicken started bouncing in our cylinder like an exploding popcorn kernel. It flew into my field of vision, a blur of orange feathers and sharp, pointy objects. Suddenly, I was back at the petting zoo being attacked by not one, but a flock (Or is it gaggle? Brood? Oh, who the fuck cares?) of chickens, all seeking to tear my skin off to get at my wormlike intestines. I didn't want to die this way. I couldn't. I started kicking my attacker, hoping to make contact and break one of its legs or wings to keep it from advancing on me. But the little fucker was too small and kept darting away, leaving my foot to collide with a two-by-four, knocking it loose. At this point, I didn't care. Better to be buried alive under a waterfall of wooden beams, tissue paper, and an angry homecoming queen than have my liver pecked out by this *pollo loco*.

"Lawrence!" Dawn cried from above. Hearing her frightened cry snapped me out of my panic like a slap in the face. I suddenly realized that I was about to take this rickety structure down. The note's prophecy was coming true. This float wouldn't make it to halftime. I was the bomb and this insane chicken was the fuse.

This time when the chicken attacked, I leaped up instead of away. I grabbed ahold of the ladder leading to the top of the tower where Dawn stood and started climbing. I could hear the chicken's angry clucks as I moved upward. Halfway up, I turned and saw the chicken flapping its wings and bouncing up to try to reach me. You'd think the avian would be content having the ring to itself. It had clearly bested me in the fight. It was time to take things down a notch and strut around the circumference of the ring in a kind of victory lap. But that chicken wasn't going to be satisfied until it ejected me from the building.

What I'm going to tell you next is going to stretch the credibility of this narrative. I'm aware of that. You can either believe me or not—that is your choice. I think the important thing to remember is that even if you don't think this could happen in a million years, you must know that I *thought* it was happening. Maybe in my panicked state, my vision of reality became somewhat distorted. I don't know. I won't say I haven't hallucinated things before. Regardless, this is what I saw while locked in my Viking mask, midway up a ladder in a moving tower.

That chicken started to climb.

After her attempts to reach me through flight failed, the chicken hopped onto the lowest rung of the ladder and perched there, somehow balancing its body amid the jostling structure. Then it hopped off the rung, flapped its wings, and fluttered to the next rung. After regaining its balance, it repeated the process, slowly inching its way toward me, all the time staring at me with its soulless, beady eyes. A few more rungs and it would be within striking distance. I saw it piercing my Achilles tendon, sending me plummeting to the floor, helpless to defend myself against the chicken's final attack from above. The claws would reach me first and rake open my veins on my exposed wrists and forearms.

My only option was to keep climbing upward. It didn't take me long before my head butted against the trapdoor that would give me access to the tower's roof. I looked down and saw the chicken making faster progress. Now she was leaping two rungs at a time. I had no choice but to push up and out of this death trap. I pounded my fist against the trapdoor above me and told Dawn to get out of the way.

I met some resistance on my first attempt to escape. Dawn was clearly not eager to share the stage with me, but when I started heaving my shoulder into the door to push it open, Dawn had no other choice but to step aside. The door flew open, and I squeezed the Viking head out of the tower just as the chicken reached my heels. After scrambling outside, I slammed the door down on the chicken's head, sending it back to what must seem like the tallest henhouse ever constructed.

You know that phrase "Out of the frying pan and into the fire"? That's never made much sense to me until the moment I escaped death by chicken only to face death by homecoming queen. The only thing that saved me from one of Dawn's heels puncturing my lung was the fact that we were parading in front of the entire student body and there was no way to kill me without it being witnessed by hundreds of people. Plus, we were, like, twenty feet off the ground, which makes subduing a Viking attacker a bit more problematic.

"Stay down," Dawn seethed through clenched teeth. She continued to smile and wave to the crowd, while pinning me on the floor with her patent leather heels. I was happy to stay out of sight, but when the crowd in the stands saw the mascot's head emerge from the tower, they cheered loudly. The fellow had gained a bit of a reputation through his acts of vandalism, and I suppose the students were happy to see him make such a public appearance. I realized as I listened to my peers cheer that the Viking was the only thing that had made homecoming interesting this year. He deserved to be celebrated more than any boring and predictable homecoming queen. Feeling the crowd's support, I grabbed the metal hand bar that circled the tower and pulled myself up.

The crowd went crazy. Everyone in the stands stood up and started chanting, "Viking. Viking. Viking." Dawn had no other choice but to step aside. She grabbed my right hand, nearly crushing my bones, and raised both our hands in solidarity. I felt a bit sorry for Jerry standing below us, invisible to everyone in the stands, but then I remembered how little the guy figures into these stories. *Snow White, Cinderella, The Princess and the Pea, The Little Mermaid*—they're all about the damsel in distress, never about the prince who rescues her. He's as generic and flat a character as, well, as Jerry.

For a moment, I forgot about all the trouble I had been in and was about to get in. It felt great to roll by crowds of people and have them cheer for you. This must be what trophies feel like, I realized, held aloft by winners to their adoring fans. I turned to Dawn and saw her struggling to maintain her smile. When we passed the stands, her grip on my hand loosened but she didn't let go.

"That was amazing," I said.

The tower shook and we released our hands to grip the handrail.

"What the fuck is going on up there?" Jerry yelled. I peered down and saw him with his arms around the base of the structure. "Is there a chicken up there with you?"

"Everything's fine," Dawn yelled down.

"I'm going to tell this driver to speed things up," Jerry said, bouncing off the truck bed. "I've got to get to the locker room before halftime ends."

The structure wobbled a bit as Jerry jumped off and ran up to the truck pulling us. Dawn and I gripped the railing and watched the remaining floats move slowly in front of the stands. The driver must have agreed to Jerry's demands because we accelerated somewhat as we approached the curve of the track. We were about to pass between the goalposts and scoreboard.

"Lawrence," Dawn said, staring at her hands. "Do you think people like me?"

"Of course they like you."

"I don't think they do," Dawn said. "I think they admire me, but I don't think they like me. It wasn't until you stood up that people started to cheer. To see the change in people's faces, it was dramatic, you know? They were bored looking at me. I'm boring. I pretend to be perfect and all, you know for colleges, and I'm just boring."

"I don't think you're boring," I said. "People just think you're perfect. When they saw you holding hands with the Viking, I don't know, it made you more like us. I think that's what they were cheering for. Their homecoming queen was showing them she was a little weird."

I looked down. Jerry had returned to the float and was now facing off with the chicken. He must have let the blood-thirsty creature out, thinking he was doing it a favor. Now they looked like two wrestlers circling each other, trying to find the best limb to grab to execute a quick pin on the mat.

"You don't really want to go to homecoming with Jerry, do you?" I asked.

"Not really," Dawn said. "It's expected, though."

"Don't do what's expected of you. Do something a little weird."

As if on cue, Eddie appeared, running behind us on the football field.

"I know someone who would kill to take you to the dance," I said.

Dawn looked up with tears in her eyes. She put her arm around me and gave me a friendly squeeze. "Oh, Lawrence, that's so sweet."

I saw that she had misunderstood me. Not only that, but she was about to "Let's be friends" me and I didn't need to hear that right now. "Not me," I corrected. "Him." I pointed down to the field, where Eddie was trailing us like a puppy chasing after his abusive master.

"Carlos?" Dawn said, squinting her eyes.

"Eddie," I corrected.

Eddie was waving his hands and shouting something, but with the marching band playing and us being a good twenty feet above him, he might as well have been one of those air traffic controllers who direct the DC-10 aircraft into their slot with their glowing batons.

Jerry was preoccupied chasing the chicken around the truck bed and was ignoring Eddie completely. Dawn cupped her ears and yelled, "What?" I hoped Eddie wasn't about to ask her to homecoming. It would be a dramatic proposal, sure, but the timing was all wrong. He needed a Jumbotron screen to make himself understood. He kept pointing up at us, yelling something that sounded like "banter."

"Good one!" I shouted, congratulating him on his use of an SAT word to identify my conversation with Dawn.

Eddie shook his head and pointed to the stretch of track

just behind us. We turned around just in time to see it. A homecoming banner stretched out in front of us with the phrase, *And they all lived happily ever after* written in cursive script. It had been hung between the goalpost and scoreboard, I suppose, as a final farewell to the homecoming royalty riding on the floats, or as a final bit of irony because the message might be the last thing we saw before we fell to our doom. The banner was just low enough to catch the tower on which we were standing. Depending on the strength of the line, it would either break like runner's tape or knock the already weakened tower down to the ground.

We screamed to the driver to stop, but he was in deep conversation with his passenger. We tried to get Jerry's attention, but he had just captured the chicken and was holding it up proudly for us to see. "This fucker is dinner!" he screamed in victory.

The wire caught the tower and sent it teetering backward. Jerry, sensing the crash, tucked his chicken prize under his arm and leaped from the truck bed. Dawn and I both grabbed hold of the railing but the force of impact sent us flying backward. I heard wood creaking and then splintering and the tower tipped backward. We were hanging on to the railing like Leo and Kate did on the sinking *Titanic*, waiting to be taken down by our collapsing tower. Someone below us yelled, "Jump!" I turned and saw Eddie waiting with open arms below. Just to clarify things, he added, "Just like we do in practice, Dawn."

Dawn executed a brilliant dismount and fell into the waiting arms of her cheerleading compatriot, who caught her and eased her onto the ground. Dawn threw her arms around Eddie and hugged him tight. "My hero!" she squealed. Eddie, locked in a tight embrace, gave me the thumbs-up sign.

"Uh, I could use a little help here," I said, but it was too late. The tower was crashing to the ground. Eddie whisked Dawn up again and ran her out of the path of the falling debris. That left me with two options: I could go down with the ship or grab on to the banner and hope it held my weight. I chose the latter because given the choice between certain injury and potential injury, I think it's wisest to hedge your bets. I grabbed the rope and held on as the structure beneath me toppled into a mass of lumber, cloth, and tissue paper.

THIRTY

I hung there for what felt like hours. As soon as the tower fell, the driver stopped the truck and got out of the vehicle. A crowd of people gathered underneath me. At first I thought they were there to break my fall, but when they started throwing things, I began to see that I was just an oversize piñata they wanted to bring down. One water bottle hit me in the side of the head, and I'm sure it would have hurt a ton if I didn't have the Viking mask to protect me. I hoisted myself up and draped both arms over the banner. It was taut and secure enough for gymnasts to use. Unfortunately, I was no gymnast.

Someone's shoe hit me in the butt. I heard another person suggest bringing me down with one of the color guard's flags. "Stop," I heard a familiar voice in the crowd say. I looked down, and through one of the mask's eyeholes, I saw Audrey push her way into the crowd. She was dressed in full battle gear and looked like a kickass maiden dreamed up by horny illustrators at Marvel Comics. Rather than make fun of her getup, the crowd murmured appreciatively.

"Hi, Audrey." I waved from above.

"Lawrence," she said. "You can drop. I'll catch you."

"Let him fall!" someone shouted. It sounded like Chester McFarland. Audrey silenced the heckler with a swift blow to the guy's nether regions. "Fuck off, you dicktard," she said, unsheathing her sword. I'm not knocking Shakespearian insults, but when it comes to getting people's attention in this day and age, you can't go wrong with a modern classic like that. The crowd quieted and stepped back to give her some room.

"You sure?" I said.

"Hold on to the banner with your hands," she said. "You're only five feet from the ground."

The crowd of people surrounding me started to chant, "Drop. Drop. Drop." I swear, I wouldn't have been surprised if someone swung at me with a stick while blindfolded. When I finally let go, my free fall lasted half a second. I fell on the soft rubbery track, knees buckling at the sudden appearance of solid ground under my feet. Audrey helped me stand and then draped her arm around my shoulder to make sure I didn't drop again. "Thank you," I said. I wanted to kiss her right there and then but all I'd get was a mouthful of poly-foam.

I thought for a moment of attempting an escape, but realized I wouldn't get very far with this Viking head stuck to my body. Most likely, I'd trip over the toppled tower lying in the end zone and knock myself unconscious. When Stone pushed his way through the crowd and grabbed my shoulder, I accepted my fate.

"Everyone back to the stands," he barked to the crowd. He turned to the scattered members of the marching band and ordered them to play something. A few seconds later, the band members regrouped and began their less than faithful rendition of Rihanna's "Rude Boy."

Stone whipped out a switchblade and held it to my neck. "I confiscated this today from a gang banger," Stone explained to anyone wondering what a high school administrator was doing with a concealed weapon.

He brought the dagger to my neck. This is it, I thought, Stone's finally going to get his revenge by stabbing me in the jugular. It doesn't even bother him that he's surrounded by all these witnesses. He's going to claim I'm some teenage Osama bin Laden and cut me down in front of everyone. Maybe he'll complete the homecoming parade with my head on a stick.

I felt the sharp stab of the dagger on my collarbone and then an upward thrust as Stone removed my head from my body. My Viking head, as it turned out. Stone tossed the battered mascot costume aside and looked at me in mock surprise. "Lawrence," he said. "It's you!"

"I can explain," I said, more to those surrounding me than Stone. "I was locked in the tower with a chicken."

You can safely assume your alibi is not believed if it's met with a chorus of laughter. Even to me, my explanation sounded like the ravings of a madman.

With my vision restored, I was able to scan the crowd. There, standing toward the back, was Crystal, smiling at me like a cat with a defenseless field mouse in its mouth. "It was her," I said, pointing in Crystal's direction. "And I can prove it."

I snatched the switchblade out of Stone's hand and walked over to where Jerry was cradling the chicken. I know chickens don't growl, but I swear the sound coming from the avian sounded more like the low rumblings of a rabid dog than any birdcall I've heard. I stopped a few feet away and handed Jerry the knife.

"Jerry is going to cut this chicken in half and divide its body between the two people claiming ownership." I remembered this trick from a childhood story about a very wise king. For some reason, my idea was met with revulsion and a chorus of boos.

"You're a sick fuck, Larry," Jerry said, dropping the knife

and snuggling the chicken closer to his chest.

"Let's go, Lawrence," Stone said, reclaiming his weapon and using it to point me in the direction of his office. "You're finished here."

Suddenly, Spencer emerged from the crowd. My little mentee raised his hand, as if he were trying to answer the teacher's question in a rather boisterous class.

"If I'm not mistaken, the breed of chicken Mr. Tortelli is holding is a Ga Noi, an extremely rare breed found mostly in Vietnamese communities. It is extremely aggressive with other chickens. My guess is that Lawrence has some chicken feathers placed on him, of which he is unaware."

I dug around my person and sure enough found my back pockets stuffed with chicken feathers. I held them up as Exhibit A just as Jerry decided to release his hold on the angry, redheaded beast. Oh God. Please, no! was all I heard in my head as the Ga Noi conducted a swift backward kick of its talons and took off in my direction.

The thing was bloodthirsty. I once saw a piranha attack on the Discovery Channel and it was nothing compared to what was steamrolling my way. The chicken's dead eyes seemed to glow fire red as it charged in my direction; its beak, sharpened from years of pecking at rocks, stabbed the air like it was reenacting the *Psycho* shower attack. I tried to run away, but the crowd found my distress hilarious and blocked my exit with their bodies. I was trapped in this inner circle with the chicken rushing me and pecking at my ankles. When it started launching itself into the air, I screamed, ran behind Stone, and used his body to protect me.

"Crystal's family's from Vietnam," I screamed. "This must be her chicken."

"That's so racist," Crystal said.

The chicken seemed to agree with her because it renewed its attack with fresh vigor. I dropped the chicken feathers at Stone's feet and the Ga Noi went after his loafers.

"Mr. Stone," Spencer continued. "I believe if you look at the soles of Miss Nguyen's shoes, you'll find trace amounts of chicken manure, I can see a streak of it from where I'm standing, indicating that Miss Nguyen has a chicken coop at home. I'm sure if you call home, they will tell you that one of their chickens is missing."

"Who *are* you?" Crystal asked.

The crowd surrounding us seemed equally puzzled. Spencer had emerged from nowhere with information Wikipedia probably hadn't discovered yet.

"This is Spencer," I said with authority and conviction. "He's my friend."

For once, I didn't stumble in explaining my relationship with Spencer. I put my arm around the little guy and pulled him close. I was proud to call Spencer a friend, even though he was clearly uncomfortable with this public display of affection. His whole body went rigid, and he whimpered softly every time I squeezed his shoulder. My former friends would see this moment as a humiliating defeat, but it didn't feel that way to me. It felt like I was finally standing up for what I believed in, and I believed in Spencer.

Audrey pushed her way through the crowd and tried to be heard above the people's chatter. "She . . . she . . ." she spluttered, pointing at Crystal.

"Say it in Old English!" I screamed.

"By my troth, she is the maiden to whom I gave the Viking head," Audrey said.

"Crystal's been working in Coach Harkness's office all week," Eddie said, coming to our rescue.

"Audrey must have given her the mascot head after she repaired it."

"You want me to call home, Crystal?" Stone asked.

Crystal hesitated, scanning the crowd for supporters. There were none. "I want you to call the ACLU," she said defensively. "This is a clear example of racial profiling."

The Ga Noi must have broken the leather skin of Stone's loafers and pierced his actual skin because Stone jerked his leg outward and punted the chicken a good five feet.

"Mr. Winkles!" Crystal screamed, and ran after her injured animal. She cradled the dazed bird in her arms, petting its ruffled feathers and cooing softly near its head. Standing up slowly, Crystal addressed the crowd that was eagerly awaiting an explanation.

"Okay, it was me who put Mr. Winkles in the float. I knew Lawrence had some weird chicken phobia and I thought it would be funny."

A murmur of disapproval rang throughout the crowd. "How could you do that to a chicken?" someone said nearby. Clearly, the people's sympathy was with Mr. Winkles.

Crystal wiped an imaginary tear from her eye. "I didn't want anyone to get hurt. I just . . . I just wanted homecoming to be special."

"Excuse me?" I said. "How does framing me for destroying floats make homecoming special?"

"No one really cares about homecoming. It's supposed to bring our school together but it's become such a boring, predictable ritual that no one pays attention to it anymore. We needed something more than floats and rallies and football games to unite us. We needed a common enemy."

"Me?" I said.

"Well, not you specifically. Someone who attacked everything we hold dear."

"Is that why you vandalized my parking space?" Stone asked.

"You're our beloved leader, Mr. Stone," Crystal said softly.

"I thought people would rally together when they saw you were under attack."

I laughed out loud at this one. Stone shot me a look as if I were the criminal making a confession. "Come on," I said. "You can't believe this, can you?"

"Miss Nguyen has always demonstrated school spirit, which is more than I can say for you, Lawrence," Stone said.

"But don't you see? That's why she tried to destroy home-coming. She was angry that she wasn't nominated to be on the court. Plus, she's totally obsessed with Jerry." I pointed to our quarterback, whose attention was entirely focused on Mr. Winkles. They seemed to have developed a strange bond since their wrestling match. "I'm sure this has more to do with her jealousy of Dawn than anything."

"That's not true," Crystal said. "I love Dawn."

"Oh, that's so sweet," Dawn said. "I love you too, Crystal."

"Crystal, can I hold Mr. Winkles?" Jerry asked, approaching her like a shy eighth grader asking a girl to dance.

"Sure, Jerry," Crystal said, handing Mr. Winkles over. Jerry cradled him in his arms and the two head butted each other. "This dude's a fighter," Jerry said. "He should be our new mascot."

The crowd seemed to like this because they all started chanting Mr. Winkles's name over and over again. "I think we're losing sight of what's important here!" I screamed.

"Crystal tried to kill me."

"Oh, lighten up, Larry," Jerry said. "It was just a harmless prank. Pretty fucking hilarious if you ask me."

"Dawn almost fell to her death!" I screamed.

I looked over and saw Dawn and Eddie regaling a small crowd with the story of their escape from the falling tower. Dawn hadn't let go of Eddie's hand since he rescued her. "I'm fine," Dawn said. "Thanks to my knight in shining armor." A collective "Awww" rose from the crowd when Dawn leaned over and kissed Eddie on the cheek. The band, sensing the moment was ripe for a rousing rendition of Journey's "Any Way You Want It," started playing. Pretty soon, everyone was dancing and hugging one another.

"We'll discuss your punishment at some other time," I heard Stone say to Crystal over the din of the celebrating.

"Thanks, Mr. Stone," Crystal said. "You're the best." She gave him a quick hug.

It was like being stuck in a demented musical where everyone breaks into song and dance to celebrate the survival of the serial killer.

I pushed my way through the crowd and found Spencer walking back to the stands, dragging his suitcase-like backpack along the Astroturf.

"Spencer," I said, running up to him. "Can you believe this?"

"It's the boomerang effect. When you wanted the Viking to be loved, it was hated. When Crystal wanted the Viking to be hated, it was loved."

"And now she's a hero."

"History may prove differently."

"She's yearbook editor," I said. "She's in charge of history. Anyway, I just wanted to say thank you for your help back there."

"I only pointed out the obvious," he said.

"Obvious to you, maybe."

"At least you no longer have to take Miss Cosmos to the dance tonight."

"That's right," I said, looking around for any sign of Zoe. Other than a murder of crows pecking at some roadkill in the parking lot, I didn't see her anywhere.

Right when I felt like dancing, the music ended and the crowd dispersed into the stands to watch the second half of the game. Before taking the field again, Eddie rushed over. He was still beaming from rescuing the homecoming queen.

"Dude, I'm off the hook with Zoe," I said, holding up my hand for him to high five. "We can totally hang out tonight if you want."

"Sorry, Lawrence," Eddie said. "I'm taking Dawn to the dance. She said yes!" He slapped my hand really, really hard.

"Congratulations," I said, wincing. "Your dream's come true."

"And it's all thanks to this little guy here," Eddie said, ruffling Spencer's hair, which was about as rigid as Spencer.

"What do you mean?"

"Just after the homecoming parade started, he comes up to me moping on the sidelines and suggests I follow the float. He points to the banner at the opposite end of the field and tells me I should go rescue Dawn when the thing topples the tower. I wouldn't have been there to catch her if he hadn't warned me."

"Spencer, how did you know the banner was hung too low?"

"It was a simple calculation," Spencer said. "Anyone with a basic understanding of geometry and physics could have figured it out."

But of course, it was only Spencer who had. I slapped him on the back. He seemed to like this display of affection as much as the other forms of PDA he was receiving.

"I should get going," Eddie said. "Dawn's suffering from a little post-traumatic stress and doesn't want her 'knight in shining armor,' that's what she calls me, to leave her side. She can be a little clingy, I'm noticing. Also, I don't think that dress suits her at all. I hope she's not planning on wearing it tonight." Eddie smiled weakly and then returned to the love of his life.

"I give 'em a week," I said.

"I wouldn't be surprised if he finds someone new at the dance tonight," Spencer added.

"I wonder who Jerry's going to the dance with?" I asked.

"It would appear he's developed an interest in Miss Nguyen's chicken," Spencer said, nodding in the direction of the sidelines. Jerry and Crystal were cooing over Mr. Winkles, who Jerry still had tucked into the crook of his arm.

"Excuse me a minute," Spencer said. He left his rolling backpack in my care and walked over to where Jerry was standing. Most freshmen would be reluctant to approach Jerry Tortelli unless they were offering up their lunch money in some exchange for protective services, but Spencer marched right up to him, said a few words, then returned to where I was standing. Whatever he said had some effect, because Jerry looked like a hyper dog that'd just been taken off leash.

"What did you say?" I asked.

"I told him that if he cradled the football the same way he held Mr. Winkles, then the chances of him fumbling would be significantly decreased."

"Looks like he agrees with you," I said. Jerry relinquished control of Mr. Winkles to Crystal and tried the new hold with the game ball. He ducked left and right and then straightened up and gave Spencer a thumbs-up sign.

"You're amazing," I said, deeply in awe of Spencer's powers. I guess my mentoring hadn't been the failure I thought it was.

The players took to the field and it was clear from the kickoff that our team was energized in a way it hadn't been before the jubilant halftime show. Within the first five minutes of play, Jerry moved the team downfield and ran twenty yards for a touchdown. The fans went wild. The cheerleaders went wild. The band went wild. The corners of Spencer's lips lifted slightly.

"Lawrence," I heard a voice from behind me say. I felt a thousand tiny spiders crawl across my skin and immediately identified the speaker.

I turned around and saw Zoe holding Audrey by the wrist. Audrey's pale, soft skin seemed almost ghostly next to Zoe's funeral attire. For a moment, I thought Zoe had killed my maiden and conjured her spirit as a final insult to me.

I left Spencer and shielded Audrey from this villainous harpy.

"You can't blackmail me anymore, Zoe. The Viking's been caught."

"That doesn't mean I don't have any power over you," Zoe said, taking a few steps back and removing the dog collar from her back pocket. She started mumbling some incantation under her breath and flopping around like a bird who's

just flown into a window.

Normally, I'd expect the world to go dark at this stage, but the lights didn't dim, the world retained its color, and the living didn't drop dead and resurrect as Zoe's zombie horde. I clasped Audrey's hand and together we stared Zoe down. Her Latin curse died on her lips and she looked around like a little girl who's just realized she's grabbed the hand of a stranger at the mall.

"All I wanted was a date to homecoming," she whimpered.

"I'm sorry, Zoe," I said, feeling sorry for her for the first time in, well, forever. If you could see past the black shroud, sinister makeup, and threatening manicure, Zoe was just a cute little girl who wanted to be loved like the rest of us.

"You will bow down to me, miscreant!" Zoe said, doing a spot-on imitation of an Orc from the *Lord of the Rings* movies. She stretched the leather collar between her two fists and approached me slowly, like a dominatrix dog walker.

She was within inches of us when Lunley suddenly called from the sidelines of the game. He was holding his cell phone aloft like he had just intercepted it. "Zoe!" he said, "the Rotary Club just announced the finalists for their Future Business Leaders of America award. You made the list! Congratulations!"

"That's awesome!" Zoe squealed, whipping the dog collar above her head like a lasso. She turned to us, as if suddenly

broken from her hypnotist's trance. "Sorry, guys. Gotta go." And she skipped off to where Lunley was waiting for her.

Audrey and I stared at each other, struck dumb by what we had just witnessed.

"That girl is whack," Audrey said.

"M'lady, thou dost speak the truth," I replied. Now it was my turn to struggle for words.

"Hey," I said, just to get the ball rolling.

"Hey," she said, tucking a stray curl behind her ear.

"Thanks, you know, for saving me."

"You were only five feet above the ground," Audrey said in an oddly normal voice. She spoke with a slight British accent, but the words were twenty-first century. "You were hardly in any danger."

"I wouldn't have dropped if you weren't there to catch me."

"I'm happy to be your safety net, Mr. Barry," Audrey said, curtseying.

"And I yours, Miss Sieminski," I replied with a bow.

Another cheer came from the stands. I wanted to think the crowd was rooting for our happy ending, but they were just responding to an interception.

"I'm sorry for thinking you were the Viking," I fumbled.

"'Tis nothing."

"Will you go to the dance with me tonight?"

"It would be my honor, kind sir," Audrey said. "Why don't you pick me up at eight?" She dropped her voice to a whisper. "Grannie should be asleep by then." She kissed me on the cheek and walked away, nice and slow.

I turned to Spencer and raised my hand for a high five. His expression turned sour as if I were holding up a piece of roadkill for him to examine. I extended my hand instead and double pumped him.

"You want me to teach you some dance moves?" I asked.

"I already know how to waltz, thank you," he said.

"Nobody waltzes at these things, Spencer," I said. "You need to get funky."

Spencer raised an eyebrow at the word "funky."

"Here, let me show you." I went through my repertoire of dance moves. After performing the Spaghetti Monkey, I detected a smile on Spencer's face.

"My father looks like that when he's having one of his seizures," he said.

"Show me your waltz, then."

"I would prefer not to."

"Okay, well you can get away with just bobbing your head to the music." I thought it best to forget about trying to move his lower body. "Try it."

I whipped out my iPhone and played "Low Rider" by War. I showed him how to move his head and adopt a bored expression of someone waiting for a cooler song to cut loose. When Spencer attempted to imitate me, he looked like someone reluctantly agreeing to an unreasonable request. He nodded his head to the beat, but his expression was wary. "That's it," I said, trying to be encouraging. With freshman mentees, it's important to boost their confidence, even if you have to lie a little.

ACKNOWLEDGMENTS

The book you've just read began with an image of a home-coming queen leaping from a crumbling float into the arms of an enamored male cheerleader. I started writing toward that ending and ended up with a bunch of nonsense, as you might imagine.

Luckily, I had a ton of people to help me shape this non-sense into something that resembled a story. These people are not listed in order of importance (they're all important) but in the order they intervened and kept me writing.

First off, there's my sister, Sheila Grau, whose book deal inspired me to work a lot harder at this writing thing so she wouldn't be able to brag at Thanksgiving. (Not that she would. She's modest to a fault, despite being a hilarious writer with way more imagination than I have.) Her encouragement and guidance were critical.

Then there are the people in my writing group, who always found at least one nice thing to say about dreck I submitted every month. Eileen Bordy, John Foley, Ann Gelder, Shelly King, Julie Knight, Katy Motley, Rich Register, Cheyenne Richards, Beth Sears, and Mary Taugher have been the best support group ever. We're like Writing Anonymous, only the meetings encourage participants to do the thing they want to stop doing.

Lyn Fairchild Hawks read the early drafts of this book with a microscope and provided detailed feedback to help me channel my inner sixteen-year-old. Robie Spector and Poppy Livingstone also kept me going with their enthusiasm and lots of chocolate babka for energy.

Then there was my agent, Adriann Ranta, who was smart enough to reject the book when I first sent it to her, but kind enough to encourage me to revise further. It's thanks to her that Lawrence isn't a dissolute alcoholic at the end of the novel. The fact that this book exists at all is due to her.

Because of Adriann, I got to work with the brilliant Karen Chaplin and her team at Harper Teen. Karen's insight helped me see that this book is really about being true to yourself and that those 200 pages where Lawrence wanders in the desert contemplating his own mortality could be cut from the story. She also let me keep the things important to me—like the talking squirrel and the phrase "fuck off, you dicktard"—despite her better judgment.

Anne Battle and April Oliver found errors at the last minute that everyone had overlooked. My street cred as an English teacher would have suffered significantly if these had made it to print.

All this represents four long years of work, none of which would have been possible without the love and support of my family. Mom, Dad, Lisa, Jeff, Charlie, Cooper, Juan, Rachel, Ricky, Alex, and Daniel are the best clan to be connected to.

And finally, to Kathleen and Henry, neither of whom read this book but provided all the inspiration, thank you for giving my life purpose and so much joy.

JOIN THE
Epic Reads
COMMUNITY

THE ULTIMATE YA DESTINATION

◄ DISCOVER ►
your next favorite read

◄ MEET ►
new authors to love

◄ WIN ►
free books

◄ SHARE ►
infographics, playlists, quizzes, and more

◄ WATCH ►
the latest videos

◄ TUNE IN ►
to Tea Time with Team Epic Reads